EVE
IN THE BEGINNING

EVE
IN THE BEGINNING

USA Today Bestselling Author

H.B. MOORE

Mirror Press

Interior design by Rachael Anderson
Edited by Kelsey Allan, Micala Downs and Melissa Marler
Cover design by Rachael Anderson

Cover Photo Credit: 2014 © iStock.com/Olena Vizerskaya,
 #13310899

Published by Mirror Press, LLC
ISBN-10: 1941145450
ISBN-13: 978-1-941145-45-6

For my mother, Gayle Brown,
a noble daughter of Eve.

Also by H. B. Moore

Finding Sheba: An Omar Zagouri Thriller
Lost King: An Omar Zagouri Thriller
Beneath: An Omar Zagouri Short Story
The Moses Chronicles
Esther the Queen
Daughters of Jared
The Out of Jerusalem Series

Publications under Heather B. Moore

Heart of the Ocean
The Fortune Café
The Boardwalk Antiques Shop
The Aliso Creek Series
The Newport Ladies Book Club Series
A Timeless Romance Anthology Series

Author's Note

I've been writing historical novels based on scriptural characters for many years. When I decided to look for a female heroine in the Bible for my next subject, it seemed to make sense to write about Eve, our first mother. Through researching Eve and Adam, I became impressed with their noble characters and their difficult and brave choices. This novelization is not meant to represent any specific religious organization or religious doctrine. The plot points are a compilation of various theories with added fictional elements and do not necessarily represent my personal religious beliefs.

There are yet many unknowns about the life that our first parents led in the Garden of Eden. I believe one day our questions will be answered, yet the purpose of this story is not to answer those questions, or even speculate on new possibilities. I wrote this story to bring to life an incredible man and woman who sacrificed immortality to start the human race . . . A man and woman whom I esteem as my first parents and will be eternally grateful for.

 **I**

In the beginning God created the heaven and the earth.
— Genesis 1:1

"**W**e can't live like this forever," I say.

"Yes, we can." Adam's fingertips brush my bare arm.

We are lying on our backs, looking up at the golden-green leaves that filter just enough of the sun's rays to make the air only a warm, fragrant whisper around us.

A quiet afternoon in our unending days of tranquility.

I close my eyes as Adam's fingers stray along my arm, moving down to my wrist, until his long fingers interlace with mine.

Serenity.

I tell myself that I want nothing more than to lie in the cool grass next to Adam, surrounded by sweet flowers while listening to the melody of the nearby stream.

I could stay here forever with him. And perhaps we have. Time moves forward, yet it never seems to move at all. The garden never changes. Even the fruits stay the same, never growing old. We never change.

I don't desire to change anything . . . not really. But the

thoughts press against my mind—thoughts that have been more and more frequent over the past moon—until I have to speak again. "Do you really want to stay here forever?" I say. "I mean the garden is lovely, but . . ." My thought hangs in the air between us.

Adam rolls over onto his side and tugs my hand to his lips, pressing his mouth on my knuckles. This captures my attention. He smiles when I look at him, his eyes changing with the light—first green, then darker. His hair is nearly black today, although I know out of the shade it will glow bronze—a bronze that extends to his skin, matching the color of my own. Our bodies are different though, as must be between a man and a woman, and I've been curious more than once to know why.

Everything with Adam has always been mysterious.

This is why I find myself thinking more and more about what it would be like to *know.*

I get lost in Adam's gaze for a moment, forgetting my questions, although I've heard his answers many times. Of how Elohim commanded Adam not to eat the fruit from the tree of knowledge of good and evil. Of how we may freely eat the fruit of any tree, except for that one.

In fact, Adam refuses to even go near the tree of knowledge of good and evil. When we are in the center of the garden, he passes by it quickly on the path and will delay only if I persist. Most of the time, I visit the tree alone.

"Eve, you're frowning," Adam says in his low voice.

I love his voice—its deep richness vibrates through my body. He is the only man I know, the only man I ever see, but I can't imagine any other creature ever sounding this beautiful.

"You're not listening." I hold his gaze so he knows I'm serious.

It doesn't change the smile on his face. He tightens his

fingers around mine, and I feel the heat radiating between our palms. "I always listen to you."

To test him, I say, "Come with me to visit the tree."

He pulls away and sits up. He's not looking at me now, nor is he smiling. "Nothing will change," he says in a quiet voice.

Despite his words, hope blossoms in my chest. "I know." Adam is determined and stubborn, but I can be more so, though I know when to push and when not to.

I stand and hold out my hand. He grasps it in his, flesh to flesh, and I am grateful he is making this exception as he stands tall next to me. He leads me through the garden, and we pass tree after tree and thick bushes of flowers, weaving our way as our bare feet tread on the soft undergrowth and warm earth path. The scents reach out to me one by one, full and fragrant, some sweet, others sharp, until they blend together and are carried away by a breeze. We cross a sloping meadow, where the sun touches our bare skin from head to foot.

The leaves rattle around us, moved by the breeze that blows my hair against my cheek. Adam reaches over and brushes the long strands of honey brown from my face, his touch gentle and tender. I smile up at him, and he squeezes my hand.

Today he is indulging me. Today perfection will outdo itself.

The walk is not far, but it seems to take a while since Adam is in no hurry. He doesn't spend as much time in this part of the garden—past the two rivers, over the hill of crimson flowers, and next to the grove that contains the tree of life—as I do. But it isn't the tree of life that I want to see today.

We both slow at the same time. It's still a good distance—a safe distance. The tree of knowledge stands by itself, as if it's somehow cast off by the other trees that grow close together, protecting each other.

Something hitches in my chest, matching the lonely feeling I sense from the tree, though I am not alone. Adam has always been with me, but I understand what it is to feel apart.

As far as I know, I am the only woman on the earth, and although my Adam is the only earthly man, our heavenly visitors are male as well. More questions.

The tree of knowledge shimmers in the sun, perhaps acknowledging our approach. Its branches of dark leaves and its pale, swollen fruit remind me of arms and hands and seem to beckon us, but I know we won't get too close.

We start walking again, and I feel the reluctant pressure in Adam's grip. Birds scatter as we near, flying to other trees not far from us. A few of the birds flitter back toward the tree of knowledge, and I wonder at their feasting.

Do they acquire knowledge as they peck at the fruit, or is the warning for only humans?

For in the day that thou eatest thereof thou shalt surely die.

My heart pounds as we walk closer to the tree. The breeze captures the scent of the tree's fruit and steers it our way. The sweetness is powerful, stronger than that of other trees. Adam doesn't seem to be swayed by the scent. He releases me and lowers himself to the ground. I know this is as far as he'll go; the finality in his eyes says it all.

I hesitate. Should I sit by Adam and ask him my questions? Or should I walk toward the tree to get a better look at the oval fruit that's the same shape as my palm? I wonder what it would feel like to touch the tree's bark—not the fruit, of course—but the rich bark.

Today I choose to sit by Adam, if only to show him my gratitude for his leniency.

His arm goes around my shoulder as I lean against him.

EVE

He smells like the grass and the dark earth. My Adam. My loving Adam who has chosen to live with me forever.

2

And the earth was without form, and void; and darkness was upon the face of the deep.

—Genesis 1:2

"You will be my wife," Adam told me when I'd first awakened on the day my spirit gave life to my body. "We're in the Garden of Eden, created by Elohim." He had stared at me with those gold-green eyes, and my chest had expanded with what I soon understood to be love.

"What is a wife?" I asked.

"What a woman is called when she is joined together as a help meet to a man."

I had looked into his eyes then and seen gentleness, kindness.

"I will be your husband," he said.

I remember that I didn't want him to stop talking in that deep voice of his. "I am yours, and you are mine?" I whispered, touching his face. He smiled then, and I had my first taste of what my life was to be in Eden.

In those early days after Elohim joined Adam and me as husband and wife, I watched Adam closely, and he watched me. We never left each other's side, each of us fascinated

6

with the other—walking, talking, eating, sleeping. Each moment was a marvel.

We spent many moments—days—exploring the garden, hand in hand.

"Are there any other men or women outside the garden?" I asked one day, and that was when the first shadow crossed Adam's face.

I open my eyes to gentle tapping on my shoulder.

"Eve? The sun is setting."

Adam is stretched out in the grass, his gaze on me. We had fallen asleep, watching the tree of knowledge. Violet shadows have gathered, deepening the greens and browns of the grove and darkening the earth beneath. The western sky is nearly indigo, framing the final streaks of orange.

I reluctantly stand, the scent of grass lingering on my skin. "Can we come again tomorrow?"

He sighs and threads his fingers through his hair. "I don't think we should be spending much time by that tree. It's forbidden, and being close to it can't be what Elohim wants for us."

He is right, of course, but there are other things that are right as well. Something expands in my mind, then flees just before I can comprehend it. Something about another commandment Elohim gave us. Adam turns away from the setting sun, and I glance once again at the tree.

It has changed in the twilight. The once-welcoming arm-like branches seem dark and cold. The dense leaves mask the fruit, no longer offering sweet appeal, its fragrance still and heavy. Just as I turn to follow Adam, something moves near the trunk. The shape is too large to be a deer. I pause, staring through the dimness, but the shape is gone as quickly as it appeared.

Perhaps it's a reflection of the trunk in the fading light—or it's nothing at all.

"Adam, look," I say. "Behind the tree."

But he is already looking as if he too had seen it. He squints in the dimming light. I can feel his nervousness as my heart trips. Anything to do with the tree of knowledge makes him wary.

"Something was there," I whisper.

He stares for a long moment, and just when I think he might venture closer to inspect the surroundings, he shakes his head. "There's nothing." His gaze—stern—meets mine. "I don't like being close to the tree at nightfall."

As if we might wander closer and accidentally eat the fruit in our sleep? I don't say it. I have pushed him enough for the day.

"Let's go," he says, and I nod.

But my heart still races as I slip my hand into Adam's. The shadow was not like that of a beast but more like that of a human. A man or a woman, I'm not sure. What if, I wonder—what if we are *not* alone in the garden? Curiosity creeps into my breast, curiosity about more than Elohim's warnings. I don't tell Adam about these new thoughts because I, like Adam, don't want anything in the garden to change what is between Adam and me.

And if there is another human in the garden, things will definitely change.

I cling to Adam as we make our way up the slope. If he notices my tighter grip, he says nothing. The moon is a sliver tonight, making travel difficult, and I stumble twice. By the time we reach our sleeping alcove, I'm perspiring, and my breath is heavy. Tonight, for once, I don't want to talk.

3

And God called the light Day, and the darkness he called Night.

—Genesis 1:5

Adam waited until Eve's breathing evened before he quietly sat up. He studied her in the near-darkness, assuring himself that she was truly asleep. She looked peaceful as she slept, her hair curling around her shoulders and along her neck, her eyelashes and lips still . . . as if she weren't capable of construing all the probing questions she asked when awake.

He moved a strand of hair that rested against her cheek. Her skin was smooth and warm beneath his touch, but she didn't stir. Her incessant questions must have truly worn her out today.

Normally, Adam would smile to himself and brush off her persistence. But not tonight. Though he'd told Eve he hadn't seen anything under the tree of knowledge of good and evil, he'd *felt* something—a presence? He wasn't sure.

Unease formed in his stomach. He wanted to gather Eve in his arms, promise that he could always protect her, and purge the heaviness that seeped through him.

Instead he closed his hands into fists. He didn't want to disturb his wife. She might have more questions, and he didn't know if he could continue to deny what he'd felt back at the tree of knowledge. And he couldn't give her the answers she wanted.

He gave up on sleeping—again. He reluctantly left Eve's side, and their sleeping alcove, and perched on a nearby boulder that overlooked a tangle of flowering bushes. The scent of the blooms floated around him, and he breathed in deeply, wishing he could regain the peace of the previous afternoon—before Eve asked to visit the tree.

Eve hadn't been with him in the very beginning. She had been created after he was, and although he'd told her all of Elohim's instructions, Adam felt she should have heard them firsthand.

Yet she had seen and heard Elohim nearly as much as he had now. So why did she persist with questions and ideas when they both knew Elohim provided everything for them here in the garden? They needed nothing more, wanted for nothing. At least Adam wanted for nothing, for the most part.

It was complicated. No, *Eve* was complicated—more than he could have ever imagined. When Elohim had told Adam that he'd be given a wife, Adam hadn't known exactly what to expect.

But when he first saw Eve and those clear blue-green eyes of hers, he couldn't imagine a time before she came into his life. What had he done before she was created? Who had he been before he had a wife? Things seemed to hold significance only when Eve was with him.

And that's why when Eve felt restless, something he couldn't describe churned deep inside him.

It was as if she was saying to him, "This is not enough. *You* are not enough."

Adam let out a frustrated sigh and rubbed his arms. The

EVE

air held a slight chill, not so cold so as to send him back to Eve's side but sufficient to make him miss her.

He climbed off the rock and walked the perimeter of the small settlement that he and Eve had organized. There wasn't too much of a difference between their place of habitat and the rest of the garden, except for the paths they had formed. They'd also created areas where they'd grouped rocks and arranged canopies of branches to create places to sit during the mists. Their sleeping alcove provided plenty of shelter from mist or sun, and they needed to refresh the bed of leaves only every few days.

As Adam moved along the paths, he listened for any unusual sounds, but, as always, the night sounds were familiar: the rustling of leaves, the low call of an owl. He circled the alcove where Eve lay, knowing that if he joined her, he'd probably wake her in his restlessness. It was better for only one of them to be tired the next morning. He fully realized he could sleep during the morning, yet he didn't want to leave his wife unattended—not even for a short time.

It wasn't that he didn't trust her or that he feared that she wouldn't tell him every thought or action, but he couldn't stand the thought of being without her. The garden held only one danger—the tree of knowledge of good and evil—and it was that one thing he didn't trust. He didn't like that Eve wanted to visit it so often.

Especially now. Especially with what he thought he sensed earlier.

What did she gain by watching a tree? It grew like the others and produced fruit on a regular basis. Birds and small animals seemed to spend no more time there than at other trees, yet Eve remained fascinated.

Was it because of the unknown—death?

"We'll never die," Adam had told Eve on more than one occasion, "if we follow Elohim's commandments."

But the warning didn't seem to create the same feeling

II

in her as it did in him. Adam slowed his step as he neared the alcove again. He edged closer until he could see his wife sleeping. It was too dark to make out her features clearly, but he was satisfied she still slept unharmed.

Yet . . . why should she be harmed? There was nothing or no one here that could harm her.

The feelings that coursed through him weren't new, but they were stronger than he'd ever remembered. He'd do anything to protect her, even if it meant telling her a final *no*.

Adam breathed out, the idea washing over him, bringing greater comfort. That's what he'd have to do: forbid her to visit the tree. It was the only way to ensure her protection. And he meant to protect her—forever. He wouldn't let her die.

And God said, Let there be a firmament in the midst of the waters, and let it divide the waters from the waters.

—Genesis 1:6

A dam is curled up next to me when I wake. He usually stirs easily, but this morning he is heavy in sleep.

I move away from him carefully so as not to wake him. I normally wait until he has gone to wash in the pond before I walk to my stone wall. At the back of the alcove, where I've hung woven leaves to keep the space cool on hot days, I've begun to scratch marks in the stone.

One mark for each time the sun rises.

It's the only way I can keep track of the days.

"How long will we live here?" I asked Adam once.

"Forever."

"How long is forever?" I said.

"Forever will never end," he answered, as if it were obvious.

I thought about his words and wondered if there was a way to count forever. But tracking the number of days and nights with my fingers did not work. Did forever have an end? If there was a beginning—the day that Adam was created—then there must be an end.

Even if we don't die.

I move quietly to the back wall as Adam's breathing fills the silent spaces. With a broken rock that I keep tucked in a corner, I scratch a line about the length of my finger. I look over the many lines I have drawn. They reach from the ground to my waist now, spanning the width of me twice over. I replace the rock and return to the front of the alcove.

Another day toward forever is marked.

Adam's face looks tired, and I decide to let him sleep while I refresh myself. I walk to the pond that branches off the nearby river and wade into it, soaking myself in its delicious coolness. I drink my fill of the water, then wet my hair. Water drips down my back as I walk to the closest tree and gather the fruit. Adam is always hungry when he wakes, whereas I can wait to eat until the sun is halfway up the sky.

But this morning I want to nourish myself for a long walk.

Adam doesn't know it yet, but I want to visit the borders. On the way, I can check on the cattle, and if the mist has cleared past the borders, I might be able to catch a glimpse of what's beyond the garden.

Returning to the alcove, I find Adam just waking up, but I wait until we are preparing to set off for the herb gardens before I speak. "Where are you working today?"

He looks up as he places a stone tool into a basket I have woven from long grasses. "I'll be overturning the soil between the patches of herbs in the north garden."

It's something he can do by himself. "I plan to visit the cattle," I say.

He lifts the basket and straightens, facing me. His gaze is sharp. "I don't want to be separated. We'll go together to the north garden. You can help me till the ground, or you can gather herbs." Elohim has given him the task of keeping

14

the garden and tending to the herbs. I spend most of my time with the animals unless Adam needs my help.

I wait, but he offers no other explanation.

"I haven't visited the cattle for a number of days," I say.

"We can visit them together, *later*," he says.

I have never heard his voice this hard. I don't like it. But I think if I follow him today, he'll be more willing to go to the borders tomorrow. "All right."

He grasps my hand and leads the way, nearly tugging me along. Something is bothering him. My heart pounds as I realize I must be right: he did see something by the tree of knowledge of good and evil yesterday. What was it? *Who* was it?

Perhaps Adam is correct; we should not be separated.

Yet, I still want to visit the borders, and I don't want to wait until tomorrow or another day. It has been a while since we've been there. Adam didn't like my many questions the last time we went, and we haven't been back since. I want to push through the thick trees and look out at what's on the other side. Any time I've gone with Adam, it's been too difficult to decipher anything in the mist.

I glance at him, wondering how much I should press. His bronze complexion looks sallow in the morning light. "You're tired this morning," I say.

Adam stops, as if remembering that I'm at his side, and looks at me, then past me. "I slept little last night."

"Were you dreaming?" I ask.

He shakes his head, and we continue walking, more slowly now. I don't remember Adam having trouble sleeping before. If he has, he has not told me. I am the one who sometimes wakes in the middle of the night, unable to shut out my intruding questions.

The north gardens teem with activity. Bees fly among the flowering herbs that grow on the small hill leading up to a tangle of vines. I've tried to tame the vines before, but I give up when the sun grows too hot. Colorful insects hop from plant to plant, and birds chirp in a chorus of song. I hum without thinking about it, imitating the birds' sounds.

Despite all the activity, a few deer doze in the shade near a grouping of trees. I cross to them and stroke their short, sleek fur. They barely stir, cracking their eyes open only to see who approaches. "You are lazy ones today."

The deer I am stroking blinks its eyes open for a moment, and I wonder what it's thinking. It has been in the garden as long as we have, maybe even longer. All of the animals have been. They don't die either.

I can't help but glance toward the borders. We aren't too far from them, and I can see the top of the line of trees. The morning sky is clear, and I wonder if there is mist beyond the borders today. Adam says he has never seen beyond the borders without mist.

I sense Adam watching me, and I turn to see him smiling. I wave, grateful his melancholy has left. He's told me many times he loves to see me with the animals.

He doesn't want anything to happen to me, I think. And of course I don't want anything to happen to him, to us, or to any of the animals in the garden. I don't want any of us to die, but I still think he is too cautious. There is no one but us in the garden, and it's always been that way and always will be, as long as we follow Elohim's commandments.

Adam bends over and turns the rich earth with a stone tool, and I think of Elohim's commandments to us. Some of them were given before I was created, and although Adam has repeated them many times, I can't always keep them straight.

I walk over to Adam and stand near him; I am his shade from the sun.

"Which commandments were given *before* I was created?" I ask him.

Even though his face is turned down, I see his lips quirk.

"The commandment about the tree," he says in a patient voice. I have that commandment memorized.

"And the ones after I was created?"

Adam straightens, squinting in the sun. He's perspiring, and he wipes his forehead with the back of his hand. I think I might help him do the tilling, but there is no hurry to get the work done. There never is.

"Be fruitful and multiply," he says. His memory is flawless. "And replenish the earth and subdue it."

I nod. I know those ones, but I can't remember the exact order. "Are the commandments for the animals as well?"

"They are."

The sun is rapidly warming the garden. I look back at the lazing deer. "They aren't following the commandments," I say.

Adam chuckles. "They aren't doing much of anything today."

I look up at Adam. "What does *subdue* mean?"

"Just as we're doing now." He waves a hand at the flourishing herbs. "Caring for the plants."

He is right, but we aren't really doing that much. I wonder if we are *subduing* anything. The plants grow whether we tend to them or not. The sun and the mist do the majority of the work.

"Let's walk to the river and get a drink," Adam says.

"Can we continue to the border?" I ask. "Just for a short while? There is no mist today."

Adam is silent, but he puts an arm around my shoulder. Even though it's too hot to be touching much, I let his arm remain. Soon enough we step into the cooler shade of the trees. The river on the northern end runs deep and wide. Both of us like to swim like the river fish.

Adam splashes me as we step into the river, and I laugh and dive under the water. I come up near him and tug him in with me. He swallows a mouthful of water and surfaces with a sputter. I quickly swim toward the opposite bank before he can dunk me.

But Adam is faster than I am, and he easily overtakes me. I scream as he pulls me beneath the water again, and I manage to wriggle away. I stay underwater as long as possible, letting the current carry me along the bank. When I resurface, Adam is dozens of paces upstream.

At first I think he's laughing. Then I realize he is calling out to me. He dives into the river and swims toward me. I wade onto the bank and sit down, waiting for him to arrive, my toes dipped into the water.

I can't read Adam's expression when he rises out of the water, but he is by my side in an instant. "You shouldn't have gone this far without me," he says, still breathless from swimming.

"The current is fast," I say with a shrug of my shoulder.

"Eve," he says, his tone serious.

I sigh and look over at him. "Just tell me what's wrong, Adam. Why are you behaving like this? What are you worried about?"

He runs a hand through his soaking hair, and water droplets fall onto his shoulders. He is stalling, and I wonder why he has to think about talking to me.

"Has Elohim told you something?" I press.

"No," he says quickly. "Elohim hasn't visited me without your knowledge."

It's been at least one moon cycle since Elohim has appeared. I brush off beads of water clinging to the hairs on his arm. "Why can't you tell me?"

"I can," he says, but his voice is reluctant. "It's just that I'm not sure of what I saw—if it was anything."

"By the tree?" I ask in a quiet voice.

He nods.

Then he did see something too. We are silent for a moment.

EVE

When I reach for his hand, I say, "We should explore the garden, see if there are any changes."

Adam meets my gaze and squeezes my hand. "You really want to go to the borders, don't you?"

I hide a smile. "Only if it would make you feel better."

"It might," he says, and I can see the smile in his eyes. He pulls me to my feet, and we start walking toward the second river. My heart pounds in anticipation. The sky is clear blue, and there is no wind. It's a perfect day to see into the wilderness beyond.

"Do you think we'll be able to catch a glimpse of the sea?" I ask. One of our blessings from Elohim is that Adam and I have dominion over the fish of the sea. But in the garden, there are only rivers.

Adam chuckles. "Perhaps. Or perhaps not."

"What kinds of fish do you think are in the sea?"

"They are probably much like the ones in the rivers," he says, his voice ever patient.

I hear the cattle before I see them. They are scattered quite far from one another today, lowing quietly when not feeding on grass. Adam and I walk among them, stroking their backs and talking to them as if they could reply.

I love spending time with the gentle cattle, but I'm more interested in visiting the borders today. The grass grows higher near the line of trees, and as Adam and I walk through the trees, I relish the cool shade. My hair is still damp from the river. The birds stop their chattering as Adam and I pass by, and I wonder if they have ever been past the borders. Do the birds follow Elohim's commandments as well?

Adam and I stop at the low stone wall that Adam built before I was created. It circles the entire Garden of Eden and has never been crossed by either of us. "There is nothing out there for us," Adam has told me many times.

I place both hands atop the rock wall, which reaches to

19

my waist. There is no mist today, just as I had believed. The sun is stark, and it illuminates the rocky ground that slopes away from us. I look as far as I can see in all directions and see nothing but dirt and rocks in a vast plain.

"Where are the plants? The herbs?" I ask.

Adam is staring past the rock wall as well. "I don't see any. They must grow farther out."

In the distance, a dark form swells against the sky. "What's over there?" I ask, pointing.

"It's too far away to know, but it's probably a hill," he says. "A very large hill."

Shielding my eyes, I stare at the looming form and try to estimate how high it is; it is much higher than the hills in the garden. I turn to Adam. "Do you think the sea is out there?"

"It must be," he says in a slow voice. He too is staring at the large hill.

"How are we supposed to have dominion over the fish of the sea if we have never been to the sea?" I ask.

Adam leans against the wall, his back to the wilderness. He doesn't seem to have the fascination that I do. "We still have dominion over them, even if we aren't there," he says.

It makes sense, yet it doesn't.

"Do the fish of the sea multiply?" I ask.

"I don't know, Eve," Adam says with a sigh. "We can ask Elohim on the seventh day during our worship. Perhaps he'll visit us."

My heart stutters at the thought of asking Elohim my questions; it's much easier to ask Adam. One part of me is curious to know what Elohim might say; the other part is reluctant to voice any of my curiosity. But I don't want to wait until the seventh day. "The animals in the garden don't multiply," I say in a stubborn voice. "And neither do we."

Adam straightens, pushing away from the wall. "They also don't die," he says, staring at me. "You don't want the animals to die, do you?"

Of course I don't. I think of the cattle and the deer. Even the birds are innocent in their flying. I look away from Adam. I don't like the sternness of his gaze.

"Sometimes I wonder. That's all." I run my hand along the rough stone wall. "I wonder if we're meant to keep some commandments and not others."

"What do you mean?" Adam says, but I hear the sharpness in his voice. He knows what I mean.

I fold my arms and look out at the wilderness. It's not nearly as interesting as I thought it might be. The mists made it intriguing. With the mists gone and the sun revealing only long stretches of rocky dirt, I don't want to leave the garden any more than Adam does. Yet I wonder if there is more . . . beyond what our lives are now . . . and whether it can be found outside the garden.

I walk away from the wall, back toward the cattle. Adam follows me, but neither of us speaks.

5

And God called the firmament Heaven.

—Genesis 1:8

On the seventh day, we walk to the altar. Each seventh day, we rest from our labors, just as the gods did when they created the earth and the heavens. Adam has told me the story of the creation many times, a story he learned from Elohim. On the seventh day, we don't tend to the garden or the animals. We spend the day in worship and thanksgiving to our maker. We never know if he'll appear and give us more counsel; it seems that every few moons Elohim visits us.

I wonder what Elohim will see in me if he visits today. I slept little last night, thinking of the commandments that Elohim gave us—specifically the command to multiply and replenish the earth and how it will be through my body that children will come forth.

We are not keeping that commandment. Why does that not bother Adam? He knows the commandments and blessings so well. How could he not be troubled about this one?

The altar Adam has built stands in a lush field just east of our dwelling place and near the east gate. Adam once examined the garden, before I was created, and walked the length of it several times to determine where he wanted the altar. There are few trees near the east gate where Elohim enters the garden, and the grass grows low and thick.

Adam kneels at the altar of rough stones. I clasp my hands together, closing my eyes as he begins to pray. "Blessed is the seventh day. Sanctify this day that Elohim rested from his creation."

His prayers are ones I've heard many times; they're always the same prayers, ones he learned from Elohim. After Adam is finished, we both wait, but the heavens are silent today. Elohim won't be visiting us. My questions will go another day, or many days, without being answered.

Adam meets my gaze as he rises from the altar. A day of rest stretches before us, and I'm not ready to return to our dwelling. We are already halfway to the tree ...

When Adam reaches my side, I say, "Do you think the birds know that it's the seventh day?"

Adam shakes his head. "I don't think they understand the passage of time."

"Do you?" I ask.

His brows draw together, and he faces me, placing his hands on each side of my face. "So many questions, Eve."

I nod slightly, but I don't draw back. I hold his gaze steady. "How long have we been in the garden?"

Adam releases me and lets out a sigh. "I don't know exactly."

"Hundreds of days? Thousands?"

"Most likely thousands."

I agree, but I don't tell him so. I have hundreds of marks on my stone wall, marks made only since I've been tracking the days.

"How many more days will we break Elohim's

commandments?" I ask. I have deliberately irritated Adam; this I know. But I have not slept, and I find it hard to contain my thoughts.

His hands fall away from my face, and I feel the coolness between us like a sudden breeze. "Why do you persist?" he says, his underlying tone thick with impatience.

"Why can't you answer my question?"

Adam's face stills, and I step back. Perhaps I have gone too far now.

"Elohim gave us the garden for us to live in," he says. "He didn't send us here to die. If so, what would be the point of creating us?"

"So that we can multiply and replenish the earth."

"Yes, and that time will come."

"When, Adam?" I ask, my words spitting out of my mouth. "In another thousand days? Look around us. Nothing ever changes. Nothing ever dies, or grows, or multiplies."

Adam's expression is one of disbelief—disbelief at the way I am speaking to him.

There is a horrible twisting in my stomach, but I continue, "And how are we to multiply and replenish this earth? Can you tell me that?"

He opens his mouth, then shuts it. Finally, he says, "We would have to become mortal."

I want the twisting in my stomach to stop, but I must clarify to fully understand. "We would have to bleed?" I ask.

"Yes," he says. "Without blood, we remain immortal. We can live forever and never die."

I stay quiet for a moment as his words settle over me. "And until I bleed, children won't come forth, and if children don't come forth, we are not following all of Elohim's commandments."

Adam knows I am speaking true. But he turns away, his fists clenched.

My head pounds, but he must hear this—all of this. "You have been given as much knowledge as I have been given," I say in a quiet voice. "Just think on it. If you can answer my questions, then I'll stop asking them."

"You want to bleed?" His voice is low and quiet. "To do so, your body will have to change. Introducing blood into your body means that you'll also face death. This is what Elohim has taught." When Adam looks at me, his eyes are vivid green against his dark red complexion. "And the only way to do that is to eat of the tree of knowledge of good and evil. Is the price worth it just to know all the answers to your questions?"

My heart thunders in my ears. "I don't know," I say. "I don't want to die, and I don't want to leave the garden."

Adam's face returns to an almost-normal color. "Then why won't you ask your questions to Elohim?"

I swallow against my tight throat. "What if he thinks I'm not grateful for the blessings we've already been given?"

Adam exhales, and he steps forward. The calm is back in his expression. "I will ask him for you."

I nod. It's the only solution I can think of. Adam's hand grasps mine, and I let him slide his fingers between mine.

"Let's go see the tree," I whisper. "Let's make sure nothing has been changed or altered—to know that we are truly alone in the garden."

"Eve, I don't want us to visit the tree anymore." Adam's gaze finds mine. "And I don't want you going alone to visit the tree." His breathing slows. "Not ever again."

I stay very still. "Why?"

"It has been forbidden."

"To eat of the fruit," I say. "It has not been forbidden to visit the tree or to see it from afar." I release his hand. "There might be something changed or something that lets us know if our worries are justified." The brown specks in Adam's green eyes darken. His lips are drawn tight.

25

His hand falls to his side, and he clenches it. "The risk is not worth it. I forbid you to visit the tree, Eve."

"You are forbidding me?" I stare at him until he looks away. His tight jaw tells me he does not like what he is saying, but it also tells me he's more determined than ever.

Before I can think better of it, I say, "You are not Elohim."

His eyes narrow, and I regret my words. But he knows that I must say what I think.

"I am your husband," he says in a slow voice.

My eyes burn, and I'm hot inside; I don't know what's wrong with me. I say the first thing I think of. "And I am your wife."

His eyes widen for an instant. He reaches for my hand, but I don't want him to touch me. I want to visit the tree, even if just from afar, to see if there has been any change. I want to know how long we'll be in the garden. I want to know if Adam and I will be the only people here forever. I want to know how we are supposed to keep two commandments that are completely opposite.

I step back, away from Adam's reach.

"Eve . . ." Adam says, his tone imploring.

I shake my head because I don't trust my voice. And then I turn and run.

 6

And God called the dry land Earth; and the gathering
together of the waters called he Seas.

—Genesis 1:10

A dam calls after me, but his cries grow distant as I
run along the stream, the sound of trickling water
masking his voice.

As I run, the heat in my body fades, and air rushes
through my chest, making me focus on how fast I'm running
and where I'm going.

When I slow, it's not because my legs are tired, but
because I realize where I've run to.

In the morning light, the tree of knowledge is more
beautiful than I've seen it before. The green leaves, dappled
in shimmering sun rays, are moving gently in the barest
touch of wind. I walk past the area where Adam and I sat two
days before. I don't stop when I am only a few paces from the
tree.

I don't pause when I walk beneath the canopy of
branches. I don't even need to stoop when I walk under the
tree since the branches arch high and wide. I stop only when

I place my hand on the trunk. The trunk is cool and gritty like a stone, yet smoother.

I look at the ground and inspect the grass and dirt, searching for any sign of disturbance.

As I move my hand down the trunk, the leaves above me rattle in a whisper as if they are speaking to me. I gaze up at the fruit. Its pale orange color stretches tight, perfect in its ripeness. Wondering if this is the last time I'll be this close to the tree because of Adam's request, I reach toward the fruit. Touching it won't bring me harm; it's only eating it that will. At least I think so. My hand hesitates just before I make contact.

Pulling my hand away, I again stare at the fruit. Then I reach out again, more slowly, and let my hand hover near the fruit. A slight fuzz covers the outside, and I can almost imagine what it feels like. But I don't touch it. Part of Elohim's admonition was to not even touch it.

I wait for something to change, something to happen, but nothing does. There is no warning voice from Elohim, no echo from the heavens.

With my hand close to the fruit, I imagine the weight of it solid in my hand. I think of what would happen if I plucked the fruit from the branch. I wonder if the fruit feels warm or cold or if it's the same temperature as my palm.

I lower my hand and wait, listening for any sounds, but I hear nothing unusual. I look at the branches and leaves; they are not broken or torn. Then I look along the ground, examining the tufted grass. I can't find anything that has been disturbed. Perhaps no one was here after all.

I leave the canopy of branches and sit at the edge of the shade to watch the tree. It doesn't seem any different than any other tree, although its fruit is lighter, and it seems isolated from the other trees.

One thing I notice is that there is no fallen fruit on the ground near the tree. I try to remember if there has been fallen fruit there before. Does no fruit on the ground mean anything?

I pull my legs up to my chest and sigh. I glance toward the hill that I came down. I imagine Adam running down the hill, looking for me, his face flushed with exertion. But there is no one on the hillside, and I haven't heard Adam's voice since I crossed the river.

I lie back in the grass and study the fruit hanging from the branches, wondering if it ever overripens and falls off. If I were able to come here more often, I could keep track of the different stages of growth. I would know if something is different today.

Closing my eyes, I decide I will rest for a short time. Then perhaps I'll return to Adam.

I fall asleep and dream of the tree, but this time I see the tree up close and not from a distance. I can smell the fruit, and I notice that it smells different from any fruit or flower in the garden. Its richness is hard to describe, but it's not difficult to imagine its taste.

Even in my dream, I realize my thoughts are growing dangerous. Adam is right. I shouldn't even be close to the tree. But I have no intention of tasting the fruit and dying. I need to stay away from it. I need to stop thinking about it. I need to ask Elohim my questions—about how we are supposed to multiply and replenish the earth without the issue of blood.

A shadow falls over me, and I struggle to open my eyes, but I am still dreaming. My limbs feel heavy, and I can't move. The shadow grows darker and cooler until I think it's an actual being.

"Eve," it whispers.

My mouth opens into a silent gasp.

"Eve." It touches my shoulder and shakes my arm.

Finally my eyes open.

Adam is staring down at me.

"It's you," I say.

"Who else would it be?" he asks, but there is a question in his gaze. "What are you doing here? I thought . . ." He doesn't finish

"I was just resting," I say. I don't tell him about my dream.

The relief in his gaze is evident, but there is something more, something deeper in the way that he is looking at me. He kneels next to me. "Please don't run from me again."

It's not like his command before. It's a plea.

"I'm sorry." I sit up and wrap my arms around his neck, and he holds me tight.

He is the opposite of the shadow that formed in my dream. Adam is warm and solid and bright. I bury my face against his neck and breathe in his scent of earth and sweat.

"Eve," he whispers into my hair. "Don't come here by yourself again. If anything happened to you, I would be devastated, not just a lone man."

I draw away and slide my hands to his shoulders. "I'll always be with you, Adam."

He nods, then pulls me into another tight embrace. I am sorry for running from him, and I'm grateful he has come for me. We walk back up the hill together.

And I look back at the tree only once.

⁕

I have made ten more scratches in the stone wall when Adam tells me that we'll do some tending near the south borders. We have not been there for half a moon cycle.

I smile, and Adam grasps my hand. "We must stay together, though," he says.

"Of course." I don't want to sound too eager, but we have not walked that far from our dwelling for quite a while.

Since I ran from Adam, I have not let myself think of the tree of knowledge or the borders. Even though I have dreamed each night about the tree of knowledge and the shadow that seems to dwell there, I have become quite good at forgetting about the tree during the day.

I have kept my questions silent as well.

Adam and I head south, far from the tree of knowledge. The southern portion of the garden is where the land is relatively flat. The morning air is cooler today, and clouds hang heavy in the sky, but my heart is light. Adam's hand is warm and strong, and through his grip I can feel his concern. Since the day I fled from him, he has been more attentive, watching over me continually but also letting me do things in my own way.

Once we reach the southern part, the sky has changed to brilliant blue, and the green of the trees shimmers in the sun. It's hard to believe we were ever worried about a shadow. We stop for a few moments to watch a lion sunning himself.

"He loves the garden," I say.

Adam squeezes my hand. "So do I."

I look up at Adam. His green eyes are flecked in gold today. I brush back the dark hair that falls over his forehead. "Do you think the lion gets too hot with all that fur?"

Adam laughs and pulls me against him. He kisses my forehead, then says, "I was wondering when the questions would start again."

I smile and lean into him. His bronze skin is warm, and I think again of the lion sunning himself. Adam reminds me of that lion. "Well?" I press.

He speaks above me, his deep voice rumbling. "I think when the lion gets too hot, he finds a patch of shade."

"Thank you," I say.

He pulls away. "For what?"

"For always answering my questions."

A smile plays upon his lips. "Do I answer them all?"

"Or for at least trying to answer them."

He laughs at the clarification. His hand is in mine again, and we continue past the lion.

When we emerge onto a wide field characteristic of the southern portion of the garden, I slow. Adam stops next to me.

The trees at the far end of the field have low-hanging branches, heavy with fruit. "Why haven't the animals eaten of all this fruit?" I ask. I have never seen so much fruit going unused on a tree.

But that is not the only thing that looks out of the ordinary in this field. The grass is not as green as I remember. In fact, it's nearly the color of the soil.

Adam stoops and tugs a few pieces of grass, which come up by the root.

"Has there not been enough mist?" I ask.

"I don't know," Adam says and looks toward the sky. The brilliant blue has darkened, and clouds are moving in. He drops the clump of grass and surveys the field. Brown color has crept in among the green as far as the grass spreads.

"Maybe the mist has affected the trees as well," I say.

"Let's try the fruit," Adam says in a quiet voice. He releases my hand as if he can focus on only one thing. I follow him across the field, my feet stepping on the new roughness of the grass.

We stop at the first tree we get to. The fruit looks healthy enough. Its deep red color contrasts with the green leaves and rich brown of the tree's branches. Adam plucks a fruit that is pale red in color. He takes a bite and chews, then shakes his head. "The fruit's sweet. I don't know why the animals are not eating it."

I reach for the fruit in Adam's hand and take my own bite. Juice runs down my chin, and I wipe the fluid away. After another bite, I realize how quiet it has been since we came to the field.

Slowly, I turn around, scanning the trees, the flat meadow that stretches to the north, and the ankle-high grass. When we walked through the field, I hadn't noticed it, but now I realize that no grasshoppers had jumped out of our way. No butterflies had flown to and fro.

And there are no bees. That's when I realize that the flowers have changed from lavender to light brown. Many of them are drooping while the rest have given up and turned themselves over to the soil.

The sky overhead darkens slightly, and I look up at the gathering clouds, then over to Adam, who has started plucking the excess fruit.

Then I realize the most disturbing thing of all. "Where are the birds?"

His hand stops midmotion. He looks up into the tree he is picking from, then out toward the field, as if seeing the field for what it really looks like for the first time. "The flowers are wilted," he says in a quiet voice.

I nod and move toward him, suddenly not wanting any space between us. My stomach feels strange, as if I've eaten too much of the same kind of herb. Adam puts an arm around my shoulders. We both listen for several moments, but there is nothing to hear. And that's exactly what's wrong.

Adam's face is pulled into a tight frown as he looks down at me. I know he is feeling as I am. Something has happened in this part of the garden that not even he can explain.

He guides me through the trees as he examines each one, looking for evidence of fruit pecked by birds or other animals. Soon, I'm doing the same. I allow only a short distance to fall between us, reluctant to be apart.

Maybe the impending mist has driven away the birds and the insects. But when Adam stops and turns to face me, I know that the answer is not so simple.

"Someone's been here," he says, his voice low.

"What?" I ask, not sure I understand him, not wanting to think about what he's suggesting. "How could someone be *here?*"

He motions toward the fields. "Someone has scared the animals away, down to the crickets in the grass."

"How can someone besides Elohim cause the grass to turn brown?"

"I don't know," Adams says, his mouth going into a tight line. He stares past me to the evidence of rot.

"Perhaps all this is because of the coming mist." I know as soon as I speak that I'm wrong. "Would Elohim send another person to the garden without telling us?"

His gaze meets mine, but he is not looking at me; it's more as if he's looking through me, feeling as confused as I am.

"Adam?" I say.

He walks from beneath the trees into the open space. "Hello?" he shouts.

I scurry to join him. Suddenly, I don't want to be in the shade of the trees anymore. I want to be out in the open air, beneath the sun. Except the sun is concealed by heavy clouds now, and the field seems to match the dull-colored sky. My arms prickle as Adam calls out again, "Hello? Who's here?"

"Adam, there's no one here," I say, but my heart is pounding with curiosity. "Wouldn't Elohim have told us? Wouldn't we know? He, or she, must have been created by Elohim . . ."

But Adam isn't listening. He starts running along the tree line that parallels the borders, calling out from time to time.

I run after him. He seems to have forgotten me, he is so determined to discover someone else in our garden.

Finally, he stops, breathing heavily. He crouches low to the ground as if he's examining something in the grass.

In a moment I've caught up to him, wondering what's

captured his attention. My step slows when I see the long, dark shape. A snake. The snake is larger than any I've ever seen. It's nearly as long as Adam, and its shiny scales are a deep black, unlike the scales of the dark green snakes that populate the garden.

I crouch next to Adam, fascinated. Where has this creature come from? Strangely, it's not moving, but it's also not coiled as snakes usually are when sleeping. In fact, its body is twisted at sharp angles, something foreign to a snake, which naturally curves.

"Is it sleeping?" I whisper.

Adam shakes his head and reaches a hand out. He releases a breath of air as he touches the scales.

The snake still doesn't move. Adam's fingers come away with a dark red stain on them. That's when I notice there is also red coloring the grass. How does a black snake make the grass red?

"It's not sleeping," Adam whispers, his hands hovering over it, as if he doesn't know whether to touch it again.

"Then why isn't it moving?" I ask. I reach my own hand forward and lightly touch the scales. I haven't touched too many snakes, since I like to spend time with other animals, but this snake doesn't feel right.

Suddenly, I feel as if someone else is with us. I withdraw my hand sharply and look around. Adam notices my movement.

"What is it?" he asks.

The sky darkens as if to answer. "I . . . I feel as though someone is watching us."

Adam stands and walks a few paces away, scanning. When he returns to my side, his eyes are more brown than green, darkening with the sky.

"Do you think Elohim is watching us?" I ask.

Adam starts to shake his head, then stops. I can see that he too is unsure. He crouches next to me again, his gaze

35

drawn toward the unmoving snake. He still has the red stain on his fingers.

"Something crushed it," Adam says, the disbelief in his voice echoing the disbelief in my mind.

"In the garden?" *Had a few deer raced through the meadow? Or had a lion became too playful?* I don't make any of these suggestions as we stare down at the snake. This has never happened in the garden. The grasses have never turned brown either, and the animals have never abandoned a field.

I breathe out, trying to lessen the tightening of my chest. I don't know what to think. The garden is changing around us.

"Are you sure it's not just asleep?" I ask, although I don't see how it could be sleeping.

"Its blood of life has spilled," Adam says, turning over his hands, showing the red stain on his fingers.

Blood? "Are you sure?"

"It must be," he says just above a whisper.

Although neither of us has seen blood before, we know that our bodies don't have it. The animals in the garden don't possess it either. With blood, we can die. And now, this creature, this snake, has blood.

This means that something has just died in our garden, a place where nothing has ever died. Or perhaps it died before coming to the garden, but that would mean someone brought it here.

It seems Adam is thinking as I am. He straightens, his eyes trained toward the southern wall. "I have never seen such a snake. It must have come from the wilderness."

I shiver and glance around, as if expecting whoever brought the snake to reappear. The wind picks up, and Adam crouches to wipe his hands on the brown grass. Then he stands up and grabs my hand. He pulls me to my feet, and I burrow my head against his chest. I cling to him as the first mist drops fall.

"What should we do?" I say. I don't like looking at the broken snake, but it's difficult to not look.

"We'll take it to the river and release it into the water, where the current will carry it outside the garden," he says, "back to the wilderness."

"It's so large," I say, wondering if we can carry it.

Adam releases me and slides his hands beneath the limp form and lifts it from the grass.

"Do you need help?" I ask, hoping he won't. I have now touched a dead thing, and I don't want to do it again.

"I'll let you know if I do," he says with a grimace. "Come on."

As Adam carries the snake, its blood of life smears on Adam's hands and arms, and I look away from the sight.

We walk toward the river that extends beyond the borders. The drizzle is growing denser, and a mist is forming. My heart is heavy as I think of the death of the snake. What killed it?

First, the brown grass, then the heavy fruit, and now this.

I see the tension in Adam's shoulders as he walks a little ahead of me, cradling the snake as if it's fragile. We head east until we reach the river. The sun starts to break through the clouds, and I think that things aren't as bad as they seem. With the sun out, the garden looks beautiful again. But I can't forget the rot that we've left behind.

We walk beneath the overhanging trees, and the sun is blocked again. It's cool in the shade, and I remember Adam's comment about the lion finding his own shade. The lightheartedness I felt when we spoke of the lion is no longer.

Adam and I kneel on the riverbank, and he stares at the dead snake in his hands for several moments, as if he can't believe what he is holding.

I can't believe it either.

I touch the scales as if to say good-bye to a creature I

37

never knew. I don't know what will happen to its body once we release it into the river.

Slowly, Adam lowers his arms and immerses the black body into the moving water. He releases the snake, and it hovers at the surface for a short moment, then sinks below the green-blue water.

Adam whispers some words that I don't hear. Then he turns his hands over, looking at the blood stains on them. I want to reach out and rub it off, but I am repelled at the same time. After a moment of watching the spot where the snake disappeared, Adam plunges his hands in the water. When he pulls them out, there is no trace of blood on them.

But I won't forget the blood. I have seen death now.

7

And God said, Let the earth bring forth grass, the herb yielding seed, and the fruit tree yielding fruit after his kind.
—Genesis 1:11

Adam couldn't stop thinking about the snake and the fresh liquid on his hands. The snake had been long and heavy, its weight solid in his arms. He and Eve stood on the bank for a while, staring at the river together.

Finally, he knew it was time to go. They needed to get back to the borders . . . to see what they could do for the trees.

Adam grimaced and wrapped Eve's smaller hand in his. She was quiet now, but he knew her thoughts were moving rapidly as well.

"We must return to the laden trees," he said. Eve only nodded. "Perhaps the birds and insects have returned since we removed the snake."

They left the river and headed toward the south borders again. The mist had lightened, and by the time they emerged from the protective canopy of trees, the mist was barely noticeable. The sun pierced through the clouds, quickly drying the wet grass and leaves.

It didn't take long for Eve to regain her voice. It sent a jolt of relief through him when she said, "Do you think that snake had a spirit?"

That question he could answer. "Yes. All animals have spirits."

"But that snake could die—if it had blood."

"Having blood doesn't change the nature of our spirits—just the nature of our bodies." Adam was already looking forward to the next seventh day, when he could ask Elohim about the snake.

It was easy enough to keep away from the tree of knowledge, but now finding the dead snake presented new worries. What if it had something to do with the shadow he saw beneath the tree of knowledge? And what was wrong with the southern trees? Until Adam could ask Elohim his questions, he'd have to stay with Eve every moment to protect her.

Eve interrupted his thoughts. "Where does the spirit of the snake go? Is it still in the garden?"

"It will return to Heaven."

"To be with Elohim?" Eve asked.

Inwardly, he groaned. He knew what was coming next.

"So if *we* died, our spirits would dwell in Heaven?" she asked.

"Yes, I think so." He dulled his answer, not wanting to grow Eve's interest in the tree of knowledge.

"Then, although our bodies might die, our spirits can still live forever?" she said.

Adam stopped walking. They'd reached the field where he'd found the snake. He met his wife's gaze. "If we died, then this life would be over—forever. We'd no longer have our bodies—the ones that Elohim so carefully created."

Eve folded her arms and shivered. "I know, but I'm confused over what happened to the snake."

He wrapped his arms around her. "So am I," he

whispered against her hair. He closed his eyes for a moment, listening for the return of the birds and insects. But there was nothing.

When Eve pulled away, she turned her face upward. "Let's pick some fruit to help relieve the trees of their heavy burden. Then maybe the birds will return."

They spent most of the afternoon picking fruit from the trees and placing it into small piles along the edge of the field. Adam never let Eve out of his sight. If something could harm a large snake, something could harm her. His wife was strong but not strong enough to have lifted the snake if she'd been by herself. She helped him tend the herbs, but she wasn't able to work as much as he was. She needed to be protected. She needed him.

As the sun descended in the western sky, Adam crossed to Eve. She had rearranged the piles of fruit so that they were laid out in neat rows. "Let's return to our dwelling. We can come back tomorrow and finish harvesting."

Eve straightened and looked toward the setting sun as if trying to make a decision. "All right."

Adam was grateful she didn't offer any argument. He hurried as much as Eve had the strength for, and as they traveled back to their dwelling, he kept one eye on the sinking sun. The night had never bothered him, even if the moon was only a sliver of light, but every shadow they passed now made Adam wary in a way he hadn't been before.

As soon as they reached the dwelling, Adam said, "Wait here. I want to enter the alcove first." The sun had set now, the sky only a purple remnant. There was just enough light to see to the back of the alcove where Eve had draped mats of leaves.

Nothing looked out of place. The bed of soft leaves didn't appear to have been disturbed. Regardless, Adam ran his hand along the entire area, feeling for anything that might be different. He walked to the back of the alcove and pushed against the mats until he felt the solid stone wall behind them.

"It looks undisturbed," he said, stepping out of the alcove. But she wasn't where he'd left her. "Eve?" he called out.

"Over here," her voice came back.

Adam released his breath that he'd been holding. She was leaning against a boulder that he often sat on. He tried not to reveal how nervous he'd just been, but he couldn't help but walk over to her. "Come inside."

She slipped her hand in his and followed him into the alcove.

They lay down, and he pulled her into his arms, not willing to let go even when he fell asleep. Eve nestled against him with a sigh. Adam looked forward to the next day's light more than ever now. Perhaps then they could find answers about the snake. But in the dark, he wanted nothing more than to have his wife safe, close to him.

A bird's call woke Adam. First he noticed that the dark had barely lightened, that it must still be very early. During the night, Eve had moved away from him, but she was sleeping peacefully . . . and that was all he cared about.

He sat up, then saw that Eve had something draped over her—something that at first looked like a mat of some sort. But it was an unfamiliar mat. Heart pounding, he reached over to touch it. It wasn't made of grasses or leaves but of something smooth and supple.

Adam had never seen it before and doubted that Eve could have procured it without him knowing about it. He looked around the alcove, his body tense as he searched for anything else amiss. Then he gazed at the alcove entrance. All seemed quiet without.

He leaned over his wife and sniffed the covering. Its smell was sharp, and he drew back, trying to decide what it smelled of. *Where did it come from?*

Then he noticed there were little pieces poking up from the mat—like grass, but finer. He recoiled when he realized it was animal fur. The mat covering Eve was not made of grass or leaves but of an animal—a dead animal.

He lifted it off her, the touch of death making his stomach wrench. Carrying it out of the alcove, he draped it on the boulder. He wanted to throw it into the trees and never look at it again, but it had once been a live animal, and as much as he didn't want to touch it, or smell it, he couldn't completely discard it.

Adam perched on the boulder, above the skin covering. How had Eve come to have the covering? As he waited for his wife to awaken, he watched the sun rise and the sky's colors change from violet to azure, but his gaze kept moving to the animal skin. What did she know about it? How had it come to be in their alcove?

He thought about the questions Eve had about multiplying and replenishing the earth. He didn't have a satisfactory answer, but he hoped that Elohim would provide them with one on his next visit. Eve was right, he realized, that the commandments seemed to contradict each other. Their bodies would continue in an eternal state, with no issuance of blood or death, if they stayed away from the tree of knowledge. But their bodies also wouldn't be able to multiply if there was no issue of blood.

When there was sufficient light, he checked out the dwelling, not straying too far from the alcove should Eve awake and wonder where he was. He wanted to question her first thing. He walked to the pond where he and Eve refreshed themselves in the mornings. The fish swam around, flashing their silver backs as they arced toward the water's surface.

The birds were just beginning their chatter as Adam plucked a couple of pieces of fruit from a nearby tree. The birds had amply pecked much of the fruit in this area. He hurried back to the alcove, not wanting to be away too long. Checking inside, he found Eve still asleep. He settled beside her and ate one of the fruits while he watched her sleep.

His throat tightened as he remembered coming across the dead snake. Where had the snake come from? Were there other animals in the garden that could die? He shook his head, knowing that Elohim had created all things in the same state as he and Eve. What did the appearance of the snake mean? Where had it died? And who had killed it?

Adam let out a frustrated sigh before he could stop himself. The sound caused Eve to stir. She blinked at him, a slight smile on her face. "What are you doing?"

Of course the first thing she said in the morning had to be a question. He reached over to smooth her tangled hair from her face. "Come with me. I have to show you something." Eve followed him outside, where he pointed to the skin covering. "Where did you get this?"

Eve crossed to the pale-colored mat. She bent over it, then gasped. "It smells. And it . . . looks like . . ." She turned and stared at him.

"It was draped over you this morning," Adam said. "Where is it from?"

"I don't know," Eve said, taking a step away from the mat. "Did you find it somewhere?"

He met her confused gaze, feeling as if his heart had just leapt from his chest. "You didn't bring it into the alcove and drape it over yourself?"

"No," Eve said, her voice a whisper.

"Then who did? Because I found it on you," Adam said,

barely able to choke out the words. The sun had crested the horizon, and suddenly it felt too hot on his skin.

Someone had been in their alcove. Someone, or something, had touched his wife. He walked to where Eve stood, and with her, he examined the mat carefully, his stomach twisting with each moment.

Again, he knew it was from an animal. A deer? The pale color was similar to the color of the deer in the garden, although it was lighter and not quite the same color. Did that mean this deer came from outside the garden, from someplace in the wilderness? Did whoever brought it come from outside as well?

Eve touched his arm. "It looks like—" Her voice broke off, as if she couldn't say what she thought aloud.

"Perhaps cattle or deer." He stared down at the mat stretched across the boulder. "It was made from an animal's skin."

Her grip tightened on his arm. "How can that be so? That would mean . . . something else has died."

Adam nodded. He hated looking at the thing, hated that it represented death—and a torturous death, no doubt. He turned to face Eve. Her normally light blue-green eyes were gray and troubled. "Another beast has been killed," she said. "What does this mean?"

"I don't know," he said in a toneless voice. He quickly dismissed the possibility of Elohim visiting in the night and placing a covering over Eve. It had to be someone else. He crossed to Eve and took her hands in his, looking her in the eye. "Do you remember anyone coming into the alcove last night?"

She shook her head, but she didn't meet his gaze.

"What is it?" he asked. "Please tell me."

She hesitated, which alarmed him even more. When had she ever kept her thoughts to herself?

"I had a dream," she said slowly. "Or at least I thought it

was a dream." She looked down at their intertwined hands. "I've been having the same dream for many days."

Adam waited. Her hands were moist in his, and her breathing increased in tempo.

"In my dream is always a shadow, although I'm not sure of what. I don't know if it's a person or some sort of animal."

"What does it do in your dream?" he asked.

"It's just there, and if I wake up right after, it's as if the shadow is still near me, although I can't see it anymore."

"But how can a *shadow* kill animals?" Adam said. Eve didn't answer him; he was not surprised. He didn't have the answer either.

8

And God made two great lights; the greater light to rule the day, and the lesser light to rule the night.

—Genesis 1:16

My hands tremble as I smooth them over the mat made of animal skin. I have never seen anything like it, nor could I have imagined it. The bristles of hair that remain on the skin are stiff and prickly. The smell has faded a little beneath the sun. Today, Adam has told me we are not leaving the dwelling. Tomorrow is the seventh day, and he hopes that Elohim will visit.

I have many questions to ask Elohim.

My heart cries out for the poor beast that met its death. I don't like to consider how the animal died, what methods could have possibly been used to remove its entire skin, or who could perform such an act.

It's unfathomable, yet it happened. It's real. The evidence is before me.

Adam is within sight, as he always is now, watching me from time to time. I know that he is thinking about all my questions, and I know that he's added his own to them now. In the past two days, we've come across two instances of

47

death—in our Garden of Eden, where there is no death. The impossible has happened.

It troubles me, but I believe that Elohim wouldn't put us in direct danger. We are his creations, and he knows all things. He must know what is happening in our beloved garden. He *must*.

Then I wonder if Elohim knows about my dreams . . . and of the shadow that haunts them. When Adam calls my name, I turn slowly in the direction of his voice as if in a daze. I feel weary today, and I think it's because of the wondering. Is the shadow in my dream a real, tangible thing? How can a shadow have the form and agility to bring death to the garden?

I leave the skin mat behind on the boulder and walk over to where Adam's looking out over the pond. When I reach him, he points to the far side of the pond that cuts into a grouping of bushes and vines.

"Do you see the vines, how they've been cleared?"

I stare across the water, trying to remember how that area looked the morning before, when I last bathed in the pond. I probably wouldn't have noticed the vines if Adam hadn't drawn my attention to them. But now I realize the blooms on the vines have been crushed, and some of the blooms have fallen to the bank of the pond.

"Wait here," Adam says. He wades into the water, the quickest way to reach the other side. I step into the water to follow.

"Has someone been living here?" I ask as we reach the opposite bank.

Adam helps me out of the water, locking his hand over mine. Up close, there is more visible disturbance to the vines. It's almost as if someone, or something, had trampled a pathway through the foliage.

Adam looks at me, and I know what he wants to tell me.

"No," I say before he can speak. "I'm coming with you."

His jaw tenses, but he faces forward, and we walk through the crushed opening separating the tangled vines—he in front, I behind.

The ground starts to slope upward, and we follow the trail that seems to have been freshly made. I look behind me frequently, wondering who or what we are about to encounter.

When Adam stops, I move to his side to see what he sees. The grass and plants have been tramped down to create a circular space. The flattened space is not large enough for someone—at least someone our size—to sleep on. But it still appears that someone has been sitting here—and not just once.

Adam releases my hand and crouches down to inspect the ground. He runs his fingers along the collection of leaves and grass, turning over leaves as he goes. I don't know what we are looking for, but anything different, we should notice—like a mat made of a dead animal.

As he searches, I look at the surrounding bushes. I try to imagine what might have been here and what might have been strong enough to kill animals. I listen for any unusual sounds but hear nothing except a few birds in the trees above and the sound of Adam brushing through the bed of leaves.

Finally, he stands. The expression on his face tells me that he's very worried, and I grab his hand. "We'll stay together," I say.

When the darkness of night comes, Adam refuses to lie by my side or let sleep claim him. He keeps watch at the opening of the alcove. At first I sit by him for a long time, but when the moon is high in the sky, my eyes grow heavy.

I fall asleep watching Adam's back, the shadows of the trees turning into shadows in my dream.

୧୨୧

Adam moved toward the boulder draped in the skin mat. He thought he'd seen a shadow—the form of a man or a woman just beyond the border of the dwelling. One moment it was there. Then it was gone.

As reluctant as he was to leave Eve alone in the alcove, he had to see what passed between the trees beyond the boulder. Adam crouched behind the boulder, waiting and listening. Something rustled. A leaf? A branch? And then he saw it—not *it* but *him.*

It was not a shadow but a human. In the moonlight, it was clear he was a man, tall and lean. Adam tensed, disbelief and confusion colliding in his mind. How could there be another person in the garden? Had Elohim created him too? Adam exhaled, and the barest noise caused the man to turn. For the briefest of moments, their eyes locked.

Then the man was gone, disappearing into the trees without a sound.

Staring at the space that the intruder had just occupied, both curiosity and dread coursed through Adam. Should he follow the man? He had to, he decided.

Adam raced around the boulder in the direction where the stranger had stood, but there wasn't even a whisper of the man's passing. Adam crouched to the ground, hoping to hear the sound of footsteps more clearly. For there had to be the sound of footsteps, even if they were leading away.

The moon was a nearly full sphere tonight, and the stranger shouldn't have been able to disappear so completely, so swiftly. But he was faster than any animal Adam had encountered.

Who is he? And what does he want?

Adam picked his way through the underbrush as quietly as possible. Had the stranger gone toward the pond? Had he fled to another part of the garden? Adam slowly turned around, looking for any evidence of the man's whereabouts—a moving branch, a bird awakening with a start, a critter scurrying to get out of the way.

But there was nothing.

Had the man been watching he and Eve when they discovered the lair on the other side of the pond? Or would the stranger return there now, believing he was concealed from discovery?

Adam cast a look toward the alcove where Eve slept. He could just see the opening from his position. Had that been where the stranger was going until he saw Adam?

Heart pounding, Adam took a deep breath. He had to find the man—tonight.

Adam decided to check the perimeter of the pond, then return to the alcove. He didn't want to be gone too long, but he had to find out more about the intruder. Until he heard further instruction from Elohim, Adam would do everything he could to get answers from the man.

Adam made his way toward the pond, keeping beneath the trees when possible, creating more shadow for himself. He hoped to come upon the strange man unexpectedly. At one point, he stooped and picked up a rock that was long and narrow. Normally, the rock was something he'd use as a tool to turn soil, but tonight it gave him a way to defend himself. Adam didn't know what to expect from someone who had killed animals.

Creeping around the pond, Adam stopped every few paces to listen. The stream running into the pond masked a lot of sound that he might otherwise hear. He looked frequently toward the south, where Eve slept, as if he could hear her if she awakened.

He switched the rock he carried from one hand to the other. Its solid weight in his hand gave him some comfort.

Adam stopped on the north side of the pond. It was impossible to get to the newly discovered habitation without getting into the water. The stranger had picked a well-concealed place to keep his lair. Adam was about to step into the water when he thought he heard a voice—a whisper. It was incomprehensible, and he questioned whether he'd heard anything at all above the sound of the trickling stream running into the pond. Still, he waited.

Above the noise of the water, it was hard to tell where the sound came from. Should he go back to the alcove? Or should he continue through the pond? Adam slipped into the water, determined to see if the lair was empty. Then he'd return to the alcove. Just as he reached the other bank, his foot caught on something, and he splashed forward into the water. He pulled himself out of the water and onto the bank. He didn't remember large rocks being at the bottom of the pond before.

He waited on the bank for a moment, listening to see if his disturbance had attracted the man in his direction. But he heard nothing out of the ordinary.

Soaking wet, he climbed to his feet and walked through the opening in the vines. As he had the day before, he followed a trail of sorts until he reached the tramped area. Everything looked untouched in the moonlight. There was no one there, and he hadn't heard any sounds since he waded through the pond.

It was time to get back to Eve.

As Adam turned, something moved in front of him, but he didn't have time to comprehend what or who it was before a hand shot out toward his face. Adam stumbled back, trying to avoid the thrust by raising the rock he carried in front of him, swinging it wide, but he hit nothing.

And God said, Let the waters bring forth abundantly the moving creature that hath life, and fowl that may fly above the earth in the open firmament of heaven.

—Genesis 1:20

When I awake, it's still dark. I have not dreamed at all. Adam is no longer at his position, and I turn my head to the other side, expecting him to be asleep beside me. The space is empty.

Despite the sudden thudding in my heart, I get up to look outside. Perhaps he is sitting on the boulder, watching the landscape. It would give him a better view of our dwelling and the outer edge of the pond.

But there is no Adam silhouetted in the moonlight on the boulder.

A breeze touches my skin and, although the breeze is not cold, I shiver. I wonder about Adam. Where has he gone? I call out before I can think better of it. "Adam?"

There is no answer, and I wonder what might have happened to him. He's never left the dwelling during the night, even before we were wary of the two deaths in the garden. Of course I know that tonight is different: tonight we are wary, and we don't know what to expect. Not even what to look for.

I back up until I am against the edge of the alcove, halfway in and halfway out. The stone of the alcove feels cool against my skin and sends another shiver through my body. That's when I notice it: the mat of animal skin is no longer covering the boulder. Did Adam take the mat with him?

Did someone take Adam?

My breath stutters, and I can't think. Every sound seems louder, echoing in my mind—the rustling of leaves in a nearby tree, the distant chatter of some night creature, my own breathing, the pounding of my heart.

I have just called out into the unknown, and if Adam can't hear me, then maybe someone else can—someone I don't want to face alone. I move back into the alcove, believing—hoping—that it will offer me some protection should I need it.

I huddle on the sleeping mats, listening for any sound and waiting for Adam to return. Eyeing the hanging mats at the back of the alcove, I wonder if I should hide behind them, just in case. Then I realize that if Adam is caught, there is no place for me to truly hide. I will eventually be caught as well.

Still, I rise to my feet and creep to the back wall. I slip behind the hanging mats of leaves and feel grateful that they offer some seclusion. I only hope it will be enough. Closing my eyes, I lean against the wall, scratched with my marks, and listen as carefully as I can. I don't know if I'll hear much coming from outside the alcove, but I keep my eyes shut and listen.

I almost miss the shuffling sound because I am focusing on the stiffness in my legs and back. I hold my breath, trying to decide if the shuffling is Adam or some other creature. Maybe it's an animal or the shadow?

The sounds stops, and I slowly let out my breath. After a

moment, I decide that I may not have heard anything or that whatever made the sound is now gone. I move soundlessly until I have parted the hanging mat and have a view of the alcove.

Adam stands at the alcove opening, looking outside—certainly for me—and I am about to step between the hanging mats when I notice something. A mat of skin is wrapped around Adam's waist and hangs to his knees. Why would he wear that vile, dead thing—that which represents the death of an innocent creature?

I take a step forward then halt. Adam has turned his head toward the left, and in the moonlight that silhouettes his profile, I realize that the man standing at the front of the alcove is not Adam.

I move behind the hanging mats, hoping to not make any noise to draw the strange man's attention.

My heart is pounding wildly, and my breathing stalls in my chest. I can't inhale or exhale. Every part of my body is cold.

We are not alone in the garden after all.

The shadow I've dreamed about is *real*.

I mouth a silent prayer. *O Elohim, protect me from this living shadow. Bring Adam back to me safely.*

Does Elohim hear my prayer? I don't know. Adam and I usually pray at the altar on the seventh day.

The shuffling sound reaches me again, and I sense that the shadow is walking toward me. Every part of my body prickles in perspiration. It will be only seconds until I am discovered. I think about the man who is not Adam. The shadow is taller and leaner than my husband. The shadow's hair is long, past his shoulders, and as dark as the night. I did not see his eyes, but I imagine them as black as his hair. The shuffling stops, and I imagine I hear breathing. Do shadows breathe?

Will the shadow speak to me? Will he tell me what's

happened to Adam? I smell a collection of herbs, as if the shadow has been sleeping among the vines. Perhaps he has been sleeping, or at least hiding, where the trampled circle is.

Shuffling again—this time moving away. Can the shadow not detect my presence? Have I been all that quiet?

I let out my breath when all is silent, and I wait as long as I can bear it. Finally, I peer around the mat. There is no one in the alcove. I wait a little longer before leaving the hanging mats. My hands tremble as I wonder what happened to Adam.

I want to call for him, scream out for him, but I can't. I walk along the edge of the alcove until I near the opening. I dread looking outside, seeing the barren boulder, seeing no Adam. What if the shadow is waiting for me?

But I can't stay here, not with Adam gone, not with the shadow looking for me—for us. What does the shadow want? Why did he come?

I move to the front of the alcove, listening, moving slowly. When I see the boulder, I don't know if I'm relieved or disappointed that it's empty. The animal skin is again on it, seemingly untouched. I take a step, then another. I am now fully outside the alcove, but there is no sign of Adam.

Exhaling, I close my eyes, wondering in which direction he might have gone—or where the shadow might have taken him. I decide to start by the pond, reluctant as I am. Just as I open my eyes, decision made, the hairs on my arms stand up.

Someone is watching me.

"Eve," a voice whispers. The sound filters into my mind and body, and it's as though I feel its reverberations down to the bottom of my feet.

I don't turn around. I don't want to see the man that is not Adam. I want to cry out for my husband, but somehow I know he won't hear me.

"The mother of all living," the voice speaks in a low whisper that is perfectly audible.

"Who are you?" I'm surprised that I can speak at all.

Then he is in front of me. I stare at the man in the moonlight. He studies me, his mouth twisted into a half smile. His eyes are indeed black; even in the light of the moon, I can see their void. His face is more angular than Adam's, his cheekbones prominent, and his eyebrows thick and dark.

"I am your brother," he says.

My stomach jolts. *My brother?* That means Elohim is his father too. Where has this brother been? Does Adam know we have a brother? I ask none of these questions.

"How do you know my name?" I ask.

His face lifts into that crooked smile again. "I have kept my knowledge."

I blink rapidly. He has *knowledge*. Has he eaten of the forbidden fruit? I want to ask him about it, but his gaze is penetrating. Something shudders through me as if he touched me, although he has not. He takes a step forward, and I move back toward the alcove. I can see the length of his body now, and it is covered with something like an animal skin—yet his body doesn't seem to be solid.

He nods slightly, as if expecting my reaction to him.

"Where is Adam?" I ask.

He doesn't answer but steps closer. I want to ask him why his body is covered, if he is the one who placed the covering on me the other night, and if he killed the snake.

But I fail to ask any of this as he walks around me, circling. My stomach knots. This is a man who's killed animals. Even if he is my brother, I don't like him here, in my garden.

He stops close to me, not touching me, but it feels as if he is. I have never touched another person besides Adam. It's strange to be near this human. How many others are there like him? Do I have more brothers?

"Tell me where Adam is," I say. It's impossible to hide the tremble in my voice.

"He's not far," my brother says in a low voice, his breath brushing against the top of my head. I move away from him, and he chuckles.

I turn to face him. "How far?"

One of his eyebrows lifts, and his smile returns. "I see . . ."

I wait for him to finish what he is saying, but he only watches me with that amused look on his face. "*What* do you see?" I finally press.

He is moving around me again. "That you are curious with many questions . . . that you seek knowledge."

It's as if he's pressed a rock against my stomach and the air has been forced out. How can this brother of mine know my deepest desires? I never thought that when I finally met another person I would feel this way—both fascinated and repelled at the same time. I want my brother to leave, yet I want to learn everything he knows. He seems to know even more than Adam.

Before I can move again, his hand is touching my face. At least it seems he is touching me, but I don't feel his fingers as they move lightly along my cheek. It's as if his touch is merely a breeze and nothing substantial that I can grasp, so that if I were closing my eyes, I might think his touch was a dream—the shadow in my dreams. "I can help you find the knowledge you are seeking," he whispers.

I move my hand to his, to see what his skin feels like, but he pulls away quickly, and I touch nothing.

"Do you know what my name is?" he asks, standing at a distance again, breaking the haziness confounding my thoughts.

I shake my head and hold his black gaze, waiting for his answer.

"It's Lucifer."

I test the new name out. "Lucifer?" It twists, yet slides, off my tongue, like a whisper.

"Yes, Eve," he says, his mouth lifting into a smile. "And I've come to help you obtain what you most desire."

🔖 10

*And God created great whales, and every living creature
that moveth, which the waters brought forth abundantly, after
their kind, and every winged fowl after his kind.*

—Genesis 1:21

A dam opened his eyes, then winced as pain seized
him. The memory of being smashed in the face
returned, and he brought his hand to his face,
gingerly feeling the effects. He had never felt this sensation
before. It was unpleasant, he decided.

Then he remembered Eve. He didn't know where the
stranger had gone, but Adam needed to return to Eve. His
heart pounded as he stood. He blinked a few times, looking
around, checking for any lurking shadows. Then he pushed
through the vines and plunged into the pond. He half swam,
half ran through the water until he reached the other side.

He ran toward the alcove, realizing that he no longer
held the rock in his hand, but he didn't want to take the time
to find another one. He had to get to Eve. Adam passed the
last group of trees before the alcove and stopped.

Eve was standing in front of the alcove, looking at something he couldn't see.

"Eve!" he called out over his pounding heart.

She didn't turn as he ran to her but continued to look south.

Adam breathed out in relief: Eve appeared unharmed. But what was she looking at? And why didn't she respond? He grasped her arm when he reached her, and finally she turned.

"Was he here?" Adam asked.

Eve's eyes were wide. "Yes," she said, appraising him. "What happened to you?"

"I fell on the pond bank, and he knocked me to the ground." Adam took a breath. "Did he speak to you? Did he touch you?"

"He . . . he said he's our brother."

Adam stared at her. "Is he newly created?"

"He didn't say." She lifted her hand and brushed back the dripping hair from Adam's forehead. "Did he speak to *you*?"

"No," Adam said. "I don't think he wanted anything to do with me." Eve was looking away from him again. "What did he talk to you about?" he asked, trying to keep his voice even.

She took a few steps away from him, then turned. "He has *knowledge*, Adam. He said he could help me gain knowledge as well." Her eyes were bright in the moonlight. Adam felt as if he'd just fallen into the pond again.

"We don't even know who this man is," he said, taking a step forward.

Eve held her hands up. "He's our brother, and his name is Lucifer."

Adam grabbed her hands and held them fast. "He's killed animals. Did you ask him about that?"

"Not yet," she said.

He stared at her in disbelief. "You mean to speak to him again?"

She looked away. "There's so much I want to know," she whispered.

Adam released her hands with a sigh. He wrapped his arms around her, and she leaned against him. "We'll get your questions answered. I don't know that Lucifer is the one who should be teaching us. We'll inquire of Elohim on the seventh day."

Eve nodded, moving her head against his chest.

"Where did he go?" he asked in a quiet voice, even though he could probably guess the answer.

"South—where the garden is rotting."

Adam exhaled. "I think that should tell us something, Eve. If Lucifer can make the garden rot, what will he do to us?"

Eve didn't answer, but he hoped she was thinking about the answer to his question. He wished that he knew her thoughts and that he knew what to say to her so she'd understand the danger posed by Lucifer. Adam didn't fully understand the danger himself, but the fact that Lucifer spoke to her and that she tried to hide it worried him.

Adam doubted that the strange man would return again tonight, so he led Eve into the alcove. He wrapped his arms about her protectively and finally fell asleep.

The sun is high in the sky when I awaken. Adam isn't next to me, and for an instant, I wonder if he's returned. Then I remember the events of the night. And Lucifer.

In the light that filters in from the outside, it's hard to believe that Lucifer's real, that I truly have a brother, that there is another man in the Garden of Eden.

I rise to my feet, my body feeling tired, as if I haven't slept at all. I peer outside and see Adam not too far away. Before he notices me, I slip back inside and scratch another line on the stone wall.

I study the wall for a moment, running my finger along all of the scratches. I marvel at how the days are adding together. There are so many days where nothing has changed. The past several days have been different. And Adam doesn't like it.

Do I like the changes, though? Do I welcome them? Meeting Lucifer has made me think even more deeply and has added to my questions. I wonder if the changes are good. I wonder what Elohim will say about them.

I know what Adam thinks. Even though he spoke very little last night, I knew Adam's thoughts. And perhaps he is right: we should not converse with a man who brings rot to the southern portion of Eden. I don't know how Lucifer brings rot, or how he killed the snake and the animals from which the skin mats were created, but we'll never find out if we don't speak with him.

I leave the alcove and find Adam leaning against the rock. Of course he wouldn't go far, I realize—not after the appearance of Lucifer.

"How did you sleep?" Adam asks, watching me carefully.

My lack of sleep must show on my face. "Fair enough," I say. A silence forms between us, and I know that Adam has plenty to say to me, but he is waiting for some reason.

Adam hands over a piece of fruit that he must have plucked earlier. I accept it and bite into the yellow-orange flesh. It's tart, and I wrinkle my nose. "These are not my favorite," I say.

Adam nods. "It gets better with the next bite."

But why should I take a bite of something I don't like when there are so many other fruits that I do enjoy?

I toss the fruit away. He doesn't like the waste, yet he says nothing, and that makes me wonder anew.

"How long have you been awake?" I ask. His fatigue is plain, and perhaps his tiredness explains why he doesn't want to admonish me for throwing away a tart fruit.

"I'm not sure," he answers, and I sense he has slept little.

"I can stand watch if you want to sleep," I say, but he's already shaking his head.

He holds out his hand, waiting for me to take it. When I oblige, we walk toward the pond.

"I'll wait while you wash," he says. "Then we'll go to the altar."

"But it's not the seventh day." I look up at him—his eyes are reddened.

"We can't wait that long." He slows his step. "Why did our brother speak to you and not to me?"

I don't have an answer, but I don't think Adam expects me to know.

His other hand touches my face briefly. His touch is so unlike the whisper of Lucifer's touch. Adam's touch is solid and warm.

Does our brother not know that if he can explain things to Adam, we won't have cause to wonder about him any longer?

"Perhaps Lucifer thought I was more ready to listen," I say.

Adam narrows his eyes, but he is not upset in the way that I think he might be. "That's what I'm worried about," he says in a slow voice. "This brother of ours wanted to speak to you—alone."

My throat constricts. It seems to be true. If it is, what does that mean?

I don't know why Lucifer sought me out and avoided Adam. "Why wouldn't Lucifer want to talk to both of us?"

Adam blows out a breath of air and tightens his hold on

my hand. "I wish I knew, but I don't know anything about him. I wonder why he's in our garden."

Perhaps Lucifer knows that Adam is not willing to risk our existence in the garden to obtain knowledge. That is the difference between us, I think—a difference that I don't know if I like or if I'm willing act on.

I think about Lucifer's words, and they echo in my mind over and over: *I've come to help you obtain what you most desire.*

A man who brings rot to the garden has the ability to help me obtain knowledge? I wonder how he means to provide it. By answering my questions? That must be it, I decide. He says he has *kept* his knowledge, and now he intends to share that knowledge with me.

"He said I could ask him my questions," I say.

Adam's gaze hardens. "I don't want you talking to him."

"There is no harm in doing so," I say.

Adam stares at me with what I realize is fierce protectiveness. "Eve . . ."

"He is our brother, and Elohim created him," I say. "Certainly Elohim sent him to the garden."

Adam's eyes are still hardened. "Elohim has seen fit to instruct us only himself."

I run my hand up Adam's arm. "Don't you want to have more knowledge? Then you can answer all of my questions yourself."

His mouth curls slightly. "I don't want him in our garden," Adam says. "No matter how much knowledge he has, he's bringing rot to the trees and plants. We'll be satisfied with what we already have."

I lean into him and close my eyes. I can't argue with that. Elohim has created us and given us, not our brother, this garden to inhabit. But I don't know the full will of Elohim, for he has not told us.

I pull away from Adam. "Let's hurry to the altar."

When Lucifer left my side last night, I saw the intention in his eyes. He isn't planning to leave the garden.

 **II**

And God made the beast of the earth after his kind, and cattle after their kind, and every thing that creepeth upon the earth after his kind.

—Genesis 1:25

Adam placed both hands on the stone altar and stared down at it. The color of the altar had changed from pale to dark gray as the sun dipped below the western horizon. He'd been praying to Elohim all day, and still there was no answer. Adam wanted to cry out to Elohim and demand his attention, but he didn't want to be disobedient or demanding.

The clouds had come and gone, and now the sky was clear of cloud and mist. Adam felt as if the heavens were as empty as they looked. Discouragement flowed through him. If there was ever a time when Adam was desperate for Elohim's counsel, this was it. *O Elohim, I need thy counsel*, he thought. Adam couldn't give up yet.

Again, Adam raised his voice to the heavens in prayer but was met with only silence. He looked over to where Eve sat in the grass not too far off. She nodded at him, as if encouraging him to continue trying.

She was being more patient than usual and alternated between sitting in the grass and walking around, always staying within his sight. It was as if she too hadn't wanted to be separated from him.

When they'd arrived in the area of the garden where the altar sat in the open field, he and Eve had inspected their surroundings carefully. There was no sign of rot or neglect. The insects and birds were present, and several deer were settled in the shade of the trees at the edges of the field. The white and yellow flowers looked bright and healthy.

Now, Adam lowered his head and breathed out. They heard from Elohim only every few moons, but still Adam had hoped to have his cries answered. He'd decided that if Elohim intended him and Eve to have special instruction regarding the new man in the garden, Elohim might take exception and visit the garden.

A hand touched Adam's shoulder. Eve leaned next to him. "It's getting dark," she said.

Her voice was patient and accepting. He thought she might plague him with questions about why Elohim wasn't appearing, but she only touched his arm and said, "Come on, Adam. Tomorrow is the seventh day. We'll come back in the morning."

The altar had taken on a dark gray hue in the fading light, and the grass had become cool beneath his knees. Adam rose to his feet, feeling reluctant to leave, but he'd done everything he could.

The encroaching darkness was moving in faster than he expected. He grasped Eve's hand, and they hurried back to the dwelling. Adam kept watch for any sudden shadow moving through the trees. The moonlight filtered through the branches of the more dense areas of the garden, giving them plenty of light, but Adam was still nervous. Why had their "brother" been so determined to speak to Eve alone? The question bothered Adam, and he wasn't looking forward to meeting their brother in areas of the garden Adam was less familiar with.

All was quiet when they arrived at the alcove. Adam kept Eve's hand gripped in his as they made a cursory inspection. There were no dead animals or new skin mats. Nothing looked different or disturbed.

It was with relief that Adam settled in the alcove with Eve. Although Elohim hadn't visited them, Adam knew he'd done all that he could for the day.

"I'll keep watch if you want to sleep." He expected that Eve would want to go to sleep soon.

"I want to stay with you," she said. She followed him to the front of the alcove and sat next to him. He put his arm around her as they watched the darkness claim the last bits of land.

She leaned her head on his shoulder, and the sun-touched scent of her hair reached him.

She had been so quiet all day, making no suggestions, asking no questions, that he wondered if the stranger had said more to her than she was telling him. "What are you thinking about?"

Eve turned her head, and her eyes met his. Her quizzical expression was clear—he'd never asked her questions before.

"Nothing that I haven't spoken of before," she said, her gaze full of meaning.

Adam looked away. He knew what she wanted to know: the answer to the question that he couldn't exactly answer. Why had Elohim given them two opposing commandments? Elohim had been so adamant that they not partake of the fruit of the tree of knowledge, yet . . .

Eve's sigh broke into his thoughts, and she pulled away from him.

Adam studied her profile in the moonlight. He didn't know why she persisted in all of her curiosity. Why couldn't she be settled with their life? He brushed her hair back from her shoulders, but she still didn't look at him.

"When Elohim visits, we'll ask—"

She moved away from him and stood. "You spent all day praying, Adam." Her eyes bore into him. "And tomorrow, we'll be at the altar again. Do you think Elohim will see fit to answer us just because it's the seventh day?"

"It's my hope," he said, rising to his feet.

She turned away from him, her hands clenched at her side.

"Will Elohim's answer make a difference? Or will he give us another conflicting commandment?" she asked.

Adam stared at her. "What do you mean?"

"If we don't have knowledge—if we don't have blood— we can't fulfill all of the commandments given to us," she said in a trembling voice.

He moved to her side. "You can't mean that you *want* to die?" He touched her arm, her shoulder, her cheek. "Look at me," he whispered.

When she finally did, Adam said, "You can't desire death. Everything would change—not only us but the animals." Still her gaze was determined. "Remember the snake we found." Even now, Adam couldn't forget the lifeless form that he'd carried to the river.

She closed her eyes, and for a moment, Adam thought she agreed.

But when she opened them again, she said, "I'm not reluctant to face death."

Adam felt as if something had struck him, and he inhaled a steady breath. "This is because of our brother, isn't it?"

Eve shook her head, but the truth couldn't be hidden in her eyes. "He has only confirmed what I've already been thinking."

He let out a frustrated breath of air. "What else did he say to you?"

"Lucifer has *knowledge*, Adam," she said. "And he is not dead."

The name that she called their brother bothered Adam, although he didn't know why. Perhaps their spirits knew him from before when their bodies were created. Adam wished he could remember . . . but then he stopped himself. That's exactly what Eve desired, and gaining that knowledge would be too much of a sacrifice.

"I won't let him teach you *his* knowledge," Adam said. "Our knowledge should come through Elohim."

Eve's eyes widened. "Lucifer is only providing answers," she said. "Elohim is not here right now. Do you think Lucifer would tell us something that isn't right?"

"He might," Adam said. "He makes the garden rot. How can that be right? He's killed animals." He held Eve's gaze. "How can you want knowledge from a man who does those things?"

Eve took a step back and folded her arms. "The garden isn't dying. It's just . . ."

He waited for her answer, but she bit her lip, indecisive. Adam knew this was his chance to convince her to turn her attention away from their brother.

"If we let him stay in the garden, what else might happen? What else might die?" He plunged on when she didn't answer. "I can't lose you, Eve. You're my wife. You're . . . everything to me . . ."

She was quiet for a moment. Then she lowered her head.

"This brother of ours has proven to be elusive when he wants to be," Adam continued. "I can't stay awake constantly, guarding you. I need you to promise me, Eve—promise me you will stay away from him."

Eve raised her head and looked at him. She walked to

him and placed her hands on each side of his face. "Adam, I will never leave you."

He pulled her into a tight embrace. "Promise me."

"I'll never choose Lucifer over you," she whispered.

I know someone is watching me even though my eyes are still closed. At first I think it might be the shadow—my brother Lucifer—returned to the alcove. But when there is no coldness, I open my eyes. Adam is sitting with his back against the wall, watching me. His expression is one that I have never seen before.

I sit up, stifling a yawn. I'm surprised I slept at all. I vaguely remember Adam bringing me inside sometime in the middle of the night. Now the sun has risen, and the alcove is filled with light. I pull my knees to my chest, as if to brace myself against what Adam is about to say. I do sense one thing: that I won't like it.

Adam rises to his feet and stretches his hand toward me. Still, he doesn't speak. I take his hand and allow him to pull me to my feet. Then he leads me to the back of the alcove.

My pounding heart tells me what he wants to show me. He's discovered my secret.

Adam moves the hanging mats to the side to reveal the back wall, where I've marked the days for many moons. I can barely endure looking at each mark that I carefully scratched into the stone.

"What is this?" Adam asks, his voice quiet, yet firm. "What have you been doing?"

I don't want to look at him, but I must see his expression. Is he angry? Will he forbid me to make the marks? Does he know how many there are and what they mean? I slowly turn my head and meet his gaze.

In his dark green eyes, there are no warm streaks of gold.

I swallow and wish I could drink long and deep from the river. I wish I could plunge into the cool pond and swim to the bottom, staying submerged and blocking out all light and sound—including the way Adam is looking at me now.

I breathe out, then in. "I have been tracking the days."

Adam's gaze flickers away from mine and back to the wall, to the hundreds of marks. "One scratch for each day?"

"Yes," I whisper.

He doesn't say anything for a moment. My hands are perspiring, and I want to go outside in the moving breeze. I want to feel the air around me, for it seems the air has left the alcove. I had not considered what Adam would think when he found the marks; I had assumed he might never find them. But *never* is a long time.

His gaze is on me again. "Why?"

"I . . . Because I wanted to know how long we've been in the garden." It's an answer that I know he's expecting but may not believe.

He kneels before the wall and traces a few of the lines. Then he runs his fingers along the rows that are similar to the rows he makes when cultivating the plots of herbs. "So many days," he says. His fingers continue on their path, moving across the wall, then up and to the other side of the wall. Just watching him slowly trace the marks makes me realize that we have been in the garden a very long time. Not quite forever but nearly so.

Suddenly, he has straightened and is staring at me. I look up at him, waiting for what he may or may not say.

"Are you displeased with the garden, Eve? Do you reject what Elohim has provided for us?"

I have never heard this tone in his voice before. It's more than being upset or frustrated.

"I am not displeased," I say with a sigh. I wrap my arms

around his waist and lean against him. "I am grateful for this garden Elohim has placed us in." My eyes burn, and I'm thankful he can't see them. His arms wrap loosely about my shoulders, and my breath returns. "Adam, we can't live here forever."

He draws away, and I feel the separation between us is as if we are on opposite sides of a valley. "It's Lucifer, isn't it? What else did he say to you?"

"Adam," I say over my thumping heart, "I was tracking the days long before our brother showed up." I point to the wall. "Look at how many I've done—one for each time the sun rises."

But he doesn't look at where I'm pointing. "Tell me why you want to leave the garden so much."

My eyes are burning again. I look again at the wall and its many marks. "I have tried not to think about all the days, but these thoughts and questions keep coming to my mind." I touch my chest. "Or maybe it's from my heart. Can you tell me you are content to stay here . . . until that wall is filled with marks? Or until the next wall is filled with marks?"

Adam takes my hand and brings it to his mouth, pressing his lips against it. His eyes are bright and intent on mine. "If it means we can live forever, yes."

"Then we'll live forever in disobedience," I whisper. I pull away and walk to the front of the alcove. So Adam knows that I am tracking the days. It doesn't change anything. The only changes in the garden have come with Lucifer, and no matter how much Adam wants to be rid of him, I wonder if Lucifer is exactly what we need.

"Eve . . ." Adam begins. "We can't disobey Elohim."

I stop near the opening of the alcove and turn to face him. "We already are disobeying Elohim." I know he can't deny it because he can never explain how we are to multiply and replenish the earth without blood in our bodies.

"Elohim created us," Adam says, his voice sounding

tired. "Elohim also created our brother. Elohim can continue to create in order to multiply."

Adam's suggestion does nothing to satisfy me. I think of Lucifer and how when he touched my cheek, I felt only a whisper. I think of how his body is concealed and of the way he looked at me—as if he knew me better than I knew myself. Then I understand that Lucifer's body is not like ours. There is something different about him—even though he is our brother and has been created by Elohim. Why couldn't I feel his hand?

"He touched me," I say. Adam's face loses color. My hand goes to my cheek as I remember. "He touched my face, but I didn't feel anything. He has no . . . solid flesh."

Adam's eyebrows lift. "What do you mean? He's a man just as I am. He struck me to the ground."

"Elohim may have created him," I say. "And he has some sort of physical power, but I don't think he's in the same form that we are."

Adam is quiet for a moment.

"What does it mean?" I say. "How can he be our brother if he is not made of flesh?"

"More questions," Adam says. He walks past me and stands at the opening of the alcove. The day is a clear one, the sky cloudless. There will be no mist today, I think.

12

And God said, Let us make man in our image, after our likeness: and let them have dominion over the fish of the sea, and over the fowl of the air . . . and over all the earth.

—Genesis 1:26

The seventh day has come and gone, and still no visit from Elohim. I follow Adam around, never straying out of his sight. My days of spending time with the animals on my own are past. Adam and I have slept little, alternating who keeps watch during the night. Today Adam is working in the north garden, probably because it's the farthest away from the south garden.

I help him for a while. Then I find a shady place to sit and watch. Just as I am falling asleep, someone whispers my name. I know it's Lucifer, but when I and sit up, I see no one, and Adam is no longer in the herb field.

I shiver even though the air is warm.

"Eve," Lucifer says again. I am on my feet now, and I turn. I almost disbelieve what I am seeing: Lucifer is standing several paces away. He's leaning against a tree, the shade making his dark hair blacker. In his hand, he holds a fruit.

My breath slows because I think I recognize the fruit, but then I realize I don't. It's only a fruit from the tree he is underneath.

"Where's Adam?" I ask.

One side of his mouth turns up. "Was he here with you?"

I turn and look back at the field. There's still no sign of Adam. I wonder if I am dreaming. Adam wouldn't leave me alone—not now, not this way.

"Would you like some fruit?" my brother's voice says.

I look at him, and he's holding out the fruit.

"Not now," I say, narrowing my eyes at him. Adam's words come back to me: *Are you displeased with the garden, Eve? Do you reject what Elohim has provided for us?* Another shiver moves through my body.

"What about the fruit from those trees over there? Is it good?" He points to the opposite side of the field.

I don't have to look to where he is pointing. "Yes, those are good."

His smile is slight. "Have you tried all of the fruit? Can you tell me which fruit is the most delicious?"

I study him. His voice sounds pleasing enough, no guile or anger. His expression seems curious and genuine. Perhaps Adam is wrong. If Lucifer has to live in this garden now, it's only fitting that he inquires of the different fruits.

"I've tried all the fruits of the garden, except for the fruit from one tree."

My brother raises the fruit he is holding and smells it, then says, "Which tree is that?"

I wonder if I should answer—especially with Adam gone. My heart is pounding, but then I decide there can be no harm in telling Lucifer about the tree of knowledge. "There is one tree which Elohim has forbidden us to eat of, the tree of knowledge of good and evil."

Lucifer's eyebrows lift slightly. "Interesting," he says. "Where is this . . . forbidden tree?"

"Not far from our dwelling," I say.

My brother smells the fruit again.

I feel as if time is moving just as slowly. My hands are perspiring as I wonder where Adam is. How could he leave? Does he not know that our brother is speaking to me?

"Eve," Lucifer says, drawing my attention back to him. "What's wrong with the fruit of the tree of knowledge? Is it bitter to the taste?"

"I can't say. Adam and I have not eaten of it. We're obedient to Elohim's commandments." I take a breath. "If we eat of that fruit, we will die."

Lucifer drops the fruit in his hand to the ground. He takes a few steps forward, then stops, as if he is unsure whether to come any closer. "I know about the tree, Eve."

I thought he did, but hearing him say it, I realize it only makes sense. He must know about the tree. He must have kept his knowledge after all.

"Tell me what Elohim told you."

I stare at him for a moment. "Elohim instructed Adam before I was created."

One side of his mouth turns up. "Ah. What did Elohim say to Adam then?"

I wonder why he wants to know Elohim's exact words. I'm not sure if I can recite them exactly, but I say, "Elohim said that we should not eat of that fruit, not even touch it, and that if we do, we'll surely die."

I wait for Lucifer to nod his head, as if he agrees with Elohim as well, the one who created us both. Instead he says, "You won't surely die, Eve."

A gasp catches in my throat. "Elohim created our bodies and certainly knows what effect the fruit will have on us." I shake my head, hardly believing that Lucifer could refute

Elohim's words. I take a few steps away from him, hoping that Adam will return from wherever he went.

"Elohim is only warning you and Adam," Lucifer says, his expression calm. "He knows that when you do eat of the fruit, then your eyes will be opened. You'll have knowledge again, and all of your questions will be answered." He walks toward me, and I can't move. Is what he's saying true—that we will *not* die?

"You and Adam will be as the gods, knowing good from evil," he says in a quiet voice, but I can hear it plain and clear in the stillness.

I don't move as he reaches my side. If it is true that we won't die, I have to tell Adam. This will change everything.

Lucifer is watching me, and finally I meet his gaze. They are dark circles of vast blackness, and I marvel at the knowledge that he must have—all of which I so desire to have.

"We must tell Adam." I turn and call out for him.

My brother moves in front of me faster than I could have thought possible. "Don't say anything to Adam yet." His black eyes bore into me.

"He'll want to know. This will change what he will believe."

"Just wait a few more days," Lucifer says. "Adam needs to get used to my presence first."

I find myself nodding. I am pleased to hear Lucifer's words, but I'm not sure Adam will be. Although, I wonder how he could not be.

Lucifer's hand is touching my arm, but it's like a breeze, not a hand of flesh. "Meet me at the tree before the sun goes down, and I'll tell you more."

"The tree?" I say. "I promised Adam that I wouldn't visit . . . there . . . any longer."

My brother tilts his head with a soft smile. "You'll have

to visit the tree if you want your eyes to be opened. You'll have to partake of the fruit as well."

I look away. Of course he is right. "I'm not . . ."

"If you can't come today," he says in a placid voice, "then I'll be there tomorrow too. I'll wait until you can come—no matter how many days might pass."

I look at Lucifer again. "I must tell Adam."

His eyes search mine, and I wish I could know what he knows. "Please, Eve," he says, "just wait until after we meet at the tree."

I open my mouth, then close it. Finally I nod.

"I'll be waiting for you," he says. His hand moves against my cheek like a flutter of an insect's wing.

I watch him walk away until I can no longer see him as he moves into the thick of the foliage. It's only then that I notice how hot the sun is and that I'm perspiring.

Adam pushed his way out of the heavy sleep. Eve was calling his name, and he struggled to open his eyes. The sun had climbed high in the sky, and he hoped he hadn't slept too long. He shouldn't have slept at all.

Sitting up, he brushed the dirt from his arms, then looked in the direction from which he thought he'd heard Eve's voice. She was near the trees, walking in the high grass.

"Eve!" he called out, climbing to his feet. She turned at the sound of his voice, then hurried over to him.

"I fell asleep," he said when she reached him.

Her breath was short.

"I'm sorry you couldn't see me," he said, grabbing her hand. "Let's go to the river."

"You were right here all of the time?"

"I don't know what overcame me. I couldn't keep my eyes open."

"You must sleep more at night," Eve said in a quiet voice, squeezing his hand.

"I know." But he knew he couldn't—not with their brother out there. They hadn't seen him since that first night at the alcove. Adam hoped that meant he was gone, but he'd have to make a visit to the south garden to see if there were any changes.

Nothing else unusual had happened—no more skin mats or dead animals had been sighted—so Adam hoped that meant their brother had left.

Eve was quiet as they walked through the trees to the nearest river. It wasn't too far from the border, and Adam was surprised that she didn't ask to look over the wall. In fact, she seemed content to soak in the river and stay close to him. They swam for a little while, then climbed out of the water to sit on the shore and dry off.

"Tomorrow we'll visit the south gardens," he said.

Eve looked over at him from where she was sitting on the bank, running her fingers idly along the moist earth. She looked as if she were about to ask him something, but then she just nodded.

"Are you all right?" Adam asked. He didn't like her melancholy. She must have been really worried when she couldn't find him.

"I am," she said, her voice quiet.

Adam asked her a few more times if she was all right on the walk back to the alcove. Each time she assured him that she was. But still Adam wondered.

She seemed eager to settle down for sleep once they entered the alcove, but Adam stayed up long after she'd fallen asleep. He leaned against the wall at the entrance and tried to stay awake as long as possible. If he did fall asleep, he wanted it to be where his body would block the entrance.

Just as he felt himself drifting off, a bird call sounded, but it wasn't the call of a night bird. Adam rose to his feet, suddenly alert.

Then he heard it. The flutter of wings—large wings like those of an owl. Except Adam was sure that the bird call hadn't come from an owl.

Something moved near the boulder—a shadow that quickly grew larger.

Adam stiffened as the shadow became clear.

"Hello there," the being said.

"What are you doing here?" Adam said in a quiet but hard voice. He didn't want to wake Eve. He took a step toward the man. In the dark, his hair blended with the night, and his eyes looked like deep pools of water.

"I'm just out for a walk," the man said.

"I meant, what are you doing in the garden? In Eden?" Adam took several steps forward until he was just a couple of paces from Lucifer.

Lucifer watched his approach, then said, "I've come to give you the knowledge that you seek."

"Elohim didn't tell us about you." Adam's hands clenched at his sides. "We take instructions only from Elohim."

Lucifer tilted his head, his dark hair falling over one eye. "Elohim will tell you only what he wants to. I can help you obtain the knowledge that you and Eve desire most."

Breathing out, Adam tried to stay calm and keep his voice quiet, but just listening to the man speak made him agitated. Adam didn't fully understand why, but he didn't want the man around Eve. "We already know how to obtain knowledge."

Lucifer's mouth curved into a smile. "I don't doubt it. Both you and Eve seem very capable." He scanned the moonlit dwelling. "You have accomplished a lot here. The garden beyond is well kept."

Adam pushed the compliment to the back of his mind. "Leave my wife out of this conversation."

Lucifer's smile returned instantly. "Eve? She deserves compliments as well. She's certainly beautiful and intelligent."

Adam lunged for the man, not sure what he'd do, but Lucifer needed to stop talking and stop smiling like that. Instead of colliding with Lucifer, Adam landed on the ground. Lucifer was standing right next to him, untouched.

Adam raised his hands and looked at them. His hands had felt nothing when they touched Lucifer. Adam scrambled to his feet, coming face-to-face with the man. "You're not even of flesh. Who are you really?"

"I'm like you, a son of Elohim. It's one of the many things you'll understand once you have knowledge," Lucifer said in a smooth voice. "It's very simple, Adam, my brother. It takes only one bite, and your eyes will be opened. You'll be just like the gods, with knowledge of good and evil."

"Leave," Adam said.

"You're not considering what it will mean to have knowledge," Lucifer said, not moving.

"Elohim forbade us to eat of the fruit, and I take instructions from only him," Adam spat out. "Not you. You're some kind of strange being with the appearance of form. I may not know what you really are, but I do know I don't trust you."

"Well, perhaps Eve will think differently."

No, she thinks as I do. "She'll not be dissuaded by you—especially since I order you to leave the garden."

"You're ordering *me?*" Lucifer scoffed. "You have no authority to—"

Adam didn't give him time to finish. He attempted to push Lucifer toward the boulder, but again his hands touched nothing. Lucifer stood calmly to the side, watching Adam with amusement.

"I'll see you tomorrow, Adam," Lucifer said.

Before Adam could respond, Lucifer left, disappearing into the trees without a sound.

"Adam?" Eve's voice called out.

He spun and saw her coming out the alcove. How much had she heard?

"It was Lucifer, wasn't it?" she asked. In the moonlight, she looked vulnerable and small.

"I ordered him to leave the garden," Adam said.

"What did he want?"

Something inside of Adam twisted—like a warning. "He wants us to eat the fruit of the tree of knowledge." Adam turned to face the location where Lucifer had disappeared. Even now, Adam couldn't be sure if their brother was watching them.

Eve walked to Adam's side and slipped her hand in his. "We can't live forever without gaining any more knowledge."

He stared at her in disbelief. The tightness in his stomach spread to his limbs. "Elohim will instruct us in everything that we need to know."

She released his hand and walked away, toward the alcove.

"Eve," Adam said, trying to keep the exasperation out of his voice, "we need to be patient."

She stopped at the alcove entrance. "For how long, Adam? Until I have another wall filled with marks? Or two more walls?" She stepped into the darkness before Adam could answer.

He stared at the place where she'd disappeared. He hurried into the alcove. She was already lying down, her back turned to him.

"Lucifer doesn't belong here," he said. "And I don't want him talking to you."

Eve didn't respond, and Adam waited a few moments for her to say something. He wished that everything could return to as it was before Lucifer arrived. Even trying to answer Eve's questions was better than her silence and the distant feeling between them.

Adam sat next to Eve and moved her hair from off her shoulder and threaded his fingers through it. She didn't move, didn't speak at all.

13

So God created man in his own image . . . male and female created he them.

—Genesis 1:27

I 've said everything I can say. Lucifer has spoken to Adam, and still Adam won't consider gaining knowledge with our brother's help.

This morning, I rise quietly and walk around Adam's sleeping form. His arm is stretched out, as if reaching for me in his sleep. I walk to the back of the alcove and scratch in another mark. By the time I'm finished, Adam is awake.

I see his disapproval, although he says nothing.

After releasing the mat that covers the marks, I pass by Adam and go outside to wash in the pond.

"Wait, Eve," Adam says, but I keep walking, not speaking.

He follows me, as I expect him to, and wades into the pond with me. I force my gaze away from the path through the vines—the path that Lucifer once took when he was watching us.

I understand Adam's wishes and his concerns. They are my own . . . yet . . . I feel as if I'm being forced to choose between Adam's wishes and Lucifer's offer. And when I think about living in the garden forever . . . and ever . . . it's incomprehensible to me.

Nothing will change if we don't do anything, but when I glance at Adam, I can't imagine leaving the garden without him.

There may be no other choice if I am to gain the knowledge I so desire.

For a moment, I think about telling Adam what Lucifer said about not dying, but I heard enough of the words between Adam and Lucifer last night to know that it won't change Adam's mind. Besides, I'm not ready yet to tell Adam that Lucifer spoke with me alone yesterday while Adam was sleeping in the field.

The fact that Lucifer showed up at the only moment when he could speak to me alone makes me realize he might be watching us even now. Without attracting Adam's attention, I take small glimpses at our surroundings, my heart rate quickening. Perhaps Lucifer is in the tangle of vines, peering out from underneath. Or maybe he's standing behind a group of trees, watching through the lush of branches and leaves.

Yesterday he said he'd wait for me by the tree of knowledge. He must not have said anything to Adam about it, for surely Adam would have mentioned it.

If Lucifer isn't here at the dwelling, does that mean he's at the tree? I think of him waiting and of his dark eyes and of his curved mouth, which sees humor in almost every word I speak.

I think of the south gardens, where Adam wants to go today. I wonder if Lucifer will have any effect on the tree of knowledge. Could he cause it to die just as he somehow brought change to the southern portion of the garden?

After I wash in the pond, I sit on the boulder by our alcove to dry off. The sun is warm, but clouds are moving in.

A heavy mist looks like a good possibility. Adam has been quiet, seeming to understand that I'm not much interested in conversation.

He eats a couple pieces of fruit as he stands not too far from the boulder, keeping his gaze darting between the trees and me. When he's ready to go, I climb off the boulder and follow. I make no move to take his hand, and he makes no move to take mine.

The clouds gather fast as we walk; they fittingly augment the silence between us. I am perspiring by the time we reach the edge of the field that stretches to the southern border.

My heart sinks. The grass that was wilted and brown before is now only bits of spiked tufts. Adam notices the same thing and pulls up a clump of brown. The stalks break off in his hands.

I look across the field. It reminds me of the skin mat that Lucifer brought to the alcove—a wide expanse of brown. Even from a distance, I can see that the trees have changed colors as well. Instead of being vibrant green, the leaves are a mix between brown and yellow.

I set off across the stiff grass, the remaining tufts prickly beneath my feet. The heavy clouds overhead make the garden seem even more rotted, if possible. Adam is right behind me. I can hear his breathing and footsteps as his feet brush through the dried earth.

Nothing jumps or flutters before us; no butterflies or grasshoppers can be seen. If it weren't for the wind and the impending mist, this place would be silent . . . as silent as the dead snake. I watch the ground, wondering if there are more dead animals on it—another snake?—although I find myself hoping that's not so. What did Lucifer mean when he told me that we won't die if we partake of the tree of knowledge?

Stopping before the trees, I look up. Adam halts next to me and stares. Some of the trees' branches are nearly bare.

Rotting fruit hangs from them, moving faintly in the wind. Fruit that once was a supple orange is now shriveled and dark.

Adam walks among the trees, not straying too far so that I am still in his sight. I stand in one place, not wanting to venture any farther. It's hard to comprehend that Lucifer's presence could cause such torment among the plants in the garden. It must be something else, I think. Perhaps it's not Lucifer at all.

I want to ask him, but of course I can't.

Scanning the trees and the field behind, I sense that Lucifer has not followed us here. He'll wait for us someplace else. Perhaps he is waiting for me now by the tree.

The mist descends, and I shiver, but I don't seek shelter beneath the branches of the trees. Adam returns to my side. His eyes are dark like the clouds above. "Let's go," he says— that and nothing more.

He doesn't seem to mind the mist. Usually, we'd take some shelter but not today. There are worse things to consider now. Adam doesn't offer his hand, and I don't reach to take it. I wrap my arms around my waist as we cross the brown field and enter the part of the garden that is still green and filled with flowers.

I want to ask Adam if the mist will heal the brown field and rotted fruit, but I remember I'm not speaking to him. It seems too hard to begin now.

When we reach the alcove, the mist has increased, making everything wet. I sit inside, while Adam stands at the opening, looking out, waiting.

He isn't coming, I want to say. *He's waiting for me at the tree.*

The morning dawns clear and bright. I have not slept much, and Adam has slept even less. He watches me as I make the mark on the back wall. He follows me to the pond but doesn't get into it. I wash, yet I don't take long. Even with the sun warming the waters, it seems colder than usual this morning.

As I walk out of the pond, Adam holds out a fruit. I shake my head. I'm not hungry. He lowers his hand as I pass, resignation in his eyes, but hope doesn't enter my breast. I know what his answers will be to my questions. They are unchanging, just like the garden.

I walk toward the alcove, feeling tired. Adam and I still haven't spoken to each other, so I return to the sleeping mats and lie down. With the sun streaming in, warming my wet body, I finally sleep deeply.

And then I dream.

The tree of knowledge is in front of me, its leaves glittering green in the sunlight. The fruit's perfectly ripe, fragrant, and slightly dewy. My stomach twists, and I realize I am hungry—very hungry. I turn to look at the other trees, to choose one of their offerings, but they are gone. Looking down, I see the grass below is pure white, so bright that it's hard to look at.

And suddenly, I'm holding it—a single fruit. Its soft skin is smooth in my hand, just as I imagined it before. But this time, more than curiosity runs through me. Pure desire pulses through my body, blocking out any other thoughts.

I raise the fruit, unable to look away from it, when suddenly it's gone.

My eyes open, and it's as if I can still feel the fruit in my hand—the weight and texture, the coolness that quickly grew warm against my palm.

I sit up, taking a deep breath. During my dream, it was as if I knew I was dreaming, yet I was so entranced that I couldn't have fathomed another world except that one I exist in.

I know there must be other worlds, other existences—like the existence outside the garden. I wonder about the white ground from my dream that was too bright to look at.

The alcove feels strangely empty, and I think it's because I have dreamed about the fruit, and now it's gone. Adam isn't at the entrance, although I expect him to be nearby, as he always is.

So it's with surprise that when I step outside into the approaching twilight, Adam is not there. I perch on the boulder for several moments, expecting him back soon. If he returns, and I'm not within sight, surely he'll find a cause to break the silence between us. I find I want that silence broken, but I have been so stubborn; I don't know how to change it.

Finally, I walk the path that leads to the pond and pause when I'm halfway there, listening, but I hear nothing. I continue walking and stop within sight of the pond. Still, I see no one. When I return to the boulder, I call out for Adam. Perhaps he fell asleep someplace from exhaustion. I walk the perimeter of the dwelling, well aware that every time I call for Adam, I am attracting Lucifer's attention.

But Lucifer is at the tree.

What if Adam is there as well? I can hardly believe he'd go to the tree without me, but where else would he go? Even though we aren't speaking, I don't understand why he'd leave me unless it had something to do with Lucifer . . . or the tree.

So he must be there—if Lucifer is there.

I leave the dwelling, moving quickly, knowing that if Adam is not at the tree, I'll want to return to the dwelling as soon as possible; the sun will go down soon enough, and I must return before dark.

I look for Adam, or any sign of Lucifer, as I walk, but

when I come within sight of the tree, I see no one. I descend the hill slowly, almost reluctant to look at the tree so close. It's bigger than I saw it in my dream, and the leaves don't glitter green. They are a darker, richer shade in the fading golden glow of the afternoon.

The fruit hangs from the branches, untouched, and my heart quickens as I remember the feel of it in my dream. The fruit commands my attention, and my dream comes back vividly. I almost forget why I have come. I reach the bottom of the hill and pause, glancing around. I look for Adam, or Lucifer, but the garden is quiet. Even the birds seem silent now.

Then I again walk toward the tree, my heart thundering at the nearness. Stopping several paces away, I take deep breaths. Lucifer isn't here waiting. He and Adam must be somewhere else. I slowly turn away from the tree, forcing myself to walk.

"Eve." His voice whispers around me as if it's touching me everywhere at once.

Lucifer is here.

14

God said unto them, Be fruitful, and multiply, and replenish the earth.

—Genesis 1:28

I don't turn around for a moment, but when I finally do, Lucifer is watching me. He is stretched out beneath the tree as if he has just been asleep. I wonder if he does sleep. His body has no solid form, so does that mean he needs rest?

Blinking, I look away and look at the tree above him and at the sky above that. There are no clouds, and the sky is pale orange. I know I must hurry back before the darkness sets in, but first I must ask. "Where's Adam?"

Lucifer rises to his feet, his long body languid in its movements. "He has abandoned you?"

Even from where I stand, I see Lucifer's dark eyebrows lift. He folds his arms over his chest and leans against the trunk of the tree of knowledge.

"He's not at the dwelling," I say, trying to keep the tremble out of my voice. "I thought he might be here with you." My mind races as I wonder where Adam has gone, if

93

not in search of Lucifer. Perhaps he *is* searching for him, although in the wrong place.

"Have you come to visit the tree?"

I stumble over my words.

"Then to visit *me*?" Lucifer's mouth spreads into a smile.

I open my mouth to answer, but I stop when Lucifer reaches above himself and snaps off a fruit.

"What are you doing?" I ask. This time I don't mask the tremble.

"Eve, there is only one reason why you came here." Lucifer walks forward until he is out from under the tree. The gold-orange sun lights up his torso and face, making his hair and eyes look even blacker. "We both know it."

His earlier words run through my head: *You won't surely die, Eve.*

I don't realize I am walking toward the tree, but when I next look into Lucifer's eyes, I am standing right in front of him.

"You will be like the gods, who know good from evil," he whispers. "You will have all the knowledge you desire." His hands are against mine. Although I can't feel them, I sense his touch—cool and firm. Suddenly, the fruit's in my hands—solid and real. Just like my dream.

Ye shall not eat of it, neither shall ye touch it, lest ye die.

I am not dead, I think. I am touching the fruit, and I am not dead. Perhaps Lucifer is right.

Lucifer doesn't move even though he's standing very close to me. My gaze meets his, and it's as if I can see forever into the unending depth of his dark eyes.

For a long moment, our gazes stay locked, and then he takes a step back, then another. He walks back to the tree and leans against the trunk.

I look at the fruit in my hand. I haven't realized it until now, but it seems to be the most beautiful fruit I've ever seen in the entire garden. The aroma reaches my senses, and I know it will be sweet to the taste—most sweet above all.

I am touching it, and I still have my breath. I have not become as the dust.

The scent caresses my senses, and I realize that just one bite will make me as the gods, giving me knowledge—and with that I'll be able to keep Elohim's commandment to multiply and replenish the earth.

I raise the fruit to my lips, inhaling. If I do not partake, I will be the mother of nothing at all. If I do partake, I will be the mother of all living.

Lucifer is watching, and out there, somewhere, Adam is probably looking for me. But this is neither for Lucifer nor for Adam. This is for my posterity.

My lips touch the fruit, and my mouth opens. Then I bite into the fruit, my teeth breaking the skin and sinking easily into the flesh. The incredible sweetness permeates my mouth in an instant.

I chew the soft fruit and swallow. Its sweetness floods my entire body. This is completely different from just holding the fruit.

It has happened. It's over. Yet, I know it must all be a beginning.

I stare at the fruit in my hand. Its taste is still fresh in my mouth, echoing throughout my limbs. It has settled in my stomach, and I wait for a change to my body—for something to happen.

I exhale, then inhale, hardly believing I have done it. I have eaten from the tree of knowledge of good and evil. A tremor runs through my body, settling in my feet, taking my strength with it. I deliberately exhale again. My mind is spinning, and I wonder if I will sink to the ground, if my legs will simply give out. Am I supposed to feel this way? Lucifer said I won't die, but will the fruit have any other effect?

Lucifer shifts his position, claiming my attention.

Although he still leans against the trunk and his eyelids are half-closed, I know he is watching me.

"Is . . ." I begin, and then I remember. I remember in a way different from how I remember something I might have said or done the day before; I remember as if there was something I once knew and have recalled only now.

I remember Lucifer. Remembering comes in the smallest of pieces—not in words or thoughts but in scraps of memory.

Lucifer standing before Elohim. Lucifer speaking, his expression agitated. And another man is with him—a man who must be a brother. Lucifer and the man look very similar, although Lucifer's eyes are darker, his complexion like a thundercloud in his anger. For I realize Lucifer is angry, very angry, as he speaks to Elohim.

I blink several times, clearing the memory, and look at Lucifer in person.

His careful gaze is on me, his mouth lifted into a half smile. "How is the fruit?" His voice jolts through me, and I feel as if he's pushed his hand against my chest, stopping the air from going in and out. I gasp for breath and gasp again.

I know who Lucifer is now. He is the fallen angel who has set out to destroy all humankind.

His gaze reflects back all that I am thinking—as if he knows my thoughts.

I sink to the ground, still holding the fruit, as if it's a part of me that I can't let go. I bend over with a groan. My stomach twists and turns as if it wants to rid itself of the fruit. Without looking at Lucifer, I say, "I know who you are."

He says nothing, but he moves forward, and I imagine his feet brushing through the grass. When he stops in front of me, I don't want to look up. I know how he sees me now— as a woman, a woman who is naked and vulnerable. In my line of vision, I see his hand reach for me, then hesitate before touching me.

I shrink back. I don't want him to touch me, even if his fingers have no solid form. I don't want him near me. I don't want to hear his voice or glimpse his eyes and their unending blackness.

I feel as if a mountain of rock is pressing down on me. This new knowledge feels so heavy that I struggle for air.

Lucifer chuckles. His laugh, once intriguing, now slices through me. My arms ache from clenching them around my body, but I refuse to stand in my nakedness. I want to hide.

My eyes burn, and liquid comes from them, dripping onto my cheeks. I marvel at the moisture and touch my hand to my cheeks. My fingers are wet. I feel as if something is expanding yet constricting inside of me at the same time.

Images surface in my mind again and again. I now realize they're memories. I remember I was there when Lucifer presented his plan for humanity to Elohim—a plan that was Lucifer's alone.

And then his brother stepped forward.

I remember the other man now and know that he is my brother as well, but he is far different from Lucifer. This other man is the Chosen One. He speaks quietly, in a measured tone, as he presents another plan—the plan that Elohim wants. This plan gives each man and woman agency.

"You said we would not die," I whisper, knowing that Lucifer still hovers over me. "But Elohim didn't accept your plan. That means that we will all die." I know this now. I will not die today, or tomorrow, but eventually I will return to dust. I drop the fruit in the grass and look up, dreading to see the blackness of Lucifer's eyes, but he needs to understand that I know who he is.

Lucifer is gone. I look around in disbelief. He has abandoned me.

"Lucifer!" I call out. He can't leave me now. He must explain why he lied to me. He must explain what will happen next.

My body trembles, and my voice shakes as I call out again.

No voice answers, and all I hear is the breeze rattling the leaves above me. I stare at the fruit in the grass and its bite mark. I will die. I know that now. Lucifer has lied to me.

I want to throw the fruit at the tree and then tear down all of the other fruit and trample it. I wonder how long Elohim will wait before he banishes me from the garden.

"Eve," a voice calls.

I can't move. As the voice comes again, both relief and dread flood through me. It's Adam. I want to hide the fruit from him, bury it somewhere, but there is no time, and he will discover my deed soon enough.

"Eve," Adam says, his voice closer. I know that he is behind me. My breath stops, and I feel as though I am choking.

I pick up the fruit and close my eyes just as Adam's hand touches my shoulder.

"Why are you here?" Sharpness lines his voice. "You agreed not to visit the tree anymore."

His words tear through me into the deepest parts of my soul.

Adam kneels beside me, his arm going around my shoulders. We haven't spoken for days, yet he is here, speaking to me. He is doing what I should have done for him. He is taking care of me.

What have I done?

I open my hand, and his breathing changes. I can't look at him.

"Oh, Eve."

The pain in his voice makes me want to scream, to cry, to purge my stomach of the fruit. I will die now. I will be cast out, and I will never see Adam again.

My body is trembling, and when Adam puts his hand beneath mine, the hand that holds the fruit, I think that death could not be worse than this final touch.

"What have you done?" His voice reaches me, but it sounds as if he is very far away, as if he is speaking to me from the other side of the garden.

"Lucifer beguiled me," I say, the words barely audible.

I wait for his harsh words, his cries of agony, but none of that comes. He is still for a long time, the whole of the evening perhaps, but it's only a moment.

Then he moves away from me. I feel the loss of his touch, the absence of his body next to mine, as if I have already been cast out of the garden and submerged into a lonely existence.

But something else changes.

Adam is holding the fruit. I raise my eyes to his. Holding the fruit is not the same thing as eating it. This may be the last time I'll look upon my husband.

I almost can't breathe as I think about living without him—living until I die alone.

Adam is gazing at me, and I am surprised there is no reprimand in his gaze but there is the determination that I have been a witness to many times. My heart clenches. Maybe Adam will cast me out himself.

When Adam raises the fruit to his mouth, I stare at him in disbelief as he bites into it.

He holds my gaze as he chews, then swallows.

The moisture drips down my face as he takes another bite, chewing and swallowing a second time. He drops the fruit on the ground, then holds out his hand toward me.

"Adam . . . I . . ." I can't finish. I want to tell him I'm sorry. I want to tell him he shouldn't have eaten of the fruit.

He grasps my hands and pulls me to my feet, and then I'm in his embrace. I feel his lips pressed against the side of my head. His arms are warm and strong and safe, but still I tremble.

I have brought this upon Adam. Now he will die too.

15

And God saw every thing that he had made, and, behold, it was very good.

—Genesis 1:31

Adam stared into Eve's wide blue-green eyes as she looked unblinkingly back at him. The sweet tastes of the fruit still pinged on his tongue. The fruit of the tree of knowledge was sweeter than anything he'd ever tasted, and strangely, he desired another bite.

But he had dropped the fruit and now held Eve. The breeze stirred around them, lifting Eve's hair from her shoulders.

"I remember Lucifer now," Eve said. She spoke of the council in Heaven involving Elohim and Lucifer and the Chosen One.

The memories were coming back to Adam as well. Eve's cheeks were wet, and Adam wiped away the moisture with his fingers.

Her mouth quavered as she said, "I didn't know Lucifer came to deceive us, Adam. I thought . . ."

"Shh," Adam said, pulling her into his arms.

"He said that we wouldn't die," she whispered against

his chest. "He was lying. How could I not know he is the Deceiver?" Her arms tightened about him. "Our deaths will come, but it will be worth it. We'll now be able to multiply and replenish the earth."

Adam closed his eyes and rested his chin on top of her head. "We'll start the human race." He ran his fingers through her hair. Knowledge was flooding through him faster than he could comprehend it all. "This is what Elohim's plan included." He felt Eve sag against him.

"I wish I'd had fuller knowledge about the plan earlier," she said in a quiet voice. "Then I would have made the choice without giving Lucifer the satisfaction of deceiving me."

Adam drew away and looked directly at her. "He was part of that plan too."

"How?" she asked.

Even though he knew that both of their memories were returning, Eve seemed too distraught to analyze them all. "Lucifer was sent to tempt us," Adam said. "If we hadn't been tempted, we may not have made this choice—not in the eternal state we were living in."

"Do you mean Elohim intended us to partake of the fruit from the beginning?"

"Not from the beginning, but eventually." Adam kissed her forehead, and their bodies brushed against each other again. The touch of his wife's body against him made Adam realize why Lucifer had clothed himself.

"We should cover ourselves," he said in a soft voice.

Eve's face flushed in the fading light. "We should."

Suddenly, Adam felt strange looking at her, and he tried to look at only her face. He was grateful for the gathering twilight.

"We can use the grass mats. Or . . ." She hesitated. "The skin mat Lucifer left at the alcove."

"We'll find something," Adam said. He wanted to pull

her close again, but he hesitated now. They had embraced many times, and he'd never thought too much of it. But now it was different. He saw her nakedness just as she certainly saw his.

He looked around, making sure Lucifer wasn't standing somewhere, watching them, watching his wife. Adam felt exposed, and the sooner they covered themselves from the eyes of Lucifer, the better.

Adam grasped her hand, and they walked up the hillside in the gathering darkness, away from the tree, away from the half-eaten fruit on the ground. As they walked, Eve clung to his hand, and he was sure that memories of their existence before Eden flowed through her mind as well.

His stomach clenched as he thought about Lucifer, and who he really was. Even before Adam's eyes were opened, he knew he didn't like the fallen angel. Before Adam even knew who Lucifer truly was, Adam had wanted him to leave the garden.

The sun was well below the horizon now, and the sky was a deep violet. The moon rose, giving them plenty of light to find their way back.

Adam slowed as they neared the field that contained the altar of prayer. He wondered if Elohim already knew what had just happened in the garden. What would he say to them? How soon would they be banished from the garden?

Once they arrived at the alcove, Eve took down the hanging mats that covered the marks on the wall. Adam took one and wrapped it around his waist. Eve took the other one and wrapped it around her waist.

Adam crossed to her and pulled her into his arms. She leaned against him with a sigh.

"Can we finally sleep tonight?" she whispered.

Adam's heart thudded. "I'll stay awake for a while, just in case."

Eve lifted her face. "What more can Lucifer do to us?

Adam brushed the hair back from her face and her neck. He leaned down and kissed her neck and felt a shiver go through him. He pulled away abruptly. He'd kissed Eve plenty of times, but kissing her now was somehow different. The kiss echoed throughout his body.

"I should keep watch," he said, reluctantly releasing her. He felt he had to put some distance between them. He didn't completely understand the new sensations flowing through him as he thought about his wife. Perhaps the knowledge would come in time. She seemed reluctant to let go of him too.

He sat at the opening of the alcove, staring into the night, for a long time, as long as it took for him to be sure that Eve had fallen asleep. Then he crept onto the sleeping mats next to her. He watched the curve of her shoulder as it moved with each breath. Then, careful not to disturb her, he scooted next to her and buried his face in her hair, closing his eyes. He'd never realized how flawlessly their bodies fit together.

It was a long time before he finally fell asleep.

I am warm in Adam's arms, and they have never felt so perfect against my skin. I could lie here forever, but then I remember that we no longer have forever.

A chill weaves through me, and I know it's more than the realization that I've eaten from the fruit of the tree of knowledge. I feel Lucifer's presence as I've never felt it before, and his presence is far from a dream.

I open my eyes to find Lucifer staring down at me.

His lips are curved into a smile. The morning sun spreads plenty of light inside the alcove. My hand goes to my hip, and I'm grateful that I wrapped myself in the mat last night. I don't want to be exposed to Lucifer ever again, even if he is my brother, even if he has seen me in my nakedness before.

My other hand is entangled with Adam's. He slept with his arms around me all night, and I did nothing to move them. I pull my hand from Adam and sit up, keeping my gaze on Lucifer.

"Why are you still here?" I whisper.

His eyes are no longer intriguing to me now that I see who he truly is. And although I know his deception was part of the greater plan, I still don't want him here—in my private alcove that I share with my husband—observing us as if we are mere foolish things.

Lucifer's gaze moves from my face down the length of my body, and I feel my skin grow hot. I stand and back away from him until I'm against the wall. I know he can't touch me, but that doesn't stop the sting of being in his presence.

"Your task is finished here," I spit out.

Adam awakens and is on his feet in an instant. He stands between Lucifer and me, and although he has no idea what's going on, I'm grateful that he's blocking me from Lucifer's gaze.

"Leave," Adam commands, moving closer to Lucifer.

Our brother puts a hand on Adam's shoulder, and even though I know Adam can't feel it, he flinches. Does he feel Lucifer's touch twist his heart as it's twisting mine?

"I've come to discuss your new knowledge with you," Lucifer says, his voice pleasant and smooth.

I can't believe I had ever found Lucifer's voice pleasing, for now it claws at my skin.

"We'll take our instructions from Elohim," Adam says.

"Do you think Elohim will speak to you *now*?" Lucifer answers, and I can imagine his black eyebrows arching in disdain. "Not only will both of you be cast out of the garden but you will be cast out of Elohim's presence as well."

I know Adam well enough that although I can't see his face, I sense that this pains him.

"Leave," Adam repeats, this time his voice harsher.

Lucifer takes a step toward the alcove entrance, and his gaze roves over me as he passes by, his expression arched in amusement.

"I'll see you both very soon," he says.

Adam stays in one place until Lucifer has left. Then he turns to me. The sleep has long fled.

I realize I'm shaking. Adam's arms go around me, and he holds me tight. "Why is our brother still here? Hasn't he done enough?" I ask.

Adam's expression is grim when he pulls away. "We'll go to the altar. Surely Elohim knows what has happened. He has to visit us now."

I nod, my questions colliding. Emotions rock inside me, fighting for recognition. What will Elohim say—to Adam . . . to me?

It's done, I think. There is no changing my choice now.

I let out a sigh and follow Adam out of the alcove, clinging to his hand. Lucifer doesn't seem to be hovering around the dwelling, for which I am grateful.

On the walk to the altar, my eyes grow wet. More than once, Adam stops and dries my cheeks, absorbing the wet with his hands. I see that his eyes are reddened, and I wonder if that is how mine look. The closer we get to the altar, the harder my heart pounds.

We haven't even reached the clearing when we hear the voice of Elohim.

"Where art thou, Adam?" Elohim's voice seems to penetrate my very soul.

I stop walking, and Adam stops next to me. Neither of us moves for a moment. Then Adam, still holding my hand, steps out into the clearing.

I have seen Elohim many times during my existence in

the garden, but I have never felt reluctant to meet His gaze.

Elohim doesn't actually walk on the ground but strides above it. His white robe reminds me of the white earth in my dream about the tree. Next to him is another Elohim, one whom I now recognize as the Only Begotten, our brother who said He'd follow Elohim's plan. I wonder if either of them can tell by just looking at us that we have partaken of the fruit.

"You are clothed," Elohim says.

Of course he notices our change in appearance. It certainly gives us away.

"Why do you cover yourselves?" His voice dominates the air, coming from everywhere at once, even though it's coming from only him. Adam's fingers tighten around mine as Elohim continues, "Has thou eaten of the fruit of the forbidden tree?"

"Yes," Adam says, his voice strong, but I hear the tremor inside of it. "Eve ate of the fruit . . . I ate as well so that I should remain with her."

My breath stills as I wait for Elohim's response. His eyes shift to mine, and His voice is softer when he speaks. "I commanded thee that thou shouldest not eat. What hast thou done?"

I can't hold Elohim's gaze, and I look down at my hand that is intertwined with Adam's. If only Elohim had come to visit the garden earlier to answer my questions. But if this was all part of the plan . . . and we'd need to make this choice eventually . . . I lift my gaze and look at Elohim.

My mouth feels dry, but I push through the words. "Lucifer enticed me, but I desired it before my brother came into the garden." I rush on, knowing this might be my last chance to explain before we're cast out. "I want to have knowledge, as the gods do, and I want to follow all of thy commandments, including the commandment to multiply and replenish the earth. This I cannot do without my body having blood, and I cannot multiply without my husband."

I let my breath out, hoping Elohim will be merciful. Then a movement makes me snap my head to the right. Lucifer is standing in the trees just to the side of Adam and me. He leans against a tree, his mouth curled into a smile. Sheer numbness overtakes me. Why hasn't he left?

Elohim's gaze moves to Lucifer as well, and I find myself holding my breath again.

"Lucifer!" Elohim says in a thunderous voice. "Thou hast brought death to this garden. Because of this, thou shalt be cursed above all cattle. Thou shalt also be cursed above every beast of the field."

I can't help looking at my brother to see how he receives this news. His pitiless smile lessens yet stays cruel on his face. His eyes narrow, drawing his eyebrows downward. He glances at the Only Begotten, then quickly away.

Elohim continues to curse Lucifer, telling him he will spend the rest of his days upon his belly and eating dust.

Lucifer tries to argue with Elohim, but Elohim overrides his speech. Elohim declares that there will be enmity between my seed and Lucifer's seed, that my seed will have the power to bruise Lucifer's head. Lucifer is given the power only to bruise our heels, but this does not deter Lucifer at all.

He looks over at me, his expression full of triumph. I don't understand it. Does he enjoy being cursed by Elohim? Then I realize that his triumph is because he will still be able to influence us.

The vindictive smile that transforms his face is directed at me.

☙ 16

And God formed man of the dust of the ground, and breathed into his nostrils the breath of life; and man became a living soul.

—Genesis 2:7

I move closer to Adam as Lucifer slinks away, moving past the tree of knowledge. His form blends into the grove until I can no longer make out his shape. My breath comes easier after that, although I wonder if Lucifer has truly left the garden, or if he is merely hiding someplace, watching us.

Adam slips his arm around my waist, and I realize that Elohim is speaking again. Elohim looks directly at me as he says, "Thy sorrow and thy conception will be multiplied. In sorrow thou shalt bring forth children. Thy desire shall be to thy husband, and he shall rule over thee." I nestle against Adam further, and his hold tightens.

I will be having children. At last. I know this now. It will be as Elohim says. Anticipation courses through me. There will be sorrows, but I will have Adam by my side. I look up at Adam, and his gaze is tender, open.

Elohim continues, his gaze now on Adam. "Because thou hast eaten of the fruit of the forbidden tree, the ground will be cursed. In sorrow thou shalt eat of it all the days of thy life. Thorns and thistles shall it bring forth . . ."

Adam nods, his jaw clenched tight.

"By the sweat of thy face shalt thou eat bread," Elohim says, his voice lower, gentler, "until thou shalt return unto the ground—for thou shalt surely die."

My body tenses, and I close my eyes. *We'll die.* Our bodies will no longer last forever. I want to look at Adam now, to see how he is taking Elohim's proclamations, but when I open my eyes, I can't tear my gaze from Elohim's face. His voice is softer than when he spoke to Lucifer, but it holds the same firmness and power. It also holds love—a tangible love.

". . . unto dust shalt thou return." I lower my head as Elohim pauses, then says, "I have created coats of skins to clothe your bodies."

On the ground before us I see coats of skin. I pick up one of them and touch its softness. The coat reminds me of the skin mat Lucifer put in our alcove, but this coat is much softer. I swallow against a new lump in my throat, which formed at the thought of another animal death, and cradle the coat in the crook of my arm. Adam picks up the other coat and examines it as well.

We both look up as Elohim speaks again, reminding us of the commandment to multiply and replenish the earth. He explains how our bodies must unite in order to produce a child. My mind spins as I consider what Elohim is saying. He tells us that our natural desires will take over, and the result will be the conception of a child. I glance over at Adam to see what he thinks of this information; he is gazing straight at Elohim. My heart is thumping hard as Elohim explains the pain of childbirth and the blood that will be associated with it.

I look down at my hands. *I will have blood in my body, and with blood I'll bring forth children.* I knew some of this already, but now that it will become who I am, I marvel to think about it.

Adam's arm tightens around me, and a flood of warmth sweeps through me. I exhale, realizing that this is Adam—my husband—and together we'll do as Elohim asks.

Then Elohim speaks to the Only Begotten, "Behold, Adam and Eve have become as one of us, knowing good and evil. Now I will send them from the garden, lest they put forth their hands and partake also of the tree of life and eat and live forever in their sins."

Adam and I follow Elohim's gaze as he points to the tree of life, nestled in its grove.

When Elohim's gaze is back on us, I feel every part of my body tremble in anticipation. "Thou shalt never return to the Garden of Eden. I will place cherubim and a flaming sword to prevent you from partaking of the tree of life."

Adam's arm moves from being around me, and he clasps my hand in his.

"Come," Elohim says, motioning for us to follow him.

Adam takes the first step, and I walk with him toward the east. Will we use the entrance to the garden that has been used only by Elohim?

My eyes become wet again as we walk toward the east border. Elohim has probably chosen to escort us to the east entrance to make sure we do not linger in the garden. As we pass the animals in the garden, the moisture in my eyes comes faster. I won't see these animals again. I wonder if their bodies will change too. Have I caused them to Fall? Will they die?

I think of our dwelling and all of the care we have put into it. I think of the marks on the stone wall inside the alcove and of the rivers where Adam and I swam.

With each step taken in the direction of the east border, my legs feel heavier and heavier. So many times I've wondered what it is like outside the garden. I wanted to see more of our world—to know what else it contained—but now . . .

Adam stops as I slow down. I look at him in the morning light. His eyes are nearly green today, the brown faded, and he is perspiring from our walk. "I don't want to leave," I say.

His expression is a mixture of understanding and concern. "I know," he says, touching my cheek and drawing me close to him. I lean into him, feeling his heart beat rapidly against me.

When he releases me, he looks toward the garden entrance, then back to me, hesitation on his face. Elohim is near the entrance, and when we pass him, we'll leave the garden forever.

But this must be. "We'll do this together," I say, my voice quiet but determined. "Are you ready?"

"Yes," Adam says, the hesitation faded. We clasp hands tightly and walk the last few paces to the low rock wall. I can hardly believe we are actually going to cross the border and stand on soil that is not of the garden.

Adam stops before the entrance, where there is a sizeable gap in the stone wall. A tree grows on each side of the opening, and the branches from the two trees touch one another above us. The only being who has ever crossed this way has been Elohim.

We move closer to the entrance, standing to one side. Adam runs his hands against the stones that he'd stacked so long ago. I place my hands on the stone as well, feeling the solid coolness beneath my skin. I breathe out slowly.

Before I know it, Adam has stepped through the garden entrance. I glance at his extended hand and place my hand in his. Placing one foot in front of the other, I step through the entrance and across the border. My stomach flutters, and new moisture enters my eyes.

We have left the Garden of Eden.

Adam puts his arm around me, and we take a few steps together. We both look back at the same time, and we cannot see Elohim beyond the trees.

Then it happens. My legs give out, and I collapse to the ground. I gasp for air as my breathing feels suddenly shallow. Images of rock and dirt blur before me, and one part of me realizes that Adam too is on his knees, struggling for breath.

My strength leaves my body completely, and I fall forward. My hands scrape against the rocks, bringing stinging pain.

"Adam," I call out, but no sound comes. I try to speak again, to know that Adam is all right, but I can't even whisper. He is a huddled mass next to me. The only comfort that I have is that I can hear him breathing.

I concentrate on moving my arms, but my limbs are weighed down as if I am suspended at the bottom of a river. I can't tell if Adam is trying to move as well. My eyes are open, but they feel heavy, as if I've missed sleep for several nights in a row. I force my eyes to stay open as I keep my gaze on Adam.

My stomach feels empty and numb. Then the numbness grows, moving through my body like a vast emptiness. I still can't move, but finally I can manage a whisper. "What's happening to us, Adam?"

I think I hear a whisper, but I can't make out any words. My body starts to shiver. The heaviness is lifting, but it's replaced with a hundred different sensations. Lifting my hands, I see that my skin is scraped. Lines of red peek through my palms among the grooves of torn skin.

It's blood—just like the blood I saw on the snake. I have blood.

"Adam, look at my hands," I say in a hoarse voice.

His head slowly turns. "You're bleeding," he says, his voice low and rough like my own.

Our eyes connect. His are reddened, and I know that mine must be too.

He exhales and reaches for my hands to examine them. "Does it pain you?" he asks.

"I think so." I feel the sting anew as Adam lifts my hands toward him.

He touches one of the scrapes with his finger, and the blood smears. He looks at me with concern.

I look at the blood on both of our hands. "We have Fallen," I whisper.

Adam stared into Eve's eyes that were now rimmed in red. It was unmistakable. They had Fallen. Adam's body felt different and even seemed to breathe differently. His stomach was tight with hunger, as if he hadn't eaten for more than a day, and Eve's hands were bleeding.

But the most noticeable difference was the emptiness he felt inside. Not only had he and Eve been cast out of the garden, but they had been cut off from the presence of Elohim, who was nowhere to be seen.

It wasn't something that Elohim had told him, but Adam's new knowledge circled in understanding. What they had in the garden couldn't be duplicated outside. The Garden of Eden had been a special place, an exclusive existence.

Eve was shaking. Adam's arms felt extremely tired, but he held her as they sat in the dirt. She sniffled and clung to him. Closing his eyes, he mouthed a prayer to Elohim. They may have been cut off from Elohim's presence, but that wouldn't stop Adam from sending pleas heavenward.

There was so much to learn, he was sure. *Now I am the one with the questions.*

By the time he and Eve climbed to their feet, the sun was high in the sky. Without the luxury of soft grass, walking was a slower process. The rocks jabbed into Adam's feet, and they quickly grew dirty. He and Eve continued north, staying near one of the rivers that flowed into the garden, for lack of any particular desire to go in another direction.

When Eve stopped to look back at the garden, Adam turned as well. They had traveled a fair distance, but he could still see the rock wall, the lush trees, and the incredible contrast between the garden and the landscape in which they now stood.

"I don't want to lose sight of it," Eve said in a quiet voice.

"Neither do I," he said. "We should look for a place where we can prepare for the night while there's still plenty of light." He scanned their surroundings. Large mountains rose toward the east, and smaller hills moved westward. It seemed Adam and Eve were heading into a valley of sorts.

Not far was the river they'd been following. It was narrow, and scrubby bushes grew along its banks. Beyond the river was nothing but rocky terrain dotted with thin-looking trees. The wind rushed at them in gusts, stirring up the dirt at their feet. They'd already stepped into the river a few times, but, finding it quite cold, they'd lasted only long enough to wash off their feet and Eve, her hands.

"How far will we go, Adam?"

He looked at Eve. The red of her eyes had faded, but her face was as pale as the stones beneath their feet. "Not too much farther today," he said. The base of the rising mountains was still a good distance, and they wouldn't be able to reach the mountains before dark fell. She leaned against him, wrapping one arm around his waist.

He hadn't realized that his skin had grown cold until

she pressed against him. The warmth radiated from her, warming him where they touched.

"I'd like to visit the seas," Eve said.

The words filtered up to Adam, and he nodded, realizing that this was a courageous statement for Eve. She was already looking past today and beyond the garden.

"We'll visit the seas and the rest of this wilderness," he said. "There will be plenty of days to see everything." Although he said the words, he wasn't sure how many days they'd live or how far they needed to travel. Mortality would be much different than immortality.

He smoothed the hair resting on Eve's shoulder and felt her shiver beneath his touch. "It's definitely cooler out here in the wilderness," he said. He draped the coat of skin that Elohim had given him over her shoulders.

"This is yours," she said, trying to give it back.

"I'm not cold," Adam said. He secured the coat around her shoulders.

She finally accepted it but said, "We'll need to make clothing that gives us more warmth and protection. We'll be at the mercy of the sun, it seems."

Adam let out a breath. The land was practically barren here compared to the garden. There was so much they had to prepare for, so much they had to learn. He suppressed a shudder at the thought of securing animal skins for him and Eve to clothe themselves in. Perhaps there was another way to cover their bodies without killing animals.

"Come on," Eve said in a small voice. She linked one of her hands in his.

"How are your hands?" Adam asked.

"Better," Eve said. "The cold water helped."

They'd reached a bend in the river, where it turned east. The river widened, and the current slowed at the bend. To the north, the land sloped, dipping into a valley. The trees were thicker there, although they weren't deep green like those in the garden. Instead, the trees were a mixture of pale greens, oranges, and browns.

Eve seemed to notice the varied trees at the same time as Adam did. "They are beautiful in their own way," she said. "What do you think makes the trees different colors than those in the garden?"

Just then the breeze picked up, wrapping itself around Adam. "The cold air?" he said.

Eve blinked rapidly and looked down at the ground as they walked.

"Are you all right?" he asked.

She lifted a shoulder, and Adam noticed the tiny bumps along her arms. "I'm really hungry," she said.

If Adam hadn't been so hungry himself, he might have smiled at the way she said it. He hadn't seen any fruit trees or berries growing on bushes in their travels so far. He looked farther along the river; none of the plants looked like the herbs they cultivated in the garden.

Eve followed his gaze as she rubbed her arms as if she could make the cold disappear. "I'm not hungry enough to try those plants."

He chuckled and wrapped his arms around her, pulling her close. She seemed to sag against him until he felt as if he were holding her up. "Let's stop for a while and rest. I think we've walked equal to the whole perimeter of the garden."

They sat together on the bank, just above where the water flowed. Little insects kept landing on Adam's arms and biting him. He swatted them away, but they kept coming back. "What kind of insects are these?"

Eve was busy waving insects away from her own arms.

Then something growled from behind them. Adam turned with a start. A bear, its coat matted and brown, lumbered about a dozen paces away. It was slowly moving in their direction, its wary gaze on them.

"Oh, poor creature. It looks so lonely." Eve started to climb to her feet, but Adam grabbed her arm.

"Wait," he whispered. "It doesn't look friendly."

Eve glanced at him. "What do you mean? Maybe it's just hungry like us."

"Exactly," Adam said, and Eve's eyes widened.

"You don't think—"

"Shh," Adam said, searching the ground for a rock that he could use to defend them. He picked up a rock, although it wasn't as big as he'd like. The bear was probably on its way to the river, but now that it had seen them, it might be deterred.

Eve grabbed a rock that was even smaller than Adam's. He noticed she was trembling, but she kept her chin up, staring the bear down.

"What should we do?" she whispered.

"Stand up slowly," Adam said, even though he had no grand ideas. "There are two of us, and we're bigger. That might intimidate it."

As he stood, Eve stayed right next to him. Eve had been right. The bear looked hungry—desperately so. Its eyes had a wild look to them, unlike the those of the beasts they'd known in the garden—the beasts that had never known hunger.

Another growl came from the bear.

"We're going to cross the river," Adam whispered. "Slowly walk backward with me." With his right hand, he felt for Eve's hand. He kept the rock gripped in his left hand. Eve's hold was tight as they took a step back, then another. Soon, they'd made the few steps to the river's edge.

Crossing the rocky riverbed while keeping their gazes on the bear proved difficult. Adam held Eve's arm, helping to keep her steady. Thankfully, the river reached only their knees as they pushed through the sudden coldness.

By the time they reached the far bank, Eve was

shivering. The bear had stepped into the river at the bend where the water slowed and created something of a pond, but its attention was no longer on them. Adam watched in fascination as the bear swiped at the water with its large paw.

After a few swipes, the bear caught a fish with its claw.

Eve gasped quietly next to Adam. "Did you see that?" she whispered.

The bear's mouth clamped over the fish, and then the bear left the river and ate the fish on the shore.

Eve shuddered, but her eyes remained riveted on the bear.

"It seems we were at the bear's favorite place to catch fish," Adam said. They watched the animal walk into the river again.

The bear easily caught a second fish and then returned again to the shore to eat it.

Adam let out a breath of relief. They were wet and cold but seemingly safe from the bear.

"Now where do we go?" Eve said, breaking into his thoughts.

Adam wasn't sure anymore. North had seemed to be a natural plan, but the river turned east. The earth looked so vast, and the choices were endless. Confusion hardened in his mind.

"We should just keep to the river so that we can always find our way back to Eden," Eve said.

"All right," he said. The insects seemed to have followed them across the river, so they walked a little farther away from the bank, where the insects didn't thrive as much. They continued walking at a decent pace, keeping a closer watch out for other animals.

As the sun descended in the sky, the temperature grew even cooler, colder than it had ever been in the garden. Adam, having had nothing to eat most of the day, felt his energy wane as they continued to walk. He noticed that Eve was having a hard time keeping up with his already slower pace. The mountains loomed to the east, yet they were still quite far away.

There were no fruits or berries on any of the trees or shrubs they'd passed. Adam kept glancing toward the river, thinking of the fish that swam just below the surface and the bear that caught them. Then he thought about the bear's warm coat of fur and what he'd have to do to capture and kill the bear.

Adam shook his head. He couldn't believe these thoughts were entering his head. He'd never considered killing any animal in the garden. But now . . . the endless rocks, the dry earth, the blowing wind, and the increasing cold all combined to force him to face his new world.

Eve stopped in front of him and sank on the ground.

At first, Adam wondered if she'd injured herself again, but when he crouched next to her, he saw the exhaustion evident on her face. "Should we rest?"

She blinked up at him, her face.

"Are you still cold?" he asked. She simply nodded, pulled her legs up, and wrapped her arms around them. Adam stood and looked around for anything nearby that could provide shelter. The scraggly bushes near the river would offer little protection, and the trees were sparse in this area.

"I'm so hungry." Eve's voice seemed small as it floated up to him.

Adam decided that if he could find her something to eat, she could walk farther to where they could seek some sort of shelter. "I'm going to the river," he said.

Eve barely acknowledged him, and he hurried to the riverbank, glancing frequently in her direction in case any unwelcome animals appeared.

He studied the flow of the water and looked for the unmistakable flash of gray that would indicate a fish. Several fish swam by, but he was unable to catch them and only got wetter in the process. The water started to numb his feet, and Adam let out a breath of frustration. The coldness of the water seemed to seep through his skin and slow his muscles until he felt a deep pain in them, and the wind made the skin that wasn't in the water break out into bumps. He tried again and again to capture a fish. He didn't have claws like the bear or anything sharp to catch the fish with, and he didn't think throwing a rock at a fish would make much of an impact.

He walked out of the water, shivering. As he moved toward Eve, his nearly numb feet stung with every step. "I'm going to use one of the coats of skin to catch the fish," he said when he reached her.

Eve barely nodded.

Adam removed the extra coat around her shoulders, wishing he didn't have to. Then he returned to the river. He knotted one end of the coat so that he'd have something to catch the fish in and hoped they'd swim right into it.

It took several tries to catch the first fish. It was small and gray and flopping like mad in the wet coat.

Adam carried it to the shore. Clenching his teeth together at the thought of what he had to do, he picked up a rock, then struck the helpless fish. Blood immediately seeped out of the fish, and Adam's stomach twisted furiously, but he knew it was food. He'd seen the bear eat it.

He pulled the skin and flesh apart and discovered extremely sharp bones that supported the fish's shape. Several bones poked Adam, nearly bringing blood from his fingers. Other parts inside the fish were various colors and shapes. He tossed those back into the river and made a pile of the flesh. He set aside the bone, thinking it would be useful to have something small and sharp to use at their new dwelling.

Glancing at Eve, he saw that she hadn't moved from her position. She still huddled in the single coat of skin, her knees drawn up. Adam picked up a piece of the fish and smelled it. His stomach roiled, and he wished he hadn't inhaled. It would be difficult enough to eat, but there seemed to be no other choices.

Putting the piece into his mouth, he pretended the moist smoothness was that of a fruit. He chewed quickly and then swallowed. Closing his eyes, he felt the piece travel down to his empty stomach. He waited a few moments as it settled. *I'm still alive.*

He ate another piece, then another. Moments passed, and his strength returned by a small measure. Now he just had to convince Eve to eat.

Adam laid the wet coat over the nearby bushes. It was heavy with water now, and he hoped it would dry out, even in the cold air. He walked over to Eve and knelt next to her. "Eve," he said. "I brought you some food."

Her eyebrows lifted in response.

"I've tried it myself and find it nourishing," he said.

For a long moment, Eve stared at the pieces of fish in his hand still colored with blood. Finally, she picked up the smallest piece and put it in her mouth. In an instant, she spit it out and gasped.

"I—I can't eat that!" she said.

"You have to," Adam said. "It's all there is. Our world is different now, and we have to make changes."

Eve exhaled with a shudder. "Haven't there been enough changes already?"

He put one arm around her. "I'm sure there will be a few more."

She closed her eyes. "I know. I just . . ." She opened her eyes a slit and looked at the fish pieces. "That's a *fish.*"

"It's nourishing, Eve. You must eat. It will give you strength so that we can find shelter for the night."

Eve closed her eyes for another moment. Then finally

she opened them and picked up another piece of fish. This time she didn't spit it out.

"Try another one," Adam said.

She took another piece. "This is the last bite I'll take. I can wait until we find something else after this."

17

And out of the ground made God . . . the tree of life also in the midst of the garden, and the tree of knowledge of good and evil.

—Genesis 2:9

Adam pulls me to my feet, and although I'd rather just curl up in the dirt and fall asleep, I move with him. My husband says we need to keep moving to find shelter and that the sun is keeping the air warmer now than it will be at night when there is only the moon.

My skin has never felt so dry. Neither has my throat, and my stomach is taut with hunger. I don't dare try to eat any more of the fish, and I think of the abundant fruit that I wasted in the garden. The walking never seems to end, but just as Adam does, I put one foot in front of the other, then repeat. We see another bear, but this one just watches us from the other side of the river. I'm grateful it's on that side and not our side.

A shiver trails through me, and I grasp Adam's hand, not only for warmth but because I've never felt more alone. In the garden, I knew every tree, every animal, and it was home.

But this place . . . this place does not welcome me.

The cold wind, the rocky ground, and the lack of sweet fruit or herbs are all joining together *against* me. Although Elohim warned that I would bear children in sorrow, I feel the sorrow entering my heart now.

I feel as if I have been weighted to the earth. The only reason I keep walking, despite my weakness and my bruised feet, is because I can't let go of Adam's hand. His warm, strong hand is all that I have to keep me moving forward.

Dark seems to fall fast in this new land. As the sky changes from blue-gray to indigo, our steps slow. The moon is a sliver tonight, and the rocky ground is not easy to navigate in the lesser light. Hunger prods my stomach. I wonder how just one day of little eating can cause so much pain.

This fallen body feels things much more intensely.

Exhaustion prompts my next words to Adam. "I don't care if we sleep in the open, with only each other to brace ourselves against the wind."

Adam must be colder than I am, for I am wearing the coat of skin from Elohim. Adam carries his wet one, which he sacrificed in catching the fish.

He finally stops and looks down at me. I can see his concern, which is clear even in the fading light of day.

"There is nothing here to shelter us," he says. "It can't be much farther." But he is staring ahead and, like me, sees nothing that looks promising.

"I'm so tired," I say. The changes in my body are not what I expected. I feel as if I could sleep anywhere.

"Come on," Adam says, pulling my hand toward the river. We stop at a group of low bushes. They are not enough to block the wind, but it seems that Adam's exhaustion has won out too. His coat of skin is still damp, but he spreads it on the ground, and we lie next to each other, pulling my coat over the both of us.

My back is to Adam, and he wraps his arms around me. It takes several moments, but finally I start to warm, at least where we are covered—although I don't think my legs and feet will ever be warm again. With Adam's arms around me, I am more aware of his every movement, his every breath, than I have ever been. I focus on the heat that his body brings. It's too cold to think of much else.

The morning sun has never felt better on my face. Every part of my body aches, but at last I am warm. Then I notice red bumps on my arms, and I scratch at the itching spots. The insects didn't stay just by the river after all. The torn skin on my palms is ragged and dirty. I must wash my hands again. I turn my head and realize that Adam isn't lying next to me. When I sit up, I see him near the river; he's caught another fish. My stomach twists at the thought of eating a fish again.

Adam catches me looking at him, and he smiles.

I smile back.

We've survived our first night in the wilderness.

I can see that Adam is quite wet and surely cold. How he can endure it, I don't know. I pull my legs up and tighten the coat of skin around me, protecting any warmth that might stray. The sun's rays are still early, but they're doing a marvelous job of heating my face and arms. Even if today is a hot day, I will enjoy every moment. But the clouds to the north tell me it won't be a hot day. We are about to experience our first mist in the wilderness.

Adam strides toward me, carrying a fish. His feet are covered in mud, and the mat tied around his waist drips with water. This time I say nothing and simply eat as much as I can. I know the fish will nourish my weak body, and that is the only way I can force myself to swallow.

"Are you feeling better?" Adam asks.

"I love the sun," I say, and he laughs. I enjoy hearing it, and I laugh with him.

"Did you see any bears this morning?" I ask.

"No. I think they must sleep late, like my wife."

I shake my head with a smile. Adam returns to the river to wash off his hands, and I watch how the muscles in his shoulders and back work as he moves. I had never really noticed before how there is definition to each muscle in his arms. I know that I've touched them many times, but the thought of touching his arms now makes my chest warm, and I wonder if that is another characteristic of my changing body.

As I watch Adam, my face feels hot, as if I've stood facing the sun too long. I want him to come back to my side and put those arms around me. I realize I am now warmer than I've been since leaving the garden, and it's because I'm watching my husband in the river.

Before he can turn and see my hot face, I stand and shake out the coat of skin that we lay on during the night. A cloud of dirt and leaves falls off it. The coat is still damp, so I drape it over the bush we slept next to.

When I look up, I find Adam watching me. No, staring at me. I don't understand the look in his eyes, but it makes my face go from warm to hot.

"Thank you for catching the fish," I say, because I need to say something to get him to stop staring at me.

He looks down as he walks out of the river, shaking his hands dry. "We'll find something better today."

"As long as it's not fish or bear." I expect him to laugh, but when he looks at me, his expression is serious.

"This is certainly a different world," he says in a quiet voice, continuing his walk toward me.

I can't look away now, and I focus on his shoulders, then his arms. I wonder if he's always been as tall as he seems, or as strong.

He stops before me, and I swallow against my dry throat. His eyes are nearly golden this morning. I need a drink from the river.

"Eve," he says in a quiet voice as he touches my hair. He pauses, and I wait for him to tell me about our changing bodies. I want to know if he is feeling what I am. I think of what Elohim told us about multiplying and replenishing the earth—about *how* we are supposed to fulfill that commandment. Is Adam thinking of this too? He steps back, his hand falling to his side. "I'm glad you're doing better. Tonight, I promise, we'll have a warmer place to sleep."

I allow myself to only nod when I really want to wrap my arms around his neck and pull him close. I can only predict his surprise. He'd think I am faint from hunger again, and perhaps I am.

"Then we'd better set out soon," I say.

He grabs the coat of skin perched on the bush and throws it over one shoulder. I walk into the shallow part of the river, washing my feet and hands. The water is cold, but it soothes the scrapes on my palms. When I step out of the water, Adam is waiting for me, his hand extended. I take it, my fingers threading through his long ones, and just as I suspected, darts shoot up my arm. As his fingers close over mine, I realize that it will be very hard to let them go.

I want to know what Adam is feeling, but we have a lot of traveling to do, and I'll wait to ask my questions. I focus on the mountains up ahead. There's no real reason we are walking toward them. The mountain range just seems to be a place we should walk toward.

The distant garden, marked by tall, green trees, looks almost foreign in the morning light, as if it's a place that we haven't been to for a long time, not just a day. The space between the garden and us creates an added feeling of absence. The Eve who was in the garden is different than the woman I am now. As the bottoms of my feet throb from the bruising of walking so much, I wonder if I would make the same choice if I could go back now.

After only one night in the wilderness, I'm tired, achy, and hungry, and I itch.

But walking and moving in one direction for as far as we want to never happened in the garden. There was always a wall to keep us inside its boundaries. Now there are no boundaries. The only place we can't go now is inside the garden. Our life has become the opposite.

I let out a breath, a mixture of relief and sorrow. I already miss the animals of the garden and the beauty of the flowers and many trees. I miss the mild nights and the pond where we bathed. But we are here now, and there is no going back. With Adam at my side, I can do anything. I have to.

I look up at him and find his concerned gaze on me. I am sure that I flush, and I look quickly away.

"How did you sleep?" he asks, his voice washing over me in its tenderness.

"Fairly well, considering the cold and the insects." I lift up my arm, displaying the red bumps. "Do you have insect bites as well?"

He nods and says, "We must find something that will keep the insects away. I've been noticing that some of the plants aren't bothered by the insects." He points to a pale green plant with round leaves that's at the top of the riverbank ahead of us.

I walk over to it and examine the bush. Sure enough, I don't see any insects flying around it or crawling on its leaves. I pluck off a leaf and smell it. The scent is sharp but not unpleasant.

"Maybe I can make a coat of these leaves," I say.

Adam pulls off a leaf and examines it as well. Then he

crushes it between his fingers. The scent is strong enough that I can smell it from where I stand on the other side of the bush.

"Maybe we should rub it onto the coats."

I crush a leaf in my hand, wrinkling my nose as the sharp aroma turns bitter. No wonder the insects stay away. I touch the crumbled leaf to my arm and rub it back and forth. I lift my arm and can smell the scent on it. Adam rubs crumbled leaves on his arms as well.

"Do you think this bush is plentiful throughout the wilderness?" I ask.

"Let's take some branches with us," he says.

We each break off a few branches, and Adam bundles them together. I see that he has now collected several fish skeletons. The tiny, sharp bones will be good for something. We keep a fair pace, both of us watching the gathering clouds. They are dark gray and moving steadily toward us.

For the most part, we walk in silence, our breathing the only conversation between us.

When something cries out from the sky, I am so startled that I grab Adam's arm. A large bird with broad wings sails overhead. It cries out again. The second cry isn't as disturbing, and I stare at the magnificent creature.

Its strength is obvious as it maneuvers the sky, moving gracefully and precisely. "What is it?" I ask Adam. He has named the animals in the garden, and so I look to him, wondering if he has already named the bird above us.

Adam watches the bird with me as it cuts a path against the dark clouds.

"Is it trying to tell us something?" I say just as the wind picks up. The storm is coming quickly now. A bright light shoots through the clouds, and I cling to Adam. "What is that?"

Adam stares where the light appeared, although now it's gone. Then a low rumble sounds, coming from the earth and sky at once. The sound cracks through the air, and the bird cries out again.

"What's going on, Adam?" I ask, my voice louder than I intend. My heart thuds against my chest. "It's as if the heavens are shouting."

"It's a storm as I've never witnessed before. Come on," Adam says and pulls me toward a group of trees. The trees are nothing like those in the Garden of Eden, but their sparse branches and few leaves might offer some shelter from the angry sky.

Another crack of light sends me huddling against Adam. His arms are around me, holding me close as light after light flashes around us. It's as though the sun has made an instant appearance, coming and going at will.

I no longer hear the bird's cry as the mist starts, coming from the sky in incredible torrents. It drenches Adam and me completely in just a few moments, and it's nearly as cold as the river.

I bury my head in Adam's neck, desperate for some warmth, but even more so, comfort. "What is this place?" I ask Adam, trying futilely to steady my trembling voice. "What have we done? It's as if the very heavens are angry with us."

Adam's hand tangles into my hair as he presses his lips against my forehead. My breathing calms as he holds me, and I eventually notice that the rumbling sky has fallen silent, although the mist still drenches our skin.

Eating fish by the river in the sunshine this morning seems much more appealing now.

Adam and I sit down and pull the coats over our heads, drawing our legs up to stay covered by the coats. Adam's arms wrap around me, and I lean into him, feeling the warmth of his body matching mine. I wonder how long the heavens will rage and if we'll ever reach a place of shelter.

18

And God said, It is not good that the man should be alone; I will make him an help meet for him.
—Genesis 2:18

The night was the longest that Adam could ever remember, not to mention the wettest. He hoped Eve had slept better than he had: he'd alternated between completely awake and cold to partly awake and cold.

The heavens had tempered just before dawn, and that's when he, at last, fell asleep. By the time the sun lit the sky, he was awake again. He moved carefully so that he wouldn't wake Eve. She had been so tired the day before. Her usual golden skin had grown pale, and her hands still looked sore.

Adam moved pieces of damp hair from her face, and her eyelids fluttered, then closed again. There was dirt on her arms concealing some of the red insect bumps, and he winced as he realized that their only way to clean off the dirt was with cold water from the river. Beneath them was a mixture of mud and grass. They'd both have to venture into the cold water.

But for now, Adam let Eve sleep as long as she needed to. His arm and neck ached from being in the same position so long, but Eve was nestled against his chest. Even with the dirt and leaves in her hair, she was a thing of beauty. Just looking at her now made it difficult for him to keep his breath even.

He thought about what Elohim had said about their natural desires, ones that would result in bringing forth children, and Adam knew that, at least for him, those desires were already in effect. But watching Eve in her helpless state, subservient to the rages of the heavens and the unpredictable winds and mist, made him reluctant to do anything that might bring her more sorrow or pain.

For Elohim had said he'd multiply her sorrow when she brought forth children.

Adam's breath came short just thinking about any pain or sorrow that his wife might experience. When she'd scraped her palms, the blood had startled them both. Adam knew that in his body, just below his layer of skin, blood stirred as well. He held up his right hand and turned it over. Yes, even his skin was a different pallor. A hint of red beneath the brown belied the fact that blood was close to the surface, so that if he scraped his skin, the blood would surface quickly.

He let out a breath, and his body involuntarily shivered. They had been cold for two nights now, and they were still a fair distance from the eastern mountains. They needed warmer coverings, something to keep the mist off and the mud away, and something thicker to sleep on that would provide them with a measure of comfort.

Eve stirred and let out a soft moan. "The mist has stopped?" she asked, her voice sounding small and tired.

"At last," Adam said, running his fingers along her face. He picked out from her hair the leaves that must have fallen from the trees above during the night. At least they'd been able to take some shelter in the thin grove, although it was not enough to satisfy Adam.

"What's to eat?" she asked. "Fish?"

Adam smiled, gazing into the blue-green of her eyes. His gaze trailed to the rest of her features, including her narrow nose and full lips—the rose color of her lips reminding him of the flowers in the garden. As she looked at him, her gaze trusting, he vowed to find something more to eat today, no matter how much effort it took.

"Unless you see some fruit in these trees, we'll have fish for the morning meal," he said. "But I hope to find something new today."

Eve looked toward the trees, and he followed her gaze. There was nothing resembling a fruit among the yellow and orange leaves.

"What's that?" she asked, pointing at a branch.

Adam looked closer, seeing a small, brown shape. "It's probably part of the branch."

"But it's just hanging off, and there are quite a few of them." She pushed up on her elbows.

He moved to a sitting position. Eve was right. There were several brown shapes dangling from the branches. He stood and touched one; it was hard and quite solid. Eve stood next to him and pulled one off.

She smelled it, then shook it. A light rattling sound came from within. "There's something in there," she said, her voice warm with hope. "And if it grows on a tree, we can probably eat it."

Adam plucked one of the brown shapes and shook it as well. He turned it over in his fingers and looked for a way to open it. Finally, he bit on the hardness, but there was no malleability.

"Let's try a rock," Eve said, scanning the ground. She picked one up and, placing the brown shape on the ground, she struck it. The brown shape flew out from under the rock.

"Let me see the rock," Adam said, and he hit the brown

shape he held. There was a definite crack, and the shell was in pieces.

Eve leaned over to examine the insides. A pale brown shape was inside, although now it was crushed. She picked up a piece and put it in her mouth.

"Eve," Adam began, but she was already chewing.

"It's good," she said and promptly ate another piece. "Much better than fish."

Adam tried a piece, and although it was different from any taste he'd experienced, it was pleasing. They ate the insides of several more of the brown shapes and then collected more. Adam regarded the sparse trees with more interest, wondering how many they had passed on their journey so far. Perhaps Elohim was looking out for them after all.

Eve was all smiles as they walked to the river. They washed quickly in the cold water, but even the cold didn't seem to dampen Eve's spirit, and for that, he was grateful. He knew that this was temporary, though: they had another long day of walking ahead of them and another cold night, unless he could find shelter and a way to stay warm.

The glorious and delicious sun warmed Adam's skin as they walked toward the east mountains. He breathed in the crisp, cool air and reveled in the new warmth. The sky was free of clouds and impending mist. Tonight would be a dry one.

Eve seemed to walk with renewed energy as well. Adam caught her looking at him more than once. He was surprised she hadn't already asked dozens of questions about their new world. Finally, he laughed. "Do you have something you want to ask me?"

He was surprised to see her face redden as she looked quickly away.

Adam took her hand. "What is it? Is something wrong?"

Eve's gaze was trained on the ground, her face still red.

When she lifted her gaze, Adam's heart lurched. Her eyes were even bluer in contrast to her reddened complexion. He had the unexplainable urge to pull her into his arms. So he did.

She melted against him, nearly clinging to him.

"Tell me, Eve," he said, resting his chin on top of her sun-warmed hair. He'd never noticed how every part of their bodies seemed to blend together, and instead of being two separate people, they were like one.

Her head moved back and forth.

Adam drew away. "You aren't going to tell me what's bothering you—why you keep looking at me with questions that you refuse to ask?"

She blinked up at him, then looked to a spot beyond his shoulder.

He slid his hand behind her neck and said, "The Eve I know wouldn't hesitate." He received a half smile in return, and a jolt shot through Adam. He wanted to press his mouth against her smile. Dropping his hands, he released her, not sure where his thoughts had come from.

Was this what Elohim had said about *natural desire*? It must be, Adam decided. Then he felt his face heat up, and suddenly he knew what Eve had been thinking about.

He released a deep breath and said, "Are you thinking about what Elohim said in the garden—about multiplying and replenishing the earth?"

A deep red flushed Eve's face, and she said in a quiet voice, "Have you been thinking about it?"

He held back a smile. "Yes." When she met his gaze, his heart pounded, and it was hard to take a normal breath. "I can feel the difference in my body since we Fell. There are so many things that feel different." He stepped closer to her and moved his hands to her waist. Her hands lifted to rest on the outside of his shoulders, and she stared at his chest.

"Do you feel different?" he asked.

"Very." Her eyes closed. She leaned slightly toward him and moved her hands down along his arms, as if she were tracing every muscle there.

Adam couldn't explain what was going on inside his body and heart, but he couldn't move as Eve moved her hands down his arms and then interlaced her fingers with his.

They stood together, neither moving nor speaking for several moments, the sun wrapping around both of them.

When Eve stepped away, Adam felt as if he had just awakened from a dream, and he hovered in the moment between sleep and full wakefulness.

"Those bushes look as though they grow berries," Eve said, moving away from him.

The wakefulness came, but the acute awareness was still there. Adam followed her, seeing the high, dark green bushes she had spotted.

He took several deep breaths, trying to steady the churning inside of him. Had Eve felt as he did? Is that why she wanted space between them now?

She stopped in front of a bush dotted with small fruits that were a deep berry red and that looked perfectly good. Adam reached out to pluck one of the berries, and his hand rubbed against the stem of the bush. It pricked his skin, and he drew his hand away quickly. "That bush causes pain. We shouldn't eat of its berries."

"Let me try," Eve said, a smile on her face. "See the stems? They have sharp edges poking out. Don't touch them as you pluck a berry." She pulled a fruit from the bush and lifted it to Adam's mouth.

He opened his mouth obediently and ate the berry. It was sweet and moist on his tongue. "Very nice," he said. Eve popped another one into his mouth. He rather enjoyed her feeding him. Adam breathed out, new hope growing inside of him. They had found food.

Eve smiled as she chewed the next berry. "*Much* better than fish."

"You really don't like fish, do you?"

Eve plucked another berry and popped it into her mouth. "No."

He loved the warmth in her eyes as she ate the berries. "What about bear?" he said, holding back a smile.

Her eyes snapped to him, her face paling. "You can't mean it."

"Or maybe an insect?" he said.

She took a step back and gasped. "How can you even think of that?"

He grinned and grabbed her at the waist. He wanted to be close to her, to never let her go. "I'll never make you eat an insect . . . unless you're sleeping."

Eve pushed against his chest, both squirming and laughing. Then she stopped and lifted her face to his.

He watched her as she moved closer—the dark brown of her eyelashes and the way her tangled hair tumbled over her shoulders and down her back.

"Adam," she whispered, her breath touching his lips.

Tingling spread through him, making him feel numb and alert at the same time. He lowered his head, still watching her. Her gaze went to his mouth, and her lips moved toward his as if they had been meant to be together all along.

Adam closed his eyes, and a breeze seemed to push up from the ground and move between him and Eve. He realized that she was no longer in his arms.

He opened his eyes to find that she'd stepped out of his hold and turned away.

"Eve?" Adam asked, his words coming out strangely thick, as though he had something in his mouth he was trying to speak around.

She lifted a shoulder, but she didn't look at him. "I think I feel . . . afraid."

Adam exhaled. He knew what she was saying, and understood it even, but yet . . . "Of me?"

"No," she said in a quiet voice, then, "Yes." She turned to face him, and there was moisture on her cheeks. "Not of *you*, but of what this is . . . this desire Elohim spoke of. It's something that I'm not sure I understand."

And it's only growing stronger, Adam thought. He didn't want to tell Eve that, didn't want to concern her. He didn't comprehend it all himself, but he couldn't stop thinking about holding her and kissing her either. "Come on," he said, reaching for a berry. "Let's pick as many as we can. Then we'll finish the distance to the mountains."

19

And the rib, which God had taken from man, made he a woman, and brought her unto the man.

—Genesis 2:22

My heart won't slow its pounding. I almost touched my lips to Adam's, and he almost touched his lips to mine. Then I pulled away, and I could no longer look into his gold-green eyes. Does he understand even a small portion of what his touch does to me or how his gaze warms me from my very toes until the hairs on my neck raise up? The sun has lost its purpose when it seems my husband can warm me from now on.

I am still warm as the sun descends below the western hills and we reach the base of the eastern mountains. It has taken nearly three days to reach them, and now we'll surely find shelter.

The questions burn inside me: What is Adam thinking? What is he feeling? But I can't ask any of my questions. My heart speeds up as I consider them. I can't stop stealing glances at him, and I notice that he is looking at me as well.

My throat is tight, and my hands perspire. The journey has been exhausting, but there is energy welling up from somewhere deep inside me that continues to surface time after time. We have pressed on for an entire day, and still I could walk without slowing.

The berries that we picked are almost gone. Adam caught another fish along the way, of which I ate a few reluctant bites.

Adam is walking a little ahead of me, and I watch the movements in his shoulders and back. His hair brushes the top of his shoulders, and from time to time, the wind lifts it. I can almost feel his hair in my hands. I can't stop thinking about the way it felt to be in his arms, holding him close, feeling his heart beating as rapidly as mine.

When Adam stops and turns to face me, I wonder if he can see into my thoughts. My face warms quickly, and I'm grateful for the fading light.

"These trees will provide a decent shelter for tonight," he says, walking toward a group of trees that grow close together at the base of the slope. The mountain rises high and sharp above us.

Stopping makes me realize how tired I really am. "Those trees look fine," I say. I think of our alcove back in the garden and miss the soft bed of leaves and the protection from the heat—although now I wouldn't complain about a little more warmth from the sun.

Adam walks to the wild grove and snaps off some branches. The sound echoes against the mountain.

"What are you doing?" I ask.

"I'm going to build an alcove," he says.

"From tree branches?"

He tosses a branch to the ground, the fading sun glowing against his skin. "We need something to call home as we explore our surroundings." His eyes meet mine, and my heart thumps. The thought of sleeping next to him in a small space makes me feel hot again. The past two nights, we slept next to each other but in the open wilderness, space all around.

Although my legs ache from all the walking, I cross over to help Adam. I tug on a branch. It bends but doesn't break off. I tug harder but still don't have the strength to snap the wood. Adam comes up behind me, his arm reaching past me, and snaps the branch off.

"I'll break them," he says. "Why don't you gather them into a pile? Tomorrow we can weave the leaves together so that we can strap the branches into a shelter."

"All right," I say, moving away from his closeness.

We work quickly, and we lean the branches against a large boulder that we find. This creates a cozy, but also a very narrow, sleeping place.

"Will we both fit in there?" I ask.

"Yes," Adam says, looking a bit surprised at my question, but there is a slight smile on his face.

I exhale slowly, thinking I may not sleep much after all. The sun makes its final farewell, and darkness crowds us fast, so we finish the shelter in the faint moonlight.

Then there is nothing left to do but go to sleep. I crawl in the shelter first, pressing myself against the stone.

But when Adam peers inside, he says, "Move to the other side. The stone will be colder."

I slide over, and Adam crawls in. He stretches out, the edges of his body touching the edges of mine.

"Do you think it will get much colder tonight?" I say, folding my arms for some warmth. It has already grown noticeably cooler with the absence of the sun.

"It will be plenty cold." His voice rumbles over me. "But we should stay dry at least." Then he pulls me against him until my back is against his chest. Warmth moves through me, and my heart starts its rapid beat.

I say nothing, and Adam remains quiet. I wonder if he can hear my heart thumping and my rapid breath. I make an effort to breathe slower, to concentrate on getting warm and not on the man holding me in his arms.

"Are you hungry?" he asks after a moment.

"Not very," I say. "Not enough to eat fish or insects."

Adam laughs, and I revel in the way his chest moves with that laughter.

We are silent again, and a few times I think he has fallen asleep until he makes a slight movement or whispers a question. I'm grateful that he doesn't kiss me. I don't know what my reaction would be, and I'm not sure I want to find out.

At last sleep comes with the deepening of night and the warmth of Adam keeping out the cold.

I wake alone, but I am not cold. The sun is well into the sky, piercing through the openings between the shelter's branches. I hear a loud snap and know that Adam is breaking off more branches. The sound reverberates through me, each snap reflecting Adam's strength. In the garden we would have never broken the branches of the trees nor eaten the flesh of any fish. It seems this world is centered on destruction.

I stay quiet for another moment, missing Adam's arms around me and wondering if he slept as poorly as I did.

When I emerge from the shelter, Adam turns. There are shadows beneath his eyes, and it's as I guessed: he has slept little.

"How did you sleep?" he asks, tossing a branch into a growing pile.

"Enough," I say.

He gazes at me for a moment as if he is about to ask another question, but instead he turns back to his work. He is serious today, intent on working, it seems. I walk to the river to wash myself and to drink. Along the shore I discover that a few of the bushes grow berries. It seems we've found a good place to set up a dwelling.

When I step out of the river, I walk a little ways east, where the river tumbles down the rocks from someplace above. The thundering sound of the water fills my ears, blocking out the sound of breaking branches. I step closer to where the water falls from the mountain, feeling the water's cold spray upon my skin. The water moves so fast, never stopping or slowing, that I marvel at its power and persistence.

When I step away, I hesitate. Two black eyes are watching me from near the falling water. On the other side of the river, across the gorge, is a leopard.

This one looks gaunt; the outline of its bones at its shoulders and sides angle sharply as if there is very little flesh on the animal. Its gaze narrows in my direction as it watches me.

I have stroked the leopards in the garden, but I know that this one is not like those that I knew. With this leopard, I can almost feel its hunger as it stares. Then I notice the collection of brown fur at its feet and the stain of red on the leopard's paws and mouth. The small critter in front of the leopard has lost its life, becoming a meal.

My stomach jolts, and I want to turn and run, to scream for Adam. But I've seen leopards run, and I realize it wouldn't be much of a task for the leopard to leap the river and chase me down.

I breathe out, my heart pounding furiously. *O Elohim*, I pray silently, *I know that I'm unworthy of thy attention. But please deliver me from this beast.* As I pray, I simultaneously think of what I should do. Throw a rock? Turn and run? Not do anything? I think of the branches that Adam has collected, and I wonder how fast I could run to the pile and use a branch in defense.

The leopard tears into the critter in front of it, and even though I don't want to watch its teeth sinking into the helpless flesh, I can't take my eyes off the large feline. As I watch the animal eat, I realize the leopard is more protective of its prey than predatory, at least while there is still something left to eat.

As the leopard clamps into the next bite, I turn and start to run.

I don't dare look back, but I'm listening for any sound of following—although above the sound of the water, I may not hear anything before it's too late.

When Adam comes into view, my throat is too tight to call out. I run to the pile of branches and pick a branch up, spinning around, expecting a leopard to be running at full speed toward me.

But there is no threatening beast.

"Eve? What's wrong?" Adam asks.

My breath heaves out of me as I say, "Leopard." Adam is in front of me in an instant, gripping a large branch in his hands.

"Where?" he whispers.

It takes a couple of deep breaths before I am able to answer. "Where the river falls."

"You walked that far alone?"

He is in front of me, so I can't see his face, but his tone says it all.

"Yes, I wanted to see—"

"Shh," he says.

We both stand still, looking in the direction that I ran from. A small critter scampers across the ground, and Adam visibly relaxes, but my stomach only clenches tighter.

"It was eating one of those animals," I say in a quiet voice.

Adam turns slightly, glancing at me. "Which side of the river was the leopard on?"

"The other side, but it would have no trouble crossing."

He is now fully looking at me. "I doubt it will cross, especially if it has something to eat over there."

I look into my husband's grim face. "You didn't see how it glared at me."

Adam gazes at me for a moment, his eyes searching mine. "Don't go anywhere without me. We don't know what else is out there."

"I won't," I say. My breathing is about to return to normal, but now that Adam is staring at me, it picks back up.

He brushes the matted hair from my face, smoothing it behind my ear. "You must remember that we can die out here." His voice is quiet, almost reverent.

Something shudders through me, something I've come to recognize as fear. Our death can come unbidden. What if Adam dies first, and I am left alone? "I know." I notice the scratches on Adam's arms and hands from breaking branches. "Have you injured yourself?"

He looks down at his arms. "No. This is part of the work."

I am silent, and I can't look at him. I know he is not complaining, but we're in this wilderness suffering this cold and hunger because of my choice.

"Eve," he says, his voice just above a whisper.

I say nothing because my throat suddenly tightens.

"I couldn't sleep last night," he continues.

I only nod. I know he couldn't sleep. It was too cold, and he is probably much hungrier than I am.

"I can't stop thinking about kissing you," he says.

My head snaps up, and I stare at him. He certainly sees my flushed face and tears.

"You've kissed me many times," I say, my voice sounding raspy, as though I've just awakened for the day.

His head tilts, and he moves closer to me. "I have a desire to kiss you on your mouth."

If his expression wasn't so earnest, I might have laughed and pushed him away. But his eyes are holding mine, and there is a depth that I dare not make light of.

He is so close to me, and I'm not sure when he dropped the branch that he was holding, but his hands are sliding behind my back. His warmth consumes me as he draws me near, and I can think only that yes, I want to kiss him too.

Adam leans down, moving all too fast yet all too slow.

When his lips touch mine, I want to pull him even closer. I slide my hands up his chest and behind his neck, clutching him tighter. His mouth presses harder against mine, and a new numbness travels through my body. I feel as if I am no longer standing on the hard dirt but perhaps on a cloud, floating in the sky along with Adam.

His lips touching mine are like sunshine and mist in the same moment, warm and cool together. He breaks away slightly so that we can breathe, and then his mouth is on mine again, and we somehow manage to breathe together. Adam's arms tighten around me, and my fingers tangle in his hair.

His lips move against mine, no longer still, and I am reminded of swimming underwater in the river, floating through the absolute silence as my body moves weightlessly.

"I see you're enjoying the pleasures of this world," a voice says, cutting through my body.

I break away from Adam, my blood still pulsing hot beneath my skin. I know whom the voice belongs to before I see him.

20

And Adam said, This is now bone of my bones, and flesh of my flesh: she shall be called Woman, because she was taken out of Man.

—Genesis 2:23

Lucifer," I whisper.

He stands just within the shade of the trees. His black eyes seem to flash, even in the shadows. I feel his gaze touching my skin and moving along my body. Adam releases his hold on me, and I grasp his arm, staying close.

Lucifer wears a coat of skin the color of the earth. It wraps around his narrow waist. Across his torso, he wears a thin robe. He doesn't move. He just slides his gaze to Adam, then back to me. And smiles.

I shiver under that smile and feel my skin heat. I am no longer floating. My feet and legs are anchored to the cold, solid earth.

"What are you doing here?" Adam asks. His voice is thick, and I tremble as I remember his kissing.

I release Adam's arm but stay close. Our hands find each other, and we clench each other's fingers.

"You're in my world now." Lucifer's voice is smooth in the silence of the trees. "I can teach you everything you need to know."

Adam's grip tightens on my hand. "We aren't looking to learn from you."

I nod, but my neck is stiff, and I can barely move it. Going from the haziness that Adam's kiss brought to facing the disgraced angel who led us to fall makes me feel as if I jumped into the deepest part of the coldest river.

"You're looking for someone else?" Lucifer says. "And who will teach you how to live in this world?" He scans the pile of branches.

I breathe out. "We're waiting for communication from Elohim."

Lucifer's smile twists in laughter. "*Elohim?* I haven't seen him anywhere in this wilderness."

The darkness of Lucifer's gaze seems to press into me, making my skin feel heavy. Adam and I have been praying, but we have Fallen from Elohim's physical presence. We have been so focused on finding food and creating shelter that we have talked little of our relationship with Elohim. I do have hope that Elohim will still speak to us, but Lucifer's words are like a sharp rock against my chest.

Lucifer steps forward into the yellow light of day, his eyes muting.

Adam moves in front of me, his body a barrier between our brother and me.

"You don't need to be troubled, my brother," Lucifer says. "I've not come to separate you from your wife again."

I can't see the expression on Adam's face, but I sense the tension in his hand that grips mine. "Leave us alone," Adam says. "You have nothing to offer us."

"I have more to offer than you think." Lucifer moves forward again, and this time he keeps walking until he's near.

Adam holds his place between Lucifer and me, but I

meet my brother's gaze. Lucifer may have persuaded me to listen to him before Adam and I Fell, but I will not let him mislead me again.

"Why have you come, Lucifer?" I ask.

"To help you further your knowledge," he says, "just as I promised you in the garden."

Adam lets out his own laugh. "We don't believe any promises from you."

Lucifer's eyes are on me again, and I feel as if he's moved closer *without* moving. "We will see." His voice is slow. "I'm not going anywhere."

Adam slides an arm around me. "Then we'll leave." We turn away from Lucifer, but I can feel his gaze still on me.

"Why do you hasten from me?" His voice is slow, measured, quiet, but it reaches us all the same. I can hear the smile in his tone as he says, "You are walking away from the one who can teach you all that you desire to know."

Adam stops, and I anticipate him turning around to face Lucifer again, but he says only, "We desire nothing from you."

"Is that so?" Lucifer's voice arches.

Adam's body is tense, and he turns around, bringing me with him. The space we've put between Lucifer and us allows me to breathe more freely.

Lucifer's eyes slant as they slide over me. "I can teach you how to protect your wife from the roaming beasts and how to build a shelter that keeps her warm."

I feel it—the slightest pause from Adam. For an instant, I feel the weight of his hesitation rolling with his desire to protect me, to care for me.

And I can see that Lucifer feels it too. His voice drops to a whisper, yet it reverberates all around us. "I can teach you how to feed your wife so that she'll never feel the pang of hunger."

I tug on Adam's hand, pulling him away from our

brother—away from the lips that curl with knowledge and the dark eyes that seem to see straight into our hearts. Adam steps back with me. Lucifer makes no move to come any closer.

"We don't need your help." Adam's voice is low, resolute. "We make haste because the best protection I can offer my wife is to stay away from you."

We take another step back and turn toward the river.

Lucifer is quiet as we walk away, but that doesn't mean his voice isn't still in my head. Adam is right: the farther away from him we are, the better off we'll be. Even so, I want to bring up the possibility of the leopard still being at the riverbank, but apparently Adam prefers the danger of a hungry beast to the presence of our brother. He grips my hand so hard that pain shoots up it.

I don't protest but follow where Adam leads me. We climb up a slope, higher and higher, until we are both out of breath. Finally, he stops and turns to look over the river and the place where Lucifer was watching us.

There is no sign of the leopard, but that doesn't stop me from thinking there could be other desperate beasts nearby. Could Lucifer teach us how to protect ourselves? I dismiss the thought, wondering why I'd even consider it.

Adam and I sit together on the slope, and he says nothing about what Lucifer offered or the kiss that he interrupted. I can still feel the heat of it on my lips. My face flushes at my thoughts, and I'm grateful I'm sitting a little behind Adam. He tosses a rock down the slope.

"Should we find another place to build a shelter?" I say. "Now that Lucifer knows where we are dwelling?"

Adam throws another rock, this one landing in the river below. "He'll find us no matter where we settle."

I watch him throw a couple more rocks. "Are you trying to attract another leopard?" I say.

He turns his head. His gaze is a deep pool of sorrow,

and his jaw tightens. I realize now that he is more upset with the appearance of Lucifer than I thought.

"Maybe we should settle closer to the garden . . . in case Elohim lets us back in."

Adam shakes his head. He stands and reaches for me, pulling me with him. "We'll never be allowed back in, Eve," he says in a quiet voice.

I hate seeing his sadness. "I'm sorry," I whisper. "I wish I would have never listened to Lucifer."

"Do you really wish that?" Adam asks, surprising me.

I'm about to say "Of course," but then I stop. I know that isn't true. As cold and as hungry as I've felt for the past few days, and as confused as I've been about the changing relationship between Adam and me, I have never felt such . . . freedom. The wilderness is wild and harsh and can serve us only through destruction and death, yet . . .

I look up at Adam, and his eyes seem to absorb me in their warmth, fear, and sorrow. This is the man whom I've been commanded to multiply and replenish the earth with, and I realize I want nothing more than to do just that, even though it means I'll never step into our garden again. "Thank you for coming with me, Adam."

He nods slightly, still watching me, and I wish he would say something or even kiss me again.

Instead, he turns back to scan the valley below. There's no way to tell if Lucifer is still among the trees. If he is, he's not showing himself.

I want to wrap my arms around Adam and lean into him, to feel his strength and his warmth, but I don't move. I know that Adam is thinking beyond me, not of our kiss, and of how we are going to protect ourselves from beasts and unwanted intruders like our brother. Adam isn't dizzy with emotion over one moment of affection.

When he speaks again, he does so without turning to look at me. "We need to move closer to the garden and build an altar where we can call upon Elohim for further instruction."

"All right," I say, although I think of the days and hardships it took to get to this place and the days it would take to return to the garden. Will it make Adam miss the garden even more if we are in sight of it? Will he wake up in the morning in view of the garden with regret in his heart?

I realize that Adam is watching me when he says, "Eve."

I look up at him as he takes one of my hands. "I'm not sorry to be here with you." He pulls me in his arms and buries his face in my neck as the breeze lifts and stirs my hair around us.

Closing my eyes, I breathe him in. He smells of wood and leaves and hard work. My Adam.

"We are settling near the garden only to communicate with Elohim." His voice rumbles against my neck. "I hope it will keep Lucifer at a distance."

I exhale. To have Lucifer never bother us again would be a blessing indeed, but somehow I sense that won't be the case.

We spend the rest of the day weaving leaves together in strips and tying the branches together. Adam says that the trees are too sparse near the garden, although within the garden, the trees are abundant. So we are bringing the branches with us, to carry or drag across the vast distance.

I take a small break and gather more berries. Adam is grateful to take a break to eat too. He catches a couple of fish, and I eat as much as I can without complaint. Adam has hinted enough at eating other animals that I don't consider eating fish so disastrous now.

EVE

By the time the sky turns violet, we've completed our work.

"We'll set out in the morning," Adam says.

I glance at the shelter we slept in the night before. I don't look forward to spending another sleepless night wedged next to Adam, but the darkness sets in, and there is no other choice.

I crawl into the shelter, and a few moments later, Adam does as well. When his arms slide around me, I hold my breath. I can't seem to get a mouthful of air when he is touching me. I hold as still as possible, willing sleep to come quickly.

"How are you, Eve?" Adam whispers.

"Very tired," I say as he smoothes my hair. I hide the trembling that has started in my body.

Squeezing my eyes shut, I force myself to hold still when I really want to turn around in Adam's arms and kiss him. I ask myself why I don't turn, and I know the answer is because I am unsure. Or maybe . . . afraid. It's the unknown. Even with Elohim's explanation of how a man and woman bind together, I tremble at the unknown.

Tonight is colder than last night, and my legs grow stiff and achy, but still I don't move.

Adam's touch on my hair has become softer, and I know he is close to sleeping. I wait until I hear the even exhale of his breath before I bend my legs slightly.

I stay like that for a long time before I notice that my tightened stomach isn't relaxing. At first I think it's because of the confusion of my thoughts when I'm so close to Adam, but now I realize there is pain—hard pain.

My breathing quickens as the pain drives deeper and sharper, and I can't help but gasp. I move carefully away from Adam and slide out of the shelter. In the pale of the waning moon, I see what has brought on the pain.

I am bleeding as a woman bleeds, just as Elohim told me

153

I would in preparation to multiply and replenish the earth.

I walk toward the river, forgetting Adam's request to not walk anywhere alone. All I can think of is cleansing myself and stopping the pain. Walking eases the pain a fraction, but the pain is still sharp and hot. My head feels light, as though it's no longer attached to my moving body, and my vision blurs. When I sink to my knees, I know that I am close to the river because I can hear it. But my attention is diverted when I hear something else as well—the growl of an animal.

21

Therefore shall a man leave his father and his mother, and shall cleave unto his wife: and they shall be one flesh.

—Genesis 2:24

Adam's dream turned from walking through the lush green of the garden to stepping over the wall into a pool of black water. The cold dark wrapped around him, pulling him down, and he was surprised that he could breathe at all. The blackness increased, filling every part of his body and soul, until he realized what was wrong: Eve wasn't with him.

For the first time since she was created, he was separated from her.

His eyes flew open, and the tendrils of the dream faded away until he couldn't remember exactly what he'd dreamed about. But he did know that Eve was no longer in his arms, sleeping next to him, and it was still dark, a good wait until the first light of day. "Eve," he called out, before crawling out of the shelter. She'd be close by, he was sure.

But as he straightened and stepped out of the shelter, scouring the landscape for any sign or sound of her, the darkness from his dream returned, seeping into him.

Then the sound of a scream ricocheted through him.

Adam ran toward the river, stumbling and nearly falling twice on scattered rocks. His heart thundered in his chest, propelling him to run faster than he'd ever run before. What he saw on the riverbank nearly made his heart stop.

Eve was crouched on the ground, her hands over her head, as a ferocious animal leapt toward her. The flash of fur in the moonlight told Adam that this was likely the leopard that Eve had encountered earlier.

He dove toward Eve and the beast as it landed on her, its teeth bared, a horrible growl coming from its throat. Adam grabbed at the leopard's fur and pulled with all his strength, tugging the beast off Eve.

But the leopard was heavier and thicker than Adam expected. The beast twisted out of Adam's reach, its claws digging into his arms.

Pain exploded through Adam, and he almost lost his breath and fell back, but he clutched at the leopard, knowing that if he let go, Eve would be its target. The beast's growl turned high pitched as Adam fought to shove the leopard to the ground.

Using all of his force, Adam pinned the leopard down with his knees and elbows, his hands gripping the leopard's throat to keep the teeth out of the way. But that didn't stop the leopard's claws from lashing out.

"Adam!" Eve screamed over and over somewhere in the back of his mind. Her cries made him more determined. There were only two paths: this beast would die, or he would. There was no time for a rock or a branch to help him, so Adam did the one thing that made sense. He moved his knees up, scraping them on the ground so that he'd have a better position to turn the leopard's neck. Claws sank into his hands, causing heat to sear up his arms, but Adam kept turning until there was a sharp snap.

Just as he had done with the thickest tree branch, Adam had broken the beast's neck.

The leopard stopped moving, and Adam collapsed, exhausted, his body swimming in pain. He would welcome the dark pool of nothingness now.

Eve's voice whispered to him as he sank into a new blackness.

It wasn't until the sunlight burned against his eyelids that he awakened. Adam's first thought was: *I'm alive.*

His second thought was about Eve. He lifted his neck and realized she was nestled against him, her arm flung over his chest. She had streaks of dried blood along her arms and face.

"Eve," he said, his voice coming out as a hoarse whisper. He cleared his aching throat and said her name again.

She stirred and lifted her head, her blue-green eyes opening wide. "You're awake," she whispered in a shaky voice.

Adam sensed the fear coming from each syllable she spoke.

"Oh, Adam," she said, sitting up, then leaning over him and kissing his face over and over.

Adam didn't move because moving brought the heat of pain. With Eve's kisses, relief moved on top of the pain. She was alive. They both were, but he had ended another life in order to protect their lives. Not far from where he lay in the dirt, the leopard's bent body splayed in the dirt.

Adam pushed himself to a sitting position, his body flashing hot and cold as he did so. Pain screamed through his arms and hands.

"Be careful," Eve said, drawing back.

He looked down at his marred skin. Eve had washed the gashes, but they stung, and the skin had swollen around the long claw marks.

"I tried to stop the bleeding with the leaves," she said.

It was then that Adam noticed the leaves that littered the area around them, all of them stained with blood. "What about you? Are you injured?" he asked.

"Not as much as you." Her eyes watered, and she looked away from him.

"Let me see," he said.

Eve turned to show him her back. The leopard had clawed her, but the scrapes didn't look too deep. "Let's wash you off in the river," he said.

She turned to face him, her cheeks wet again. "I didn't think the leopard would still be here. I didn't expect . . ."

She lowered her head, and Adam touched her chin, lifting her face to look at him. "Why did you come out here by yourself?" he asked. "The beast could have ended your life . . . or mine." His breath was short again. Fear pulsed through him as he remembered Eve trying to defend herself against the leopard and how close she'd come to dying. What would have happened if the leopard had gained the best of him? How would she survive alone in the wilderness?

She exhaled. "I came to wash in the river." Her voice fell to a whisper. "My woman's blood started, just as Elohim said it would."

Adam stared at her as he thought about what she told him. "Are you all right?"

She nodded but didn't meet his eyes.

"What is it? Is there pain?"

"Yes," she said. "But Elohim said it will last only a few days."

"He said several, maybe seven," Adam said. "How much pain?"

"It's different than the gashes from the leopard—not

better or worse, just different. I don't quite feel right."

Adam wondered how he could help her. "You should have woken me up."

Her gaze met his, pleading. He ran a hand down her arm, then took her hand. "Come on. Let's get you cleaned up."

Pain shot through his limbs as he stood. There were several places where his skin had discolored from fighting the leopard. He saw similar spots on Eve as well. He kept her hand in his as they stepped into the river. He didn't want to let go of her hand or let her out of his sight. What other dangers awaited them?

Adam scooped water and washed off the dried blood on Eve's back, arms, and face. She shivered in the cool water, and Adam clamped his teeth together. He had to find something to keep them warm. He looked toward the lifeless leopard on the shore. Its thick fur looked warm and soft. The more he tried to push away the ideas circulating in his mind, the more they returned.

When Eve was clean and Adam had resoaked his wounds, he felt a measure of relief, if only because the cold water helped numb the pain. He and Eve walked onto the shore, and Eve sat on a rock, drying herself in the sun.

"I need to grab a couple of branches," Adam said. "Come with me."

She hesitated. "I don't want to be too far from the river." Her face flushed. "The bleeding won't stop."

Adam looked from her to their surroundings. Determining that there were no other wild beasts stalking them, he said, "I'll be back very soon." With Eve's nod, he hurried away, nearly running until he reached the pile of branches.

He selected a branch that was very straight, then returned to the river. He rubbed the end of the branch against a stone.

"What are you doing?" Eve asked.

He looked up at her. "I need to make something sharp enough to remove the leopard's skin and fur." Her mouth fell open. Then it closed. Her face paled slightly, but she didn't protest his actions.

It didn't take too long to get the edge of the branch sharpened, and Adam could only hope that his plan would work.

Eve walked with him to the dead animal, but before he did any cutting, she turned away. "I'll be sitting nearby," she said in a choked voice.

Adam positioned the sharp stick near the leopard's neck and pressed down. The work was more difficult and messy than he expected. His stomach churned, and he thought he might heave, but he was determined to complete the task. Once he had removed the skin, he carried it to the river and washed most of the blood from it. The underside of the skin was stained and still had parts of the animal attached to it.

With Eve completely silent and now watching from several paces away, Adam draped the skin over a rock and, holding a sharp stone, scraped away all the extra bits until it became smooth. Then he left it there to dry in the sun.

Eve brought him some berries to eat.

"Are you all right?" he asked her.

"I should be asking you that," she said. She glanced quickly at the leopard skin, then back to him as if she didn't like looking at it.

"Its flesh might be good," Adam said.

"Good like a fish?" Eve said, her face paling.

"Good for us to eat," he said.

"I don't think I can, Adam." Her voice fell to a whisper, and she turned away.

He grasped her arm, turning her back toward him. "We need to consider these alternative food sources."

Her eyes filled with moisture. She looked so thin and

160

fragile that he wanted to kill a dozen leopards to ensure that she never felt cold again. But how could he get her to eat more than just fish and berries?

"Maybe if we dry the leopard meat as well, it will be palatable," he said.

She shook her head.

"Come on. I'll try it first," he said. "There has to be more we can eat than the fish."

Eve moved away from him, her hands wrapped around her torso. "Yes," she said in a small voice. "Maybe I'll feel better tomorrow."

22

And the serpent said unto the woman, Ye shall not surely die.

—Genesis 3:4

Adam brings a piece of fish in his palm. It's just a small offering, not much bigger than the first piece of fish that I ate. I don't know if I can take another bite of fish.

It has been two days since he killed the leopard—two days of the skin drying. Adam tried some of the flesh, but I did not. By the second day, the leopard started to stink. Adam won't touch its flesh now.

I sit near a large boulder by the river, staying close to the water so that I may clean myself often. Adam has completed strapping bundles of branches together to take on our journey back toward the garden. We'll leave when my issue of blood has stopped and I have my strength back.

Adam's expression is determined as he extends his hand toward me. "Eat. You need the strength."

I know I do. I have felt my body grow thinner since we left the garden. Adam's body has become leaner as well, and his muscles are more pronounced with the hard labor.

EVE

I take the bit of fish from Adam's palm and exhale. This is a new world, and I must become a new Eve. I place it in my mouth, chew quickly, then swallow before I can consider another option.

"Thank you," Adam says, settling next to me. He has been so gentle and patient. I know he is anxious to return the way we came. I know he believes we'll be more separated from Lucifer if we are nearer to the garden. Yet he is waiting until the pain in my stomach has ceased.

"Thank *you*, Adam," I say, leaning my head against his shoulder. It's warm from his work in the sun.

"There is plenty more," he says.

There will always be plenty of fish. His arm slides around me, and I relax into him. Having him near brings me comfort, but I know that there is much to do. He can't sit with me for long.

The pain in my stomach has lessened only slightly, but I think I am tolerating it better and getting used to the differences in my body. There has indeed been pain in this wilderness, but the pleasure has increased as well. I wrap my arms around Adam's waist, nestling against him. He has not kissed me again, not as he did the day Lucifer appeared.

Now that my blood has started, we both know what may happen soon. We are both delaying, giving ourselves another day, or another seven days, to keep things as they have been so far—before we change everything together.

But it's getting harder for me. Adam is always in my thoughts, not as before, but every detail of his face . . . I close my eyes as Adam's breathing stirs my hair.

"We should leave tomorrow," I say.

"Are you sure?"

"Yes, I'm feeling better, and we can stay close to the river."

Adam presses his mouth against my hair, and I wish we

could remain like this forever, not growing hungry or cold, just sitting together while the sun warms us.

Too soon, he pulls away, releasing the warmth that encircles us. "I think the leopard skin is ready." He stands and crosses to where it has been drying. He brings it to me and drapes it over my shoulders. My nose wrinkles at the smell, but I recognize the value of warmth it will bring to us, especially on a cold night.

I look into Adam's eyes and see his anticipation. "Thank you for creating this." I know it wasn't easy for him. He loves animals as much as I do, even the unfamiliar ones in this wilderness. It's only out of protection that he has taken this animal's life.

Adam sits next to me again, and I lift the side of the skin coat so that it wraps around both of our shoulders. He intertwines me in his arms again. The combination of the sun and the leopard coat creates a warmth that I haven't experienced since the garden.

After a few moments, Adam is on his feet again, preparing for our journey.

We stay busy throughout the day, I weaving baskets that will carry berries and dried leopard skin, and Adam continuing with the lashes that will bind the branches together.

As the sun sets and the air chills, he retrieves more leaves so that I can finish the basket I'm working on. I know that he'll be gone only a short time, but as soon as he's out of sight, I start to feel uncomfortable.

"Adam," I call out, but it seems he is too far away to hear me. It's unreasonable to scream because I can't see or hear anything dangerous—no threatening beasts are growling.

And then something brushes against my arm.

I startle and nearly cry out.

"Hello, Eve," his voice says. I should have known he

would appear again—and would wait until Adam had left my side, even if for only a moment.

I barely manage to meet Lucifer's dark eyes in the fading light. He is crouched next to me, his hand moving down my arm.

Heat pulses through my chest. "Don't touch me."

"Are you sure I'm really touching you?"

I look down at his long, narrow fingers tracing my skin. Tiny bumps on my flesh stand out. "I can feel it."

"Interesting," he says, his voice soft and smooth. "Adam can't feel my touch."

I think of the times that Adam tried to defy our brother and physically remove him from our dwelling in the garden. Adam was unable to touch him because Lucifer isn't tangible.

"Why do you think that you can feel my touch, Eve?" he asks.

Inside, I want to scream at him, scream for Adam. I want to leap to my feet and escape. But I can't look away.

"I have been waiting for you, Eve," he says, his voice growing softer until it whispers all around me. "For you to become a woman."

I don't understand what he means. I have always been a woman. Then a knot tightens in my stomach and spreads fear throughout my limbs. He has been waiting for my body to change, and now it has.

Has he been watching us all this time? Listening to our conversations? Seeing me bathe in the river?

I lash out at him, trying to push him away from me. I touch something that feels like a mixture of cold mist and soft earth, but there is nothing to grab or shove away. Lucifer is still next to me, his smile crooked.

"What do you want from me?" I try to move away from him. There is nowhere to go. A boulder is behind me, but

Lucifer seems to be everywhere at once. My heart is pounding so hard that I gasp for air.

"To *teach* you, my sister," he says, his hand on my cheek. Although there is no substance to his fingers, I can feel his touch, cold and fluid. "There are so many things that I can teach you, so many pleasures of this world that you will enjoy."

His face moves next to mine, and I think I can feel his breath on me, although I know that is not possible.

"Adam and I will learn all that we need to know from Elohim," I say in a choked voice.

Lucifer doesn't blink, doesn't move at all. "Those are Adam's words," he says. "I know you are wise and understand the value of knowledge. There is much knowledge that Elohim won't teach you—knowledge that only I can share."

"I don't want your knowledge," I say. "And I won't do anything without my husband."

"I'll teach you well so that you can teach him." Lucifer's head tilts as his gaze bores into mine. "It will take you a lifetime to learn on your own. I can teach you how to keep the cold away and how to keep your stomach from ever growing hungry. I can show you the many pleasures of this world."

I am cold, and I am hungry. And the small pleasures I've had in Adam's arms have been very desirable.

But this is Lucifer—the one who was cast out of Heaven by Elohim, the one who was cast out of the garden. As Adam and I were cast out.

But unlike my brother, I don't want to live the rest of my mortal days in disobedience to Elohim.

Lucifer has moved closer to me, and I am pressed up against the boulder, trying to not let him touch me. "There is nothing I desire to learn from you," I say.

"You must think about what you want to learn." He

blinks in that languid way of his. "When Adam is stumbling around trying to protect you, think of how it might be to have *me* protecting you instead. I know this wilderness better than anyone, and I can give you all that you need." Lucifer's gaze is my face, my neck, my shoulders . . . "I can be your caretaker, Eve."

I feel as if Lucifer's both inside and outside my body, and I can't look away from him. My thoughts and my body try push against him, but I don't move, and he is only closer. "Leave me alone," I say, my eyes burning. "I don't want you near me."

Someone calls my name, and it takes me an instant before I realize it's Adam. He is kneeling in front of me. Instead of Lucifer, it's Adam.

I blink rapidly, wondering where Lucifer went. I reach for Adam and feel his solid warmth. His hands clasp around my waist. "What's wrong?" he asks.

His voice sounds far away, and I can't seem to speak. Where did Lucifer go? How can he be gone in an instant? And then I wonder if Lucifer was ever here at all.

"I think I was dreaming," I say.

Adam's hand brushes my face. "You looked as though you were trying to stand, but your face was contorted with pain."

I exhale. Had Lucifer been visiting me and Adam couldn't see him? "He was in my dream," I say. I don't need to explain who *he* is. Adam knows.

Adam's jaw tenses, and he scans my face. "Are you sure it was a dream?"

I am surprised by his question because it's exactly what I wonder. "I don't know. He was here, but as soon as you came, he was gone. How could he leave so fast if it wasn't a dream?" I say. I feel Adam's arms tighten around me, drawing me close.

I press my cheek against his chest—warm and solid. I

don't need Lucifer's instructions for anything. What Elohim doesn't tell Adam and me, we'll discover on our own.

The cold and the hunger can persist. There is no one I'd rather experience them with than Adam.

"We must leave as soon as day breaks," Adam says.

I nod against his chest. Adam leads me to our shelter, which seems far less secure now. Although I haven't seen Lucifer for several days, I realize that he has always been there, watching and listening. The hairs on my arms prickle as I think of his dark, hollow eyes gazing at me, looking through my very soul as if he knows my every thought.

Adam and I settle in for sleep beneath the rows of branches, and the thin moonlight comes in through the cracks, throwing lines across our skin. The mist has gathered again, and we lie protected underneath the leopard coat. This small comfort and Adam's protective arms about me make the night bearable as I try to push away thoughts of my brother and his words.

But Lucifer's words continue to tumble in my mind no matter how much I focus on Adam's warmth and his steady breathing as he sleeps: *I know this wilderness better than anyone.*

I wonder how Lucifer knows this world so well. Is this where he stayed while Adam and I lived in the garden? Is this where Elohim had banished him? I inhale the sharp, cool air that mingles with the warmth of the leopard skin. Although the wilderness has been difficult to adjust to, at least I am with Adam and we are together in our journey. Lucifer has always been alone from what I can see.

Lucifer has made that decision for himself, I realize. He had his freedom to choose Elohim's plan, but instead he presented his own idea—a plan that wasn't Elohim's.

It was his own plan: *I can give you all that you need.*

In the still of the night, nestled against Adam, I can't imagine feeling more taken care of. Although I know that there are many dangers out there, I trust that Adam will be equal to the task of protecting me. With the both of us determined to learn and to survive in this world, we'll find a way to stay safe. We must find a way. I don't want Lucifer to have any part in our lives.

Both of our injuries from the leopard have been healing. Elohim was right: this wilderness contains pain and sorrow, but there is also joy and pleasure I have not experienced before. These thoughts make my heart race as I think of Adam's kiss, and I can't help but wonder when he'll kiss me again. He has been more than tender these past few days as I've endured the malady.

I turn in his arms and rest my head against his chest. It moves with his breathing, and I can hear his heart beating in steady rhythm. Finally, I'm able to push all thoughts of Lucifer away and fall into a dreamless sleep.

৵ৼৄ৹

The morning brings mist and cold. I wash in the river while shivering, and Adam does the same.

"Are you all right to travel today?" he asks me.

I know that he will stay another day for me, but I also see his determination to be closer to the garden.

The earth has grown muddy overnight, and our progress toward the garden is slow. We stop to eat several times, consuming some of the fish from the river, a little of the dried leopard, and, as always, berries.

My legs ache and my breath is short, but I say nothing to Adam. We have delayed long enough. We hope to receive communication from Elohim once Adam builds the altar. Since the clouds are heavy and there is little warmth that penetrates from the sun, Adam insists that I wear the leopard coat. Obtaining the coat was a remarkable feat for Adam, and I can't help but wish that he had one too . . . but that would mean another animal would have to die.

I push the thought out of my mind, but as the day progresses, I know that Adam must be cold despite the labor of dragging the branches. As the sun sets, Adam unties one of the bundles and creates a shelter for us to sleep beneath. He is soaked, and I am half-so, the leopard coat adding some protection from the mist, but we are both shivering in the cold.

"Adam," I say, "when we set out tomorrow, let's leave the branches here."

"But there are few trees near the garden, and none of their branches were as thick as these."

"We can come back for them if we need to. We might be able to find something that will work—maybe a grove."

But Adam shakes his head. "There was nothing. You saw the wasteland stretch in all directions."

I climb beneath the shelter, and Adam follows me. "It's too much work for your body. You're shivering with cold as it is." I dislike seeing him worn out this way.

He settles next to me and arranges the leopard coat around both of us. His skin is cold, and I turn to face him, wrapping my arms around his neck. If he is surprised by my actions, he says nothing, just burrows his face against my hair. My body heats up at his touch, and I want him to press his lips to mine, but his body only relaxes, and I know he has fallen asleep.

I feel his body slowly start to warm as the leopard coat covers us both. I wonder if I'll ever truly be warm again.

23

When the woman saw that the tree was good for food, and that it was pleasant to the eyes, and a tree to be desired to make one wise, she took of the fruit thereof, and did eat.

—Genesis 3:6

The ground is white and frozen. There are flakes falling from the sky. These flakes are colder than anything I've touched before. Adam steps in the substance first, then scoops some from the ground. After a moment, he is frantically brushing it from his hands.

I run my fingers over the ground. "What is it?"

Adam looks up at the sky, which is nearly as white as the ground. The flakes land on his face, then form into water droplets. "I don't know, but it's beautiful."

"And cold." I look at my hands. They have turned red. They feel hot and cold at the same time, tingling into numbness.

He pulls out the leopard coat from the shelter and drapes it over my shoulders. "Keep this on until it stops," he says.

"What about you?"

He doesn't answer but disassembles our shelter quickly

and binds up the branches. Then he turns to scan the terrain. As far as we can see, there is white. He looks at me, his eyes trailing to my feet. "We need something to bind around our feet."

I shrug off the leopard coat. "Can we tear off strips from this?"

Adam looks from the coat to the baskets we have brought. "Maybe take apart one of the baskets."

I know the leopard coat would be warmer on our feet, but I understand his reluctance to mar our main source of warmth. I set about taking apart one of the baskets and secure the woven leaves around Adam's feet. After my own feet are bound, we set off.

The cold white is beautiful, but it isn't long before I am shaking inside and out, even with the leopard coat on. Adam's lips are purple, and I'm sure mine are too. In fact, his skin tone has taken on a purplish hue.

I remove the leopard coat and try to drape it across Adam's shoulders.

"I'm fine, Eve," he says. "You wear it. I'll feel better if you do."

"But you're so cold. We can trade off every once in a while." I hold out the coat, but he refuses to take it. Despite the wrapped leaves about my feet, my feet are so cold that it's painful to step on them. We must find more ways to stay warm. The white sky doesn't seem to be changing any time soon.

Adam releases the bundle of branches he is dragging and takes my hands in his, rubbing warmth into them. "Maybe we should take protection in a shelter until these cold flakes stop falling," he says.

My teeth chatter together when I say yes. We still have another day or two in our journey, and I can't imagine continuing in this state for much longer.

Adam and I quickly set up shelter, then burrow beneath

the roof of branches, the leopard coat draped across both of us. I think of Lucifer's words and how he said he could teach me things of this world. Could he teach us how to keep warm?

I push the thought away and focus on sitting next to Adam, sharing in the body heat that is slowly warming us. Adam's hand slides into mine, and we watch the white world fall around us in silence. As I exhale, my breath is like a cloud. I exhale again, watching my breath form white and mix with Adam's.

After a few moments, Adam says, "I'll be back soon. If you need something, just call me. I'll be in hearing distance."

He slides out from beneath the leopard coat and picks up one of the branches. It's the same branch that he used to remove the skin from the leopard; one of the ends is sharp. I didn't realize he'd brought it with us.

"Where are you going?" I say, not sure I like him disappearing someplace in this white world. What if Lucifer has been following us and appears to me again?

"I think there's a bear on the other side of the river."

I shiver as I look toward the river. The white-tipped water flows slowly, as if the cold has stalled its pace. Bushes crowd the shore, but with the surrounding white, I can't see to the other side of the river. "Why are you seeking out a bear?"

Adam's sober gaze tells me all I need to know.

"Are you sure?" I ask in a quiet voice, as if the bear can hear me where I sit.

His hand tightens around the branch he carries. "I don't see another option."

My stomach lurches. I don't see another option either, and I won't consider letting Lucifer be our instructor.

"Stay here," he says. "I don't know how the bear will react." He picks up another branch that is not as finely sharpened but would still make a weapon. "Hold onto this."

I take the branch and grip it with both hands.

Adam walks quietly away, and I wait, the leopard skin hanging off my shoulders, the branch in hand.

Everything seems so quiet as the white flakes spin and fall around me, landing on my hair, my face, my hands. With Adam's absence, the chill creeps back into my body, going deeper and deeper until I feel as if my heart has slowed and my breath has stalled in the stillness.

I imagine Adam crossing the river and walking through the icy water as the bear watches him approach. Will the bear run? Will it leap at him? My heart pounds, and the cold emphasizes my breath.

I can't stand here and think of Adam alone, facing such a great beast. I walk toward the river, careful to not make any sound. I peer through the white, expecting Adam's form to emerge at any moment, but I reach the river's edge without seeing him or any bear.

The river moves by, silent and dark, paying no attention to me. Where did Adam go? Was the bear farther down the river? I look both ways, but the white prevents me from seeing very well.

Then I hear a growl, and I nearly scream. The growl is low and deep and much closer than I imagined. I turn slowly, the branch gripped tight in my hands. I see nothing but white.

The growl turns higher pitched, and someone yells. It can be only Adam.

Where are you? I want to scream. Another yell comes, this one filled with pain. It's definitely coming from across the river. I step into the river and start moving across. The water bites into my skin, numbing it almost instantly. I realize that what I had thought was cold before was nothing compared to the feel of the river. By the time I reach what I think is the middle of the river, the water has reached my waist, and I must hold the leopard coat away from the water.

Every step I take depletes my strength more.

Even worse than the pain is the realization that all has been quiet for a few moments.

"Adam!" I call out, desperate to hear something, anything. Where is he? Where is the bear?

I push through the water until I nearly collapse on the opposite shore, but somehow I manage to stay standing. I take a step, then another, stumbling up the bank.

Not knowing which way to go, I move forward, climbing away from the river. I hold the branch in front of me while looking behind me every so often. Then I see the dark fur. I halt, my hands trembling and my heart pounding in my ears.

The bear isn't moving, so I take another step. Its thick fur is slowly being covered with white flakes. Protruding from its chest is the sharp branch that Adam had with him. Blood stains the stick bright red against the falling white.

Adam did this, but where is he now?

The bear's head is turned toward me, its eyes open but unblinking. My gaze focuses on its mouth. There are no signs of cloud-shaped breath. I take another step, looking for Adam.

Then I see him on the ground just past the bear. His body is still.

"Adam!" I cry out, hurrying to him and kneeling at his side. There is blood on his hands and arms. It's seeping from new gashes on his skin. I lean over him and touch his face. "Adam? Can you hear me?"

When a small moan comes from him, I'm filled with relief. He is alive. But I fear that he has been greatly injured. "Adam?" I say again. His eyes blink open, then close again. I touch his face, whispering to him. "Wake up. We must get you to shelter."

His eyes fluttered open. "Is it dead?"

I involuntarily glance at the bear. "Yes."

Adam's lips curl slightly, and his eyes start to close again.

"Stay awake," I say. "You must come with me." I know that I won't be able to drag or carry him. My body has started to shake from the cold and the river, and I feel as if the cold has reached the very center of me.

His eyes open, but he doesn't seem to focus on me. "You must skin the bear." His voice is so faint that I question what he has told me. I know he is right. I can't let the bear stay for too long, or it will rot like the fruit in the south garden when Lucifer arrived. *Adam will get better, and he'll be able to skin the bear.* But as I watch Adam's eyes close again, his lashes resting against his pale, cold skin, I know that I must do it myself.

But first I must warm up Adam. I gather leaves from the bushes on the river's edge and press them against Adam's wounds. I hope the bleeding will stop soon. It seems to have slowed, and I wonder if it's due to the cold air. From time to time I glance at the bear to assure myself that it's still dead.

With the leaves in place, I remove the leopard coat from my own shoulders and cover Adam with it. I look over at the bear and the branch sticking out of its chest. Although it makes me feel light-headed to think of going near the beast, I pull the branch from the bear's chest and drop the branch on the ground.

I look at Adam, and although the leopard coat must be keeping him warm, his face is still pale and tinged with purple. I sit on the cold ground and then lie down next to him, pulling the leopard coat over the both of us, using my body to warm Adam's. I wrap my arms around Adam, and begin to pray, even though I don't have an altar. I don't even have Adam's voice. I know that Elohim has been silent for many days, even a fortnight, and that we have been cut off. But I also know that Elohim is merciful.

"O Elohim, give ear to my words," I whisper, my lips

numb as they move in the cold air. "Hearken unto the voice of my cry, my Elohim, for unto thee I pray." My breath comes quickly, and my eyes sting. "I ask for thy protection and blessing of strength for Adam so that he might recover from his injuries." I continue praying and pleading over and over.

I finally exhaust myself and fall asleep for a short time next to Adam. When I awake, the world is still white, but the flakes have stopped falling from the sky. All around is a white stillness. Flakes cover the leopard coat. I look over at the bear—its brown fur is covered in white as well.

My body aches but it's warm, and Adam's body is warm. I check his injuries and find that the bleeding has stopped. I fetch more leaves and replace the stained ones with fresh ones, then rearrange the leopard coat around Adam so that the cold air won't touch his body.

Turning to face the bear, I know what I need to do, and the sooner I do it, the better. The day must be more than half-over, and I don't know how much longer Adam will need to recover. Skinning the bear can't wait until tomorrow.

With the leopard, Adam started at the neck, although I didn't watch much after that. Taking the sharpened branch in my hands, I place the tip at the bear's neck. My mouth is dry, and I have difficulty swallowing.

I stare at the brown fur beneath the point of the branch until moisture trickles down my cheeks. I glance over at Adam, and seeing his pale, still face gives me added determination. So what if my stomach heaves and sobs choke my throat? I must do this. There is no other choice.

24

And the eyes of them both were opened, and they knew that they were naked; and they sewed fig leaves together, and made themselves aprons.

—Genesis 3:7

My hands are so numb that I can barely bend my fingers. My hands are covered in blood from the bear, and the smell of the dead animal is difficult to inhale. I work as quickly as possible since dark will fall soon, and I don't want to be at this task any longer than necessary.

Once I have the fur and skin removed from the bear, I carry its coat to the river and soak it for a few moments. The water washes away the blood from my hands, although they remain red from the cold. With the bear coat cleansed, I drape it over a set of bushes. It will take a while to dry, I know, especially in this cold.

The cold is still sharp in the air, but at least the flakes have stopped falling.

My body trembles as I approach the skinned bear. The knots and forms of its muscled body are fascinating yet horrifying. Not long ago, this was a living, breathing creature. Adam will want me to save the flesh, but looking at what remains of the bear, I know that I could never partake of it, and by the time Adam is well enough to eat, the bear flesh will be rotted.

With a grimace and a lot of tugging, I drag the carcass down to the river and somehow shove it into the water. I watch it sink then move slowly away, carried by the current.

The white from the flakes on the ground has now turned a pale gray.

By the time I reach Adam's side, I am shaking all over from cold and from the tasks I've had to perform. Adam hasn't moved. He is still covered with the leopard coat, sleeping deeply. I climb under the leopard coat and nestle against him. I wait for the warmth to come, but I continue to shiver. Adam feels cooler than I remember, and I fear that he can't warm up.

I reach for his hands and rub them. Slowly the warmth comes, but it's not enough. Helplessness consumes me. Dark is gathering, and with it, the cold will increase. I think I am too cold to sleep, but eventually the trembling subsides and exhaustion takes over.

Eve. A whisper comes to my mind, and at first I think I have fallen asleep and am dreaming. But the voice comes again, like an urgent breeze, and I know I can't possibly be sleeping.

I lift my head and blink into the descending darkness. Why has Lucifer followed us now? Can he not leave us alone? I know he is close, although I can't see him. It's as if I can feel his presence.

"You're not wanted here," I whisper, wishing Adam was well and had his strength. I must protect him and get rid of our brother at the same time. I sit up, looking for Lucifer's form in the dimness, my heart pounding.

Then a spark of light as bright as the sun pierces the night. I shield my eyes, expecting the startling light to disappear as quickly as it appeared, but the yellow glow continues. My mouth falls open as I stare. Half a dozen paces from where I sit, Lucifer is crouched, holding his hands over what seems to be a circle of bright light.

Lucifer doesn't turn my way. In fact, he completely ignores me. He seems intent on the light that his hands hover over, as if it's impossible to break his gaze. I stare at the flickering light and the small spots that break off, fading into dark, only to be replaced by more bright spots.

Next to me Adam stirs, and I immediately turn my attention to him, but his eyelids don't move, and he makes no other sound. If Lucifer notices the movement, he makes no indication.

My gaze is drawn again to the flickering light. Even though Lucifer's focus is on the bright, burning light, I sense that he's watching me. Waiting. I move away from Adam and settle the leopard coat around him. Being apart from Adam's body heat and the protection of the coat, I realize how bitter the cold is.

Despite my resolve to ignore my brother and to never seek knowledge from him, I ask, "What is that?"

Lucifer is slow to respond, as if he didn't hear me, but I know he did. His hands have moved ever so slightly. Finally he says, "Fire."

I have not heard the word before, and I try it out silently to myself. "It's like the sun," I say.

"Very much like the sun," Lucifer says, raising his head. His black eyes reflect the bright yellow. For an instant he reminds me of a black leopard. It's then that I notice he's wearing a heavy fur—thick and dark—around his shoulders. It looks similar to the fur from the bear that Adam has killed.

I know that it's not the same coat I have just skinned, but I marvel at the similarity.

Lucifer watches me, his mouth turning up slightly. "Not only is Fire the color of the sun, but it also gives off heat."

I can't help myself; the questions tumble from my lips. "You can feel the heat with your hands?" What am I saying? Lucifer doesn't have a body of flesh, yet he is warming his hands against this Fire. I realize what he is doing. He is tempting me. Again.

"See for yourself, Eve," he says, his voice smooth in the utter stillness of the night. Even the sounds of the river seem muted.

I go rigid. Making this one allowance is a step in a direction I promised myself I would not go. I don't dare move but continue to stare at the Fire, mesmerized.

Lucifer chuckles, his hollow voice reaching across the night air. "You may choose for yourself, Eve. That's what's so wonderful about this world. You can make a choice, unlike when you lived in the garden. Out here, you can choose to let your husband die of cold, or you can choose to create Fire and keep him warm." His gaze slides to mine. "This cold weather will last for many moons—it's named winter. You won't last so many cold nights without extra warmth."

My throat is tight, and my breath seems to leave my body for a moment. When I gather my voice, I ask, "How does the Fire warm more than your hands?"

"Like this," Lucifer says, pulling his hands back into a wide arc. The bright light expands and grows until it's nearly the height of a man. The heat rushes across the once-cold space and feels like a hot slap on my skin, splashing against my body, leaving my back as cold as ever.

A sigh from somewhere deep inside escapes me. I don't know if it's relief or if my body is clamoring for something that isn't wet or cold.

I want to wrap myself in this Fire, to feel it on all parts of my body. Without considering what I'm doing, I rise to my feet and turn slowly around in circles. I feel as if I'm standing partly in the sunlight, partly in the shade, with the hot and the cool contrasting against each other, battling for space.

Lucifer gazes at me, but for the moment, I don't care. I lift my arms up, slowly spinning, soaking in the Fire from all sides.

"It feels nice. Agreed?" Lucifer's voice whispers, but I don't answer. I want only to feel the intense warmth.

"This will burn for most of the night, keeping you and Adam warm," he says.

I stop, feeling a smile budding on my face, despite my own caution to myself. This Fire has come from Lucifer, from the fallen angel whom I have vowed not to let teach me anything. Yet . . . if Lucifer goes and the Fire fades, the heat will be gone too. I'll be left again, cold and alone with Adam.

I glance over at Adam's sleeping form. His face looks peaceful and less pale in the yellow glow. I take a deep breath, knowing what I must do and knowing that Adam won't like it.

"Teach me," I whisper, then say louder. "Teach me to make Fire."

Deep pain twisted in Adam's arms and shoulders, and a pungent smell was in the air—a smell he couldn't quite describe. The last thing he remembered was driving a branch into the chest of the bear. Adam sat up, looking around him, surprised to see the light of morning softening the sky. Eve slept next to him, but where was the bear? They were sleeping in the open, with no sheltering branches above them.

He examined his arms, which were plastered with leaves. His wife must have treated his wounds. But he was more concerned about what had happened to the bear.

Adam looked around, searching for the beast. He was certain he'd killed it. The clouds were heavy, masking the rising sun, but there was enough light for him to assess that the bear was gone.

"You're awake," Eve said next to him. She was sitting up, her eyes wide in the gray light. "How are you feeling?"

"I'm not sure yet." The pain was deep, and he felt tired. Hungry. Cold. But none of that was new. "What happened to the bear?"

"I skinned it." Her voice sounded breathless. "Its coat is spread over the bushes by the river, and I dumped the flesh in the river."

"We could have eaten the flesh."

"I know," she said in a small voice. "I just . . . couldn't . . . not after I removed the skin." She looked down at her hands as if remembering the task.

Adam placed his hands on hers, trying not to wince at the movement. Her hands were warm, but the warmth was fading fast in the cold morning air. "Are you all right?"

She laughed faintly. "There's no need to worry about me. You're the one who fought and killed a bear." She looked at his arms.

He looked down at the plastered leaves. "Thank you for doing this. I . . ." He thought of the fight with the bear and how he'd lost the upper hand at one point. The injuries could have been much worse.

"How did you best the bear?" Eve asked.

"It was busy eating, so I crept up on it, but it turned just as I was about to use the branch." He shuddered at the memory of the bear's wild eyes focused on him. "It lunged at me, and I was able to stake it." Turning his arms over, he gazed at his open wounds. "I held the stake in place so the bear couldn't run off. That's when it clawed back at me."

She nodded, her expression solemn. "I was worried about you. I couldn't wake you last night."

He looked at her, then noticed that the strange smell was on her as well. "What is that smell?" It might be the bear, but it didn't smell at all as the leopard had.

Eve looked away from him.

"Tell me," he said. Her eyes were lowered, her shoulders slack. He glanced at their surroundings again. Everything was gray in the cloudy light of morning. The white flakes from the night before were gathered in a few places, still claiming parts of the ground as their own.

Not too far from where he sat, a patch of dark earth—nearly black—formed a round shape. There was something odd about it. It looked as though mist rose from the black patch.

Glancing at Eve, he saw that she was looking at the black space as well.

"The ground is burned," she said in a halting voice.

"Burned?"

"Burned hot," she said, "by Fire." She took a deep breath. "Adam . . . I know a way to create heat—heat like that from the sun—that can keep us warm on cold days and nights."

Something pressed at the back of his mind, a memory or a recollection of what might have been a dream, but he couldn't quite grasp it, and it faded just as quickly as it had come.

"I'll show you," Eve said. She rose and broke off some twigs and leaves from a nearby bush. Then she carried them to the middle of the black patch. Scooping something off the ground, she held up two rocks—at least what looked like black rocks. "These are used to create the Fire." She crouched down and struck the two pieces together.

Adam flinched as yellow light sparked from the black rock. It glowed bright in the gray day, and Eve held it against the twigs and leaves she'd gathered. The yellow light grew, flickering, changing form by the instant as if it were breathing in and out and then growing larger and larger.

Eve gathered more twigs and placed them on the bright light. "This is Fire," she said. "Last night the Fire was large and kept us warm." Her eyes sought his over the vibrant yellow. "Come and place your hands near the Fire."

Adam stared at her, then looked at the Fire that she had stretched her hands over. "Who taught you to do this?"

She looked past him. When she spoke, her voice was nearly a whisper. "You were so cold . . . and lifeless. I couldn't warm your body." Her gaze rose to the sky. "He told me this was a season—winter—and it would last for several moons."

"Lucifer?" Adam said. "He came last night?"

"He showed me how to make Fire, how to keep ourselves warm in this season." She rushed on, her eyes deep green as she looked at him. "I know we don't want him to teach us anything, but knowing how to make Fire will save our lives—" She broke off, and Adam struggled with the churning emotions inside him.

He hadn't expected to be rendered helpless by the bear and to make Eve worry about keeping him warm through the night. It also seemed that Lucifer wasn't going to relent, no matter where they traveled. He had shown up just when Eve was desperate for warmth and provided it for her.

Exhaling, Adam tried to make sense of his anger mixed with both confusion and relief. He could already see that Fire would be useful. If he and Eve could warm their bodies when the season was winter, they could warm other things . . . like water from the river. And they could speed up the drying of the bear skin.

The scent remaining from the Fire was still strange to Adam, though it wasn't entirely repellent. But why did it have to come from Lucifer—and not Elohim? Adam knew he and Eve had been cut off spiritually, but if the cold had held off a few more days, he would have had the chance to build an altar and begin worshipping.

He noticed the tremble in Eve's hands. She'd withdrawn them from the Fire as it had started to diminish, leaving a black mark in its place.

Carefully, Adam climbed to his feet, hesitating as dizziness drove through him. When it passed, he crossed to Eve. She looked up at him, questioning and hope in her eyes.

"Show me how to make this Fire," he said, crouching next to her.

25

And they heard the voice of God walking in the garden in the cool of the day: and Adam and his wife hid themselves from the presence of God amongst the trees of the garden.

—Genesis 3:8

Adam's exposed arms strain as he lifts the final rock to complete the altar. I have exhausted myself in carrying, rolling, and lifting rocks. We are both clothed in animal coats now: Adam wears the bear skin, and I wear the leopard skin. And we have captured and killed another bear, using its skin to cover us at night.

It has been several days since Lucifer showed me how to make Fire, and I have learned to contain it and make it grow. I haven't seen Lucifer since that night he was stooped over the bright glow of Fire, but I sense he is never far away and certainly pays attention to what we are doing.

Brushing his hands together, Adam turns and walks toward me. Today the sun is bright and the sky clear and blue. The sun provides more warmth than we are used to, although tonight we'll still be able to see our breath. The breeze stirs Adam's hair, which has grown darker since leaving the garden, and instead of catching the gold of the sun, his hair turns a darker bronze. He sits next to me on the boulder I have chosen. His breath comes fast from all the exertion, but I know that soon he'll want to begin worshipping.

We have chosen to settle east of the garden, near the entry, on the other side of the garden border from our former dwelling. The river runs beneath the wall that Adam built so long ago, giving us a connection between our new home and our old home. It's remarkable to think that we once swam in this river on the other side of the border, where the river was cool and pleasant—not bitter cold as it is now, in this winter season.

"Are you ready?" Adam asks, reaching for my hand. His grasp is as warm and strong as before the bear injured him. His wounds have healed well, and although there will be many scars remaining, he is as healthy as he's ever been.

I look up at him as he reaches over and brushes the blowing hair from my face. His touch makes my face warm, and the warmth spreads down to my neck. I wonder again if he will kiss me as he did that day Lucifer interrupted. So much has happened since then. There has been no time to dwell on those things.

And now the altar is finally built and ready.

"Let's go," I say, standing with Adam. We walk hand in hand toward the altar, and my heart pings for how life was in the garden—for how we called upon Elohim with the soft, green grass beneath our feet and the multiple trees, with their large leaves and sweet fruit, around us.

The wind tugs at my coat and lifts my hair from my neck. Small bumps dot my skin, and I glance over at Adam. He is focused on the altar and drops my hand as he kneels, folds his hands on top of the altar, and bows his head.

I kneel next to Adam and clasp my hands together as he begins to pray.

His words are thick and choked in the beginning. "O Elohim, hear our prayer on this day."

Emotion swells within my own breast. I want Elohim to hear our prayers, to answer us, and to open communication with us again, and I can hear the same desire in Adam's voice.

I stare at the east border of the garden, wondering if Elohim is within the garden or if he is in his Heaven. Does he know about Lucifer teaching me how to create Fire? Of course he does, I decide. Elohim knows all things.

I squeeze my eyes shut, adding my silent pleas to Adam's verbal ones. I wish Elohim would break his silence and give us further instruction. I think of the instruction he gave before we left—that we should eat by the sweat of our own labor and that our sorrow would be multiplied as we bring forth children.

I rest my head against Adam's shoulder, moisture sliding along my cheeks as his unanswered words echo in the silent wilderness. We have yet to bring forth children, to follow the commandment to multiply and replenish the earth. Is Elohim waiting for us to fulfill this commandment before communicating with us again?

"What are you doing?" a voice says.

I open my eyes. Lucifer stands a few paces away in front of the altar. He wasn't there a few moments ago, and I marvel at the way he travels.

Adam rises immediately. "We are praying to Elohim, which doesn't concern you."

A half smile forms on Lucifer's face. In the bright sunlight, his hair has a burnished look to it, but his eyes are as black as ever. His gaze moves slowly from Adam to me.

I keep my mouth tightly closed. I won't speak to him, even if he did teach me to make Fire.

"And has Elohim answered you yet?"

Adam says nothing, staring at Lucifer. The two lock gazes for a tense moment.

"It's as I suspected," Lucifer says. "You have been cut off, have you not?"

I nod my head and then catch myself and don't move.

The glimmer in Lucifer's eyes tells me he noticed my movement. His gaze focuses on me as Adam grasps my hand.

"You have a resourceful wife, Adam," Lucifer says, his voice as smooth as the river. "She saved your life the other night, and it was with skills that *I* taught her."

Adam swallows audibly, but still he says nothing.

Lucifer walks toward us. I feel Adam stiffen beside me, but he doesn't move, and his grasp doesn't change.

"Don't you think you should be grateful to her?" Lucifer says. "For being teachable?" He stops walking and stands on the other side of the altar from us. The carefully constructed pile of stones is no protection from his intense glare.

Why can't he leave us alone? Why does he always try to interfere?

"You are not wanted here, Lucifer. You will never be wanted," Adam said.

The smile on Lucifer's face only widens. "Maybe you should tell that to your wife. She seems to feel differently."

I can't keep my silence any longer. "I've never welcomed you, Lucifer. You twist every word and every action."

His dark brows arch high as his gaze settles on me. "I know what you want more than you do yourself. You can't deny that the Fire has been useful."

"It has," I say in a quiet voice.

"I am Elohim of this world," he says. "And the sooner you realize that, the sooner you can learn to become masters of your own lives. Fire is only one element that is useful. There is much more I can teach you."

My breath stalls, but I have been enticed by Lucifer

before and know that he gives out knowledge only in part truths. I am grateful I know how to make Fire, but I suspect there is danger to the knowledge as well, something hidden that Lucifer has not revealed.

Suddenly Lucifer is standing right in front of me. Adam puts his hand around my waist and moves me a step back, but I can't look anywhere but into Lucifer's eyes. I don't know how he manages to completely capture my gaze without my consent.

As Lucifer stares at me, it's as if Adam fades. I know Adam's still holding my hand, but I can no longer feel his touch. I feel as though the black has somehow moved inside me, like a dark thundercloud that expands and shifts, filling the recesses of my soul.

I step toward Lucifer. I think Adam may be pulling me back, but whatever pulls me toward Lucifer is much stronger than Adam.

Lucifer touches my shoulder, and I feel a smooth coolness. His head tilts, and he speaks so low that I think only I can hear. "You understand me, Eve," he says in his near whisper. "You need me just as I need you."

His face is so close to mine that I imagine reaching up and touching his cheek, his jawline, but then he draws back.

Adam's words filter into my mind, seemingly from a distant place, from somewhere behind me. "In the name of Elohim, I command you to leave, Lucifer."

Lucifer seems to shrink, even as I reach for him and try to stop him from leaving.

Adam's warm hand, strong and firm, pulls me back, and Adam captures me against his body. I gasp for air, and it rushes inside my chest. I sag against Adam, closing my eyes.

When I open my eyes, Lucifer is gone. "What happened?" I whisper.

Adam cradles me against him, his arms wrapped around me from behind. "Telling him to leave is no longer enough," Adam says. "He somehow has more power and influence in this world than he did in the garden."

My mind turns over what just happened, but I can't quite grasp it. "Is it because Elohim is not here?" I turn around in Adam's arms, lifting up my chin so I can look fully into his golden eyes. I cling to him and allow him to hold me up. Helplessness spreads through my limbs, threatening me with loss of balance. "I am so weak," I whisper. "How can I be so weak?"

One of Adam's hands goes behind my head, and he presses his lips to my forehead. "We must remember Elohim's promise. Lucifer might be able to bruise our heel, but we can bruise his head."

"So he is not leaving? He will always be around to torment us?"

Adam exhales and pulls me closer. "You must not let him tempt you again."

"I know," I whisper, pressed against the warmth of Adam's chest. "But there is so much that we don't know."

"You've always been so eager to learn everything and anything all at once."

I draw away from him. "I want to learn to survive this place—to know how to protect ourselves—and Fire will help us do that." I turn toward the altar. It's barren and silent. "Elohim has cut us off. Where else are we supposed to turn?"

Adam stands next to me, looking at the altar. "We have to be patient, Eve. We must wait for Elohim's time."

My hands clench at my sides. "We waited in the garden to ask him our questions. But he didn't come until it was too late."

"Eve—"

"I know I made the right choice." I can't look at Adam. "And you made the right choice, but this world is not what I expected." I look down at my body. "Everything has changed: our bodies, what we eat, how we spend our days.

What are we doing here? What is our purpose?" I thought I knew our purpose, but I can't help the frustrated words that tumble out.

"We can do this, Eve. We just need to do it together. Lucifer can't be a part of our lives."

Moisture forms in my eyes. I remember the night I worried that Adam would die of either the bear wounds or the cold. I'm certain that if it hadn't been for the Fire that Lucifer brought, Adam would have died. Our mortal bodies are not so strong. He seems to think he is still immortal.

On one hand, I know Adam is right. On the other, Elohim has seemingly abandoned us. We must make do with what we have.

"Elohim could have taught us about Fire, but he didn't." I say.

Adam stiffens. "We were cut off because we disobeyed Elohim."

"But in doing so, we obeyed his commandment to multiply and replenish the earth," I say, which isn't entirely accurate. We are not obeying that commandment either.

Adam turns away. I can't read his expression now, and fear builds in my heart. Does he not want to obey that commandment after all? Is that why he hasn't kissed me again?

"We should at least be able to talk about it," I say in a quiet voice. He doesn't move. "Have you not felt the physical changes in your body as well?"

"You know I have." His voice is quiet yet harsh.

Why is he upset? What have I said? We discussed this commandment plenty in the garden, but out here—where we must face it directly—he refuses to speak about it.

I stare after Adam as he walks away. I want to tell him to not walk away from me—from this—but then I look toward the garden and the lushness lying within that is no longer a part of our lives. Has the sacrifice been too great for him? Does he regret our choice but can't tell me?

I start to walk after him but change my mind. I won't push him to speak of what he doesn't care to—at least not right now. Lucifer's presence has exhausted me. I sit on the ground, pulling my leopard coat tightly about me, and lean against the cold stones of the altar.

How long must we be in this probation and remain cut off from Elohim? How does he expect us to survive this wilderness without his guidance?

I look to the heavens as if the answers lie above. The sky has changed from blue to purple, bringing with it the cold.

Loneliness settles into my heart. I have been separated from Elohim, and now my husband has walked away from me. He refuses to speak of multiplying and replenishing the earth. Why is he so repelled by the idea? Why is he so angry with me?

My throat tightens. Is this what Elohim meant by living our days in sorrow? Will every day be like this? Battling against Lucifer, struggling to provide food, wondering how to communicate with my husband.

I lower my head to my bent knees. Will my prayers even be heard if I decide to utter them? "What do you want from me, O Elohim?" I whisper. No one whispers back.

26

And [Adam] said, I heard thy voice in the garden, and I was afraid, because I was naked; and I hid myself.

—Genesis 3:10

He is swimming in the wide, slow river. The water is just the right amount of cool as his arms slice through the water. Eve watches him from the shore, laughing. Although he can't hear her laughter, he can see her expression as he comes up for air.

Then she's swimming next to him, her arms matching his pace stroke for stroke. Her long hair flows behind her, skimming the water's surface. They are back in the garden: they are surrounded by warmth, abundant fruit, and fish that don't have to die.

Adam can see the fish swimming below him. It looks as if there aren't any spaces between the individual fish as they swim together, side by side. Their silver bodies cut through the water in endless motion. They will forever swim.

He looks over at Eve as they both come up for air. He's pleased to be back in the garden, pleased to have eternity back with his wife at his side.

Back down in the water, he catches another glimpse of

the fish. As he watches them, their silver bodies turn dark. Adam stares at the changing fish, missing his time to take another breath at the surface of the river. His body aches to breathe, but he can't take his eyes from the fish. Their flesh darkens beyond black until it falls from their bones. The fish are nothing but bones now, moving through the water below him, still swimming with no scales or fins.

Adam lifts his head to gulp air, but the air is too thick to inhale. He chokes and tries to inhale again, fighting to stay above the water.

"Eve," he tries to call out, but his voice sounds only in his mind. He gasps for air, but it won't come . . .

Adam opened his eyes and realized they were burning—no, stinging. It was dark, yet the air was strange, as if there were gray clouds touching the ground. His throat hurt when he tried to breathe, and he realized he was smelling . . . Fire . . . smoke.

And the sound—it was like a low animal growl but unlike anything he'd ever heard. There was popping and hissing. A Fire burned somewhere close, and it was large.

"Eve," Adam said, reaching frantically for her. He touched the ground—where she should have been—only she wasn't next to him.

Taking a stuttered breath, he moved to his hands and knees, throwing off the animal skin he'd become entangled in. "Eve." He gasped, both to inhale some air and because of the pain that seared his chest as the smoky air made its way into his body. He groped along the ground. "Please, Elohim, let me find her." He could only hope she'd made it away from this oppressive smoke.

Then his hand touched something soft and smooth: Eve's arm. He crawled closer and felt her body. She wasn't moving. He wasn't even sure if she was breathing. There was no time to wait. Adam pulled her to a sitting position, but her body just slumped. He gathered her in his arms and stood.

The smoke was thicker, and he could see nothing with the burning in his eyes. He turned to the right, hoping he was headed toward the river. Then he half ran, half staggered, Eve's limp body in his arms.

"What have you done?" he asked her silent figure. They hadn't spoken a word before going to sleep that night. Adam knew Eve was upset, but he was battling enough with his own feelings and was trying to sort them out for her to understand . . . and not be upset over.

He didn't even know when she built the Fire. It must have been after he'd fallen asleep. Did she make it large on purpose? She was usually very careful and kept it contained. But now . . .

Adam felt the change in the ground as it sloped and grew muddy. He was close to the river.

Once his feet splashed in the cold water, he slowed his pace. The river tugged at the bear coat he wore, slowing him down even more. Cold numbness pierced his feet, but he kept pushing through the river, knowing that Eve was getting wet. She still didn't wake, not even with the water touching her.

He stumbled when he reached the other side of the river, nearly dropping Eve, but managed to gain his balance. The smoke was lighter on this side, but he kept walking and climbing, his legs aching with cold and his arms trembling with the effort to carry Eve. A faint wind blew in his face, dissipating the smoke even more, and for that, he was grateful.

When Eve started coughing, relief filled him. He set her down and supported her in a sitting position as she continued to cough. When she could speak, she said, "Why is there all this smoke?"

The smoke clouded just enough of the moon so that

Adam couldn't see her full expression. "Did you create a Fire last night?"

"No," she said before coughing again. When she could take a breath, she said, "I was tired . . . and fell asleep shortly after you did."

"Then how did the Fire start?" he said. Even as he asked the question, he knew there could be only one answer.

Eve sagged against him. "What have I done? Why did I let Lucifer teach me anything—even if I thought it would help you?"

"The Fire is not your fault." He wrapped his arms around her. "Elohim made it clear that Lucifer would exercise power over us." Adam pulled her into his lap and held her close. The air was cleaner closer to the ground. "But we must remember we have the power to resist him as well."

She nodded her head, burrowing closer against him.

After a moment, Adam said, "Come on. We must escape the smoke. Can you walk?"

"I think so." She took the hand he offered and climbed to her feet. She coughed a few more times but was able to walk farther north.

When they got to a point where the moon could be seen clearly, Adam finally stopped. They were at the base of a small hill, surrounded by scrubby bushes. "We'll rest here until morning or until the smoke dissipates."

He cleared a section of ground, making it free of rocks, and pulled Eve to sit next to him. He leaned back, and Eve lay against his chest. It would be a cold experience bathing in the river in the morning to get rid of all the smoke and dirt, but at least they were safe now.

Eve shuddered in his arms.

"I'm sorry," he said in a quiet voice.

"For what?"

"For not talking to you about . . . what Elohim commanded."

Eve lifted her head. "I just want to know why . . ." She moved away from him and straightened, as if she'd changed her mind about asking her question.

"Why what? Tell me."

"Why haven't you kissed me again?" she asked, her voice quiet and apprehensive.

He let out a breath. He'd wanted to kiss her many times, over and over, but he was unsure of what he must do. Confusion muddled his thoughts, and he didn't want to hurt Eve. Elohim had made it clear that her sorrow would be multiplied when she conceived children. She'd already endured enough pain in this wilderness.

"I know Elohim's commandments," he began. "But that doesn't mean we need to hasten into this . . . if you're not ready." She continued to stare ahead, not looking at him. "This will affect you more than me. You've already experienced pain with the changes in your body. Bearing a child will multiply that."

Her head turned slightly, and he thought he saw a glimmer of moisture on her cheek.

He continued when she didn't say anything. "How am I supposed to watch you endure more sorrow and pain? How am I supposed to protect you when I can't stop your pain?"

Now she looked at him. "I know there will be pain, and I *know* there will be sorrow. I still want to bear your children, Adam. That is why I made the choice in the garden." She touched his face, and he had to hold his breath so that he didn't drag her into his arms. "We can blame Lucifer all we want for us being expelled from the garden, but the choice was ours. I want to start the human race upon this earth with you. The pain and sorrow is part of the price, but being with you will make it worth it."

"I don't want to hurt you," he whispered.

"You won't hurt me," she said, moving her hand behind his head and drawing him in. She pressed her mouth against his, and he became lost in her kissing. He pulled her closer, and she responded by wrapping her arms around his neck.

"You taste like smoke," she said, and he laughed.

"You taste like Fire," he whispered. He kissed her then without the reservations he'd felt before, but he was still cautious. His body was responding to her in ways he hadn't previously imagined. He drew away, breathless, and stared at her.

"Are you all right?" she asked, equally breathless.

"I think I'm starting to understand."

Eve nodded, a faint smile on her face. She leaned forward and kissed his cheek, her hand lingering on his neck. Then she pushed against his chest. "I must smell horrible. I need to soak in the river."

"Are you hinting at something?" he asked, capturing her in his arms again.

She grinned. "We both need to soak."

Her eyes were growing bluer with the rising sun, and Adam brushed her tangled hair from her shoulders. There were dark smudges under her eyes, but her gaze was bright . . . so *Eve.* "I love you," he said.

"You still need to wash."

He laughed. "Let's go then."

"Not reluctant any longer?" she said.

He pulled her to her feet. "I think you're right. We can't avoid the pain and sorrow of this new life, so we might as well embrace the joy of it."

She rose up on her toes and kissed him again. This time it was the lightest touch, which left him wanting more. "You should listen to your wife more often."

27

Who told thee that thou wast naked? Hast thou eaten of the tree, whereof I commanded thee that thou shouldest not eat?

—Genesis 3:11

By the time we reach the river, we can see the devastation at our former dwelling. The ground is dark with ash, and the shelter that Adam had hauled the branches for is nothing more than a black shell. Thoughts of our shared intimacy just moments before flee as we wade through the cold river hand in hand.

All that we have labored to build is now gone. It wasn't much and definitely was not as luxurious as our abode in the garden, but it was ours and ours alone.

Lucifer has destroyed another measure of our comfort.

I stand and watch as Adam picks through the damage, seeking for anything that might be salvaged. The altar that was so recently completed is the only thing that remains. Its stones are scorched black, but not one stone has tumbled out of place. The large bear skin, which we shared during cold nights, is now a hideous lump of black. The baskets that I had so carefully woven, in which we stored various food stuffs, are now ash.

Even the dried meat that Adam spent so much time hunting and procuring is inedible.

Looking toward the garden and its untouched green billowing above the serene stone walls, I feel as if I've been mocked, but when Adam comes to my side and wraps me in his arms, I immediately chastise myself.

This was not Elohim's doing. It was not our doing. It was Lucifer's doing—and Lucifer's alone.

I must accept this as a warning and a consequence. Although Lucifer might give us something that is lifesaving and useful, it can destroy if not used with proper care. I hold onto Adam. Not only is our dwelling gone, but we also won't be able to rebuild with the ground black and dead.

The smell of smoke is overpowering, and I can't wait to leave this place behind. Yet I release Adam and help him scour the ground. It's not long before I realize we were blessed to get away with our lives intact.

When Adam turns toward the garden and gazes at it for several long moments, I want to ask him what he is thinking, but I let him have his silence. When he finally looks at me, there is redness in his eyes. I walk toward him and take his hand. "Where should we go now, my husband?"

My voice seems to bring his thoughts back to our current plight. "We'll inquire of Elohim," he says.

My heart is heavy as I walk with him to the altar, the place of worship that was so serene the day before and the site of Lucifer's noxious appearance. This time I don't let go of Adam's hand as we kneel together and bow our heads.

His voice lifts to the heavens. His cries rend the air, but still there is no answer. When both of our knees are aching and Adam's voice is hoarse, he rises to his feet.

"We'll go south until we reach the far river," he says. I don't question his decision. "We'll stay close to the garden until we receive further instruction from Elohim," he finishes.

Stubbornness may be seen as a weakness, but today it's a strength in my dear husband.

Our footsteps scuff the scorched earth as we walk. The Fire stayed clear of the garden, as if there was a power pushing it away in another direction. The burned terrain stretches for quite a distance, but the Fire seems to have died out before reaching the first bend in the north river.

We walk south, staying in sight of the garden. The memories of visiting the southern borders of the garden—and how we found the dead snake there—return. So much has happened since then that I marvel at my innocence on that day. The first appearance of death should have been a greater warning to me. It had been a warning all along to Adam, but I, of course, had refused to listen.

The cool wind cuts through my hair and blows it in front of my shoulders, but the walking keeps me warm—that and my leopard coat and Adam's hand in mine. I can now allow myself to think of our shared kisses that morning. My face heats at the thought, and soon I am too warm. My skin becomes moist with the effort of walking, and a few moments pass before I realize Adam is watching me.

He is smiling.

It seems his frustration over our burned dwelling has passed more quickly than I thought possible. "Why are you smiling?" I ask, my heart expanding because I guess the answer.

He stops and slowly takes me into his arms. "No reason."

I close my eyes as his lips touch mine. It's the middle of a bleak, cold day, and we are standing on rough, scorched earth, but I feel as if I am surrounded by the warmest breeze and standing on the softest grass. My aches and exhaustion fade in his kiss. Even the images of the dead snake and all the rotting fruit in the southern fields seem to belong to another life.

All that matters, all that I can feel, is here, now, in Adam's arms.

It's too soon when Adam lets go, and we start to walk again. When the sun is still high in the sky, we reach the southern river. It's narrower and riddled with more rocks than the northern river. Adam releases my hand and scoops up a handful of water. Rubbing his hands together, he declares, "Still cold."

I laugh. I didn't expect the south river to be any warmer than the north river. Joining him at the water's edge, I scoop a few handfuls of water and take a long drink. Then I rub the water on my arms, washing off the lingering ash and dirt. But it's not enough to crouch at the river's edge. I glance at the sky, assessing how much sunlight we have left. I walk into the river, and the cold immediately takes hold of me.

"What are you doing?" Adam asks, but he follows my lead. First he sheds the bear skin. Then he steps into the water, wearing only the covering Elohim gave us in the garden.

I wade to the middle of the river. It's not as deep as the northern river and reaches only to my thighs, but I sink into the depths, gasping as the cold surrounds me and seems to pierce straight through my skin. Fish swim by, treating me like another rock they pass on their journey.

When Adam reaches me, he immerses himself in the water and comes up almost instantly, his hair soaked and dripping. "It's much too cold!" he says.

I laugh and move away from him so that he's not tempted to pull me under with him. I dip my head back cautiously, letting the long strands of my hair sink into the water. The cold on my scalp sends tremors through me.

"Do you need help?" Adam asks.

"Not from you," I say. "I've been in long enough."

"Use the bear skin until your covering is dry."

Now I know why he left his bear skin on shore instead of washing it as well. I soak in the river for as long as I can stand the cold. My body is numb by the time I reach the bank. A glance behind me tells me that Adam is facing away. Whether he is doing it on purpose I don't know, but I'm grateful. Since we left the garden, I have not been fully unclothed in front of him. The changes in my body have made me more conscious of my nakedness.

I shed the leopard coat for the bear coat, and by the time I've draped the wet leopard coat over a bush, Adam has finished his bathing and is walking toward shore. He finds a nearby boulder to stretch out on, letting his skin dry beneath the feeble sun. I look away from his stretched out form. The heat is building inside of me again, and I can think only of the way he held me and kissed me on our walk here.

Turning my attention to our surroundings, I examine the terrain. There are a couple of lone trees on this side of the riverbank, their branches looking weak and ineffectual for building a shelter. They are mere saplings compared to the trees in the garden. My gaze strays toward the garden. It seems that the trees that had once suffered at the southern border are now fully revived. I can't see the fruit from this distance, but I imagine its sweet lusciousness among the green boughs.

"Are you hungry?" Adam's voice reaches me, as if he's heard my thoughts.

"Not for fish."

He laughs, squinting over at me. "Do you have any other ideas?"

I try not to look toward the garden, but when Adam catches me glancing in that direction, he rises up on his elbows and casts me a stern look. "We're not pilfering from the garden. Don't you remember we were cast out?" His words are serious, but there is a smile trying to emerge on his face.

"I was thinking no such thing."

He sits up all the way and climbs off the boulder. Without another word he walks to one of the scrub trees and rips off a lower branch. Within moments he's whittled away one end on a rock, creating a sharpened end. Then he crosses to the river and steps into the cold water again. I watch in amazement as he spears a fish, then another one.

He carries the fish to the riverbank, where I meet him, and while he prepares one fish, I pick up the other. Adam's eyebrows arc as I take the second fish in hand. I hide a smile and set to work, mimicking his method of preparing the fish for eating.

My stomach clenches, but I force all thoughts of revulsion out of my mind. After all, I have skinned a bear—this can't be any worse. The fish carcass slips beneath my fingers, and I lose my grip several times, but I grit my teeth together and finish removing the flesh from the bones, getting poked by the sharp-edged bones only twice.

Adam finishes with his fish first. "Do you want me to help you?" he asks.

"I can do this," I say, intent on my work and also intent to not let on how hard it is to manage such a slippery fish. Adam washes up, then leaves me to my task.

When I have finished preparing my fish, I wash my hands in the river, trying not to shudder at both the cold and handling the fish on my own. Adam waits for me, a half smile on his face. I meet his gaze with a smile. "You are certainly looking forward to eating cold fish."

Then he steps to the side, and behind him is a small Fire. At first my heart lurches. Then I see how he's surrounded the Fire with a makeshift wall of rocks. This is the first time he's made Fire without my instruction.

He motions with his hand. "Come, sit by the Fire. I want to try something."

I walk toward the Fire, and he guides me to sit on a nearby boulder.

"This boulder blocks the wind nicely and doesn't disturb the flames," he says.

I perch on the boulder. "What are you doing with the fish?" He has several thin twigs lined up on the rocks that border the Fire, pieces of fish speared through each twig.

"We're going to heat the fish."

I narrow my eyes as he lifts the first twig and holds it over the orange flames.

"I decided that if our food were warm, maybe we'd become warm as well from eating it," he says.

Sliding off the boulder, I pick up one of the twigs and hold the fish over the Fire. After a couple of moments, Adam withdraws his twig. The flesh has darkened in the process. He touches it with his finger. "It's quite hot." Then he pokes at it with his tongue. Finally, he bites into it.

"How does it taste?" I ask.

Without a word, he hands the warm fish to me, and I take a small bite. The fish, which was formerly cold and slippery, now has a warm and pleasing substance to it. "Excellent," I say, awed at the change in taste. It's still the same fish we've eaten many times, but the taste is much better. I hand the piece back to Adam, but he waves it away.

"You finish it. We'll make plenty more."

As the sun sets, the Fire becomes brighter, illuminating our faces and hands as we continue to heat the fish.

Adams stands after a while and heads back to one of the small trees. He tears branches from the tree and, after snapping the branches into smaller lengths, he feeds them to the Fire.

"We don't want it too large," I say, my heart thrumming. As the flames leap, I am both awed and fearful. I wonder how large of a Fire Lucifer built in order to have it burn wild.

Adam grabs my leopard coat and spreads it out on the boulder near the Fire. I reach over and run my hand along the fur. It's only about half-dry and will be useless to wear tonight.

With the quickly falling temperature, I know that Adam must be colder than he is willing to admit. "Do you want the bear skin back?" I ask.

His gaze meets mine over the glowing Fire. "We'll share tonight."

It's a natural solution, but my heart races. Since our intimate kissing, sharing the bear skin—which isn't nearly as large as the one that was destroyed—seems to carry new consideration. And the way Adam is looking at me, as if I am the only thing he is thinking about right now, sends rising bumps along my arms.

"Of course," I manage to say. I break off from the heat of his gaze and look at the Fire, but I know he's still watching me. My breathing is suddenly thin, and I inhale deeply.

Adam moves away from the Fire, away from me, and walks over to one of the trees. I try not to stare after him, but I watch him anyway as he picks leaves from the tree.

He comes back with fistfuls of leaves and sprinkles them on the ground not too far from the Fire. I realize he is making a place to sleep, so I stand as well and help him gather more leaves. The leaves are not as large or as soft as the ones in the garden, but they cover the ground and provide some padding.

I don't know why the act of picking the leaves and spreading them on the ground, walking back and forth between the tree and the Fire, makes my heart pound. Maybe it's the way that Adam keeps looking at me and how when I catch his look, he doesn't turn away. When I say, "I think that will do for tonight," Adam nods his agreement.

"Why are you staring at me?" I say at last.

His mouth moves into a smile. "Come over here." He is standing in the middle of the leaves we've laid down.

"I'm not tired yet."

"Eve," he whispers, looking at me with those gold-green eyes of his. He holds out his hand, waiting for me.

I know I should move, should step forward into his waiting arms. But I don't.

28

And the man said, The woman whom thou gavest to be with me, she gave me of the tree, and I did eat.

—Genesis 3:12

I listen to Adam's breathing long after he falls asleep, his back toward me.

The warmth that comes from his body heat is not enough, and I am shivering, but I refuse to move, to turn and wrap my arms around Adam beneath the shared bear coat.

I can't forget the look of hurt on his face after he extended his hand to me, inviting me to lie with him on our new bed of leaves.

I can't forget my hesitation after all that we have shared and after all the times he's kissed and held me. When the moment arrived, when I knew what he hoped for, I turned away.

As the Fire's glow dims and sputters, I listen to his every breath, how he exhales and inhales. I keep my eyes closed, but I can still remember his face: his lips curved into a smile, his dark hair falling across his forehead.

His gaze full of hope. And love.

I slip from beneath the bear skin and cross to the boulder where the leopard skin has been drying above the Fire. The fur is now dry and warm to the touch. Tugging it across my shoulders, I crouch next to the Fire, reveling in the bits of heat that reach my skin.

With the exception of Adam's breathing and the sparking Fire, there is no other sound above the rush of the river. I remember the night that was so cold when the white flakes covered the ground—the night when Lucifer taught me to make Fire. I had acted in haste, but it was out of a strong instinct to protect my husband.

And I want to protect him now, protect him from ever feeling sorrow or hurt—but I know I have caused him pain tonight. I had returned his kisses earlier in the day with as much eagerness as he had bestowed them. I'd cherished his words from his heart when he'd told me that he didn't want to cause *me* any pain.

And yet . . . what does he think of me now? What is he dreaming about as he lies alone on the bed of leaves he created for me—for us?

Tomorrow the day will bring the same cold, the same challenges, and the same hunger. And it will most likely return the distance that was between us before the great Fire. I want to tell Adam that I am afraid—more than I care to admit even to myself. I hadn't realized until the moment arrived that I wasn't sure. It would be an action that I wouldn't be able to change or return from.

Yes, I want to fulfill all of Elohim's commandments, and I have made the choice to do so, but when I realized I needed to fulfill them *now*, in that moment, my breath and my heart failed me. And in doing so, I failed my husband—his trust betrayed.

The Fire sputters in a gust of wind then settles back to its usual glow. I look toward the river, which is barely visible in the moonlight. I realize that no matter what happens, the river continues to forge onward. It moves without complaint, bringing life to the trees, plants, and animals—bringing life to us. The river is fulfilling its purpose, and it will do so until it dries up and fades from this earth.

"Oh, Adam," I whisper to myself. "Why am I so foolish?"

I stand, giving the river one last look, remembering the times that I have used it—for nourishment, for washing, for swimming—without gratitude.

Turning, I look at Adam sleeping, and then I replace the leopard skin on the boulder. I remove from my body the skin coat that came from Elohim. It's strange to be in this state again, a state that I have not been in since the garden. Being in a state that used to never cause me a second thought has now become a deliberate act.

With the glow of the Fire behind my back, I slide beneath the bear skin and turn toward Adam, not touching him yet. I watch as his shoulder rises with each breath. Closing my hands into fists, I resist touching him. He is my husband, but I am still hesitant. Everything has been different since we walked out of the garden. His tenderness has burrowed deeply into my heart, and even tonight, there was no remonstration. Just patience. And hurt.

I swallow, and my breath scrapes against my dry throat. I am perspiring with nervousness, or maybe fear—it's hard to tell the difference.

But there is no expectant hand held out to me now. There is just me and my own decision—my own choice. Adam has given me this gift of choice, and I know that I choose my husband. I'll always choose him—just as the river will always flow and give life.

"Adam," I whisper. I have spoken too quietly—to give myself another excuse if he doesn't wake. But the thudding in my chest grows only stronger, and almost against my will—yet obeying that same will—I reach out and place my hand on his back.

Sliding my fingers upward, I move my hands along his muscles, across his shoulder, and to his neck, until my fingers reach his hair. Then I rise up on one elbow, moving my hand around to his chest, and I kiss his neck.

His eyes flutter open, and just as he turns his head, I press my mouth against his. Even though he is still mostly asleep, his mouth welcomes mine. Then he turns fully toward me, his gaze finding mine, and he draws me against him.

His kissing grows deeper, possessive, until I don't know exactly where he ends and I begin. I feel as if the Fire that fades behind me has rekindled and now burns between us. And I know everything will change.

We sleep through most of the morning, our bodies entangled, our breathing as one. There is much to do today, much to decide, but we are both reluctant to get up. We have partaken of the sweetest of fruits, and it has left us only desiring more.

Adam's fingers trail along my jawline, then down my neck. His eyes are closed, but I know that he is more than awake.

"Good morning," he whispers.

"It will be high sun soon," I whisper back.

He laughs, his voice vibrating through me. I nestle my head beneath his chin and exhale.

"Why did we wait so long?" he asks.

"Because we wouldn't have gotten anything else done if

we hadn't waited." I push away his hand that is moving lower, but he captures me and kisses me until I can barely breathe.

"Adam," I say when he breaks off. "We can't stay like this all day."

He raises his head to gaze at me. "Actually, we can." Then he tugs the bear skin over both of our heads, blocking out all light.

৵৫৹

The sun rises and the sun sets, but I'm not paying attention to whether I am waking up or falling asleep. All I know is that Adam is next to me and that I am in his arms. We wouldn't even eat or drink if I didn't force Adam out from under the bear skin.

But the time finally comes when we must build a new altar.

Together we gather rocks for the altar, with Adam carrying the larger ones. Whenever we cross paths, Adam pulls me into a kiss.

"We'll never get the altar built if you don't leave me alone," I say.

He just grins and kisses me again. "I can't believe how much time we wasted."

"If you stop kissing me, then we can build much faster."

"That's not what I meant," Adam says, his hands at my waist. "We've been married for a long time, and only now do we enjoy the fullness of our union."

I shake my head. "You forget so easily."

"What am I forgetting?" he says, speaking into my ear.

"That you didn't look at me in that way until after we ate the fruit," I say. "Now are you grateful you ate of the forbidden fruit?"

Adam buries his face against my neck. "I just want to be with you—wherever you are, whatever you're doing."

"No matter the pain and sorrow?" I say as the heat between us grows.

"There's nothing more I want than to share your pain and sorrow."

"As long as you aren't inflicting it," I say.

He draws back and gazes at me, his expression serious. "Do you think you are with child?"

I place my hand on his cheek. "I hope so." Then I rise up on my toes and kiss him. He tightens his hold around me and lifts me from the ground.

Something cold tickles my heels, and I draw away from Adam and turn around.

On the ground at our feet, a large snake coils back and opens its mouth with a hiss.

I scream before I remember that I should probably stay quiet. Adam tugs me behind him, and we slowly back away.

I have never seen a snake act so aggressively. Of course I have learned that in the wilderness the animals and reptiles are focused on their own survival and that other animals, as well as Adam and I, are threats.

My heart is pounding, not just because there is an aggressive reptile threatening us, but also because the reptile is a snake. Long and black, it reminds me of the snake we found dead in the garden. Although this snake is smaller, it's still large, and I assume it would reach to my waist if it slithered up my leg.

I can't look away from the snake; its black eyes seem to be staring right into mine. "Lucifer?" I whisper. I don't know why I just called the snake Lucifer, but its eyes remind me of my brother.

"Don't move," Adam whispers as he slowly crouches and picks up something off the ground.

The snake hisses again. What does it want? We can't possibly be a food source for it.

Adam tosses something toward the snake at the same time he grabs my arm and pulls me back with him. I realize he has thrown a handful of dirt, and it has done nothing but aggravate the snake. It hisses again and lunges forward.

We leap back, but the snake keeps advancing. "We need a rock or something," I whisper frantically. The sharpened branches are on the other side of the boulders. "Should we split up?"

"Move away from me. See if you can capture its attention," Adam says.

My heart pounds faster. "What are you going to do?"

He shakes his head, and I move away from Adam and clap my hands. My palms are moist, but the sound alerts the snake.

Adam makes a wide circle, trying to get behind the snake. I clap louder, stepping backward as I do so. The snake starts moving faster, and I move faster as well. My heel catches on a rock, and I trip backward. I scream, putting my hands up to ward off the snake.

And then Adam is there. "Watch out!" I yell, but he reaches for the snake just as it turns toward him. He picks it up by the tail and swings it.

There is a rush of air, but nothing touches me. Adam brings down the snake hard onto the ground with a dull thud. The long body of the snake is still. When Adam's gaze meets mine, I feel a sob rise up in my throat, but I push it back. "You killed it."

His jaw tightens, and he only nods.

I stare at the snake, drawn to its lifeless form and the way its long body curves and twists on the ground. Just moments ago, it was advancing in an attack, alive.

I remember the sorrow and confusion I felt when we discovered the dead snake in the garden, how we reverently carried it to a river to let the current wash it away. But this snake . . . I wrap my arms around my torso and shiver. Again the thought of Lucifer filters through my mind.

Adam crouches over the snake, watching it as carefully as I am. There is no movement, no signs of life. "Do you think we can eat the flesh?" he asks.

My hand goes to my throat. "Anything but a snake. Please." I rush on to explain what I'm not sure I understand myself. "It somehow reminds me of our brother," I say in a quiet voice.

He nods once, then reaches for the snake. Without asking me anything more, he carries it to the river and deposits it into the water. He stays at the riverbank for several moments, gazing at the water, while I keep my distance, trying to catch my breath.

29

And God said unto the woman, What is this that thou hast done? And the woman said, The serpent beguiled me, and I did eat.

—Genesis 3:13

Adam watched Eve as she stood at the riverbank, her arms wrapped around her torso as if to protect herself from the cold. It was plain that the snake's appearance had left her shaken. Adam was shaken as well, but he was grateful that he was able to kill the snake without harm to either him or Eve. He worried about encountering another snake. In the garden, snakes were never aggressive, and in the garden, there was never a need to kill one.

He wondered about Eve comparing the snake to Lucifer. Was it because the snake reminded her of the dead one they'd found in the garden? Or was it something more?

Adam joined Eve at the riverbank and grasped her hand. Her delicate fingers reminded him of her touch over the past couple of days. His desire was still strong, but he knew they needed to finish building the altar.

"Do you not think it's strange that the snake appeared

just now?" Eve said in a subdued voice. "Just when we're building a new altar?"

"What do you mean?" he asked, but he felt an uncomfortable prickling of his skin growing.

"When we completed the other altar, Lucifer arrived." Eve continued to stare at the river, as if lost in her thoughts, yet she spoke again. "Lucifer put enmity between you and me."

"Then drove us out with the Fire," Adam added.

"Yes," she said, finally turning to look at him. Her eyes were rimmed in red, and the sight of her distress tugged at his heart. "Adam, do you think Lucifer meant for us to die? Is he trying to return us to dust so soon?"

He swallowed against the dryness in his throat. It made him uncomfortable how easily Eve discussed Lucifer. "I don't know," he began. "If Lucifer brought either of us death, then what would he do on this earth?"

She stepped closer. Adam's heart quickened as her other hand brushed his cheek. He tried to ignore her touch as he thought through Lucifer's motivations. "If our brother brought us death today, when we have done everything we can think of to be righteous, then our souls would be saved in Heaven."

"And what triumph would that bring him?" she said in a quiet voice.

"None," he said in an equally muted tone. "I don't think he means to take our lives. I think he means to cast doubt on our faith and to divide us from each other."

Eve exhaled and laid her head against Adam's chest. Her arms went around his waist, and he buried his face in her hair. It was as if every part of his complemented every part of hers.

"We'll never let him divide us," she said. "He's already tried and has failed each time."

Adam lifted his head. He believed in Eve's words, but he

knew they would have to be diligent. He hadn't expected Eve to partake of the fruit without Elohim's permission, and although she was more subdued in the wilderness, focusing on finding food and keeping warm, he suspected that once the winter passed, her curiosity would return in full force.

As for himself, he wasn't dismissing any power of influence that Lucifer might have over him. He'd hid it well, but since he had recovered from the bear attack and thought about how their brother had provided the one thing they truly needed—Fire—and Elohim had not, the seed of discontent had taken root in his heart.

He pushed it back time and time again before it could sprout and grow. The worst nights were when Eve slept and he had only his thoughts—and concerns—to dwell on. The past couple of nights, with Eve in his arms, were exceptions. They made him forget all else.

Drawing away from Eve, he smoothed her hair back and gave her a light kiss. He wanted to take the kiss deeper, but as enticing as spending the next moments with his wife would be, he knew kissing would just delay the progress of the altar. "I'll get back to the altar. You can take the time you need before joining me."

"I'll come with you."

Adam and Eve worked side by side, literally. It seemed that Eve was next to him every time he turned. He doubted another snake would catch them unaware, but it was obvious that Eve wasn't taking any chances.

They completed the altar before sundown, and after a meal of heated fish, Adam turned to his wife. He was beyond exhausted and could see that she was too, but he didn't want to delay their worship. "Are you ready?"

She blinked back at him with bleary eyes. "Tomorrow is the seventh day. Should we wait until then?"

"Every moment we wait gives Lucifer additional time to thwart our efforts," he said.

Her mouth lifted into a subtle smile. "And we have delayed quite a while already."

"Yes," Adam said in a soft voice. He was becoming lost in her eyes. "Let's go." He stood and held out his hand, and they walked together to the new altar. He sank to his knees and bowed his head.

Eve stayed at his side until the dark turned too cold. He wasn't sure when she crept away, but the moon was high in the sky when he finally stood and walked back to where she lay curled beneath her single coat. He lay down next to her and used his coat as an added measure of warmth to cover the both of them.

He pulled her gently into his arms, reveling in her warmth but at the same time being careful not to wake her. Her even breathing started to relax his aching muscles and the tension running through his back and neck. Elohim had remained quiet . . . again.

Adam let out a breath. He was grateful that Eve was sleeping and couldn't see the despair settling over him. What if Elohim had abandoned them for the rest of their mortality? *No,* Adam thought. *He can't have abandoned us. We are the first man and woman on the earth, and even though we disobeyed one of Elohim's commandments, we are keeping the others.* Nearly keeping the others. *It will be only a matter of time before Eve conceives and brings forth the first child.*

Adam inhaled Eve's scent—a smell of the rushing river with a faint touch of Fire—taking comfort in her presence. Even if Elohim remained silent, they still had each other, and even if Elohim stayed silent, they still didn't need Lucifer or any of his teachings. Did they?

We don't need Lucifer, Adam told himself firmly. The way Lucifer looked at his wife was enough for Adam to wish their brother would never approach their dwelling again. And the way Lucifer was able to confound their words and put doubt and questions into their minds made Adam's pulse race hot with anger. Lucifer seemed to always be around, to always be watching, and just because they hadn't seen him since the big Fire didn't mean he wasn't lurking somewhere nearby.

And he probably listened to every word of my prayers as well, Adam thought. He clenched his jaw. *O Elohim, hear our prayers. If thou needest to remain silent, please protect us from the influence of our Fallen brother.* Adam continued to silently pray until Eve broke away from his arms with a moan.

Her head moved back and forth a couple of times, and her eyes fluttered open.

"What's wrong?" he whispered, rising up on his elbow.

Eve blinked up at him. "Adam," she breathed. Her hands reached for his neck, and she pulled him toward her. "It was Lucifer again—in my dream."

"Tell me," he said, feeling the tension in her arms and back.

"It was as if he were next to me, instead of you. He was whispering to me, telling me there is still so much knowledge to be had and that he could begin teaching me now." Her voice cut off. "Oh, Adam, why does Elohim not answer our prayers?"

Adam tightened his hold on Eve, swallowing back his own complaint. He had to be strong for her. Although he worried about the same thing, he didn't want the worry to escalate and push Eve in Lucifer's direction.

"We have to accept the differences in the wilderness," he began as Eve nestled against him. He was grateful that after a dream about Lucifer, she would turn to him for comfort. "Elohim will probably communicate with us differently. He may not walk among the thorns and the thistles to visit us. He may speak to us by more subtle means." Adam was trying to convince himself as much as he was trying to convince his wife, but the more he spoke, the more new possibilities entered his mind.

"Elohim won't speak to us anymore?" she asked, lifting her face and putting space between them.

"I think Elohim's voice will be more like a whisper or even a thought." It felt right—comforting, somehow—the idea that perhaps Elohim *was* communicating with them. They just had to pay more attention. He smoothed the hair from Eve's face, then touched her cheeks, catching the wet there.

She closed her eyes. "That sounds nice. A quiet thought. Or maybe a feeling."

"Yes, a feeling," Adam said. He kissed her forehead and ran his fingers over her hair and down her back. She relaxed against him and after a few moments had fallen asleep.

Adam listened for any sound of movement around their dwelling. He looked around. The Fire had long since died, although he could still smell its remains. In the moonlight, there were no out-of-place shadows. Everything was quiet.

He lay down as he clung to the hope that Elohim was still mindful of them, still watching over them, even in his silence.

30

And God said unto the serpent, Because thou has done this, thou art cursed above all cattle, and above every beast of the field; upon thy belly shalt thou go, and dust shalt thou eat all the days of thy life.

—Genesis 3:14

I stare at the fish that I told Adam I'd prepare. He is busy praying. Again. He has prayed so much over the past two moons that his knees are bruised and chafed.

The fish's luminous dead eyes seem to stare back at me, as if to ask me why I am here, shivering at the riverbank, while my husband is at the altar. If he didn't spend so much time at the altar, he could have captured other beasts and procured their furs. We'd have something besides fish to eat, and we wouldn't have to huddle over the Fire so much to garner bits of warmth.

The loss of the bear skin in the great Fire still hasn't been made up for. The newfound intimacy with Adam has softened the cold nights, but when the cold and exhaustion set in, I desire only warmth and comfort.

Yet Adam refuses to leave the dwelling we've created on the southern side of the garden and search for a place with more ready resources. Instead, he spends day after day in supplication to the silent Elohim.

I have tried to listen, as Adam suggests, for whisperings from Elohim, but my stomach's sounds are much too loud to hear any whispering.

I pierce the fish's flesh and hold my breath as I remove the innards that we won't use. My stomach tightens, hardening more than usual. I drop the fish as my stomach feels as though it's turning inside out. I fall to my hands, my stomach violently clenching. The little food that I ate this morning comes up through my throat, and I spit it out.

I have never felt such revulsion and weakness in my stomach. I scoot away from the mess and take a deep, shuddering breath. A bitter taste is in my mouth, and I can't look over at the fish again. Just the thought of finishing the preparation makes my stomach clench again.

After a few moments, the pain in my stomach subsides, and I stand, my legs shaky. I feel as if all my strength has left me. I walk toward the altar, which is on the other side of our dwelling. Adam has his head down, praying, or even sleeping. My step falters as my stomach roils again, and I decide I can only make it as far as our bed of leaves. Panting, I try to calm myself. I feel too weak to call out to Adam, and it's some time before he notices that I've abandoned all tasks.

"Eve?" his voice floats above me somewhere. I feel his hands on my face, my neck, my arms. Then I feel a weight, a warmth, settling over my body, and I realize he's placed his bear skin over me.

You'll get cold, I want to say, but the words are too weak to leave my mouth. I hear the snapping of a new fire, then feel Adam's hands on my forehead. They are trembling, and he's calling my name.

I open my eyes. "I'm all right," I whisper.

Adam's expression is full of concern and fear. "You don't look all right."

I grimace. "My stomach is ill. I was overcome with revulsion when I was preparing the fish." Before Adam can speak, I rush on. "It wasn't the usual distaste but a violent rejection. My stomach turned out the food from this morning."

Adam's hand caresses the side of my cheek. I exhale. Each moment that passes, I feel a little better. Perhaps it's due to the extra warmth as well as Adam's attention.

"I'll finish with the fish," he says.

I nod but then say, "I don't think I can eat any of it. My stomach won't accept it."

"You have to eat something." The fear comes back into his eyes.

"My stomach hurts just thinking about it."

Adam sits back and looks over at the Fire. "What if I heat the fish again? Or find another animal to try?"

I let out a sigh. If only there were berries or some sort of fruit, but we have scoured our surroundings more than once and picked all of the bushes clean. It seems that berries aren't too plentiful in the winter season.

I sit, and Adam puts an arm around my shoulders. "I will ask Elohim to direct us."

My face heats with indignation. "That's all you've been doing since building the altar. We've neglected exploring our surroundings." My voice drops at his expression. "I don't mean to blame you." But I can see that it's too late to repair what I said.

Adam rises to his feet, his torso clothed only in the skin coat from the garden. I'm still wearing his bear coat. He walks around the Fire and grabs the sharpened branch he uses for spearing fish. He can't possibly be going to catch more fish.

"What are you doing?" I ask.

"I'll try to be back before dark falls," he says without looking at me.

I watch his back as he walks away. "Where are you going?" I ask, climbing to my feet. I take an unsteady breath. His step slows but without turning, he says, "Just rest."

He continues to walk, but it seems to be with reluctance. I would run after him, but I know I can't run without upsetting my stomach again. And I'd be no good to him in my condition. I don't know what's wrong with me, but resting sounds like the best option right now.

Adam heads north, and I watch him until I can no longer see the outline of his shoulders. I feel sad and angry at the same time—sad that I was so sharp with him, angry that I had to be sharp with him to send him into action. Yet this wasn't the way I'd intended for it to happen. I thought we could both go exploring, maybe plan to stay overnight somewhere.

But here I am, completely alone.

I move closer to the Fire and lean against the boulder. There is a long wait until dark, and I'm unsure how long it will take Adam to do whatever he is doing. Is he hunting for another animal? Is he looking for a new dwelling place?

I can't believe he's left me alone. Although we haven't seen any sign of Lucifer for a couple of moon cycles, I still dream of him. Each time I awake, it's as if he's actually been talking to me. I wonder if he really is speaking to me through my dreams. Adam brushes it off, as if he's confident that Elohim will speak to us and we won't have to rely on Lucifer for anything. But I can see the tension along the muscles of Adam's face when I tell him of my dreams.

My breath comes short as the quiet settles around me. What if Lucifer comes today? What if he's been watching all along and just watched Adam leave me? What if he heard my words?

Adam, I want to scream. *Come back!* But if I speak aloud, Lucifer will be sure to hear my cry, and he is the last person I want to hear me. I pull myself to my feet and kick dirt over the small Fire until it has no chance of spreading—not that we have much to lose in our current dwelling anyway.

I think of Adam searching for an animal as the cold increases with the setting sun while I sit here, by a Fire, with the leopard skin and the bear skin around me. All because I have a weakened stomach. I move to the river and drink a handful of water. It slides down my throat easily and doesn't produce any sharp pains. Gazing over our dwelling and the altar in the background, I think there is nothing there that would entice Lucifer. He can have it if he wants it.

As for me, I'm going to find Adam.

The last point where I saw him doesn't seem too far away, until I start walking.

Not eating a midday meal has left me weaker than I'd like. I haven't been eating as much over the past few weeks, and my physique has grown thinner. I stop many times to rest, telling myself to turn back, but I can't. I must continue on.

When I arrive at the place where Adam disappeared, I am standing on a ridge. The ground dips sharply into a valley, then eventually rises to meet the northern mountain range. To my surprise, there are thick clusters of trees, as well as bushes and all manner of tangled plants, all dried and brown. I think of the luxurious plants in the garden in stark contrast to the view that spreads before me now.

Will the brown plants renew themselves once the winter harshness has faded? At the top of the ridge, the wind is a fair contender and tugs at my coats and hair. I look for Adam's familiar shape and hope that I can see him moving through the trees. But with the gray clouds blocking out the sun's rays, all of the colors spread out before me seem to blend together.

Again, I want to call out to Adam, but I stay silent, searching and searching. I look behind me, gauging the distance I've come and making sure this is the place to where I watched Adam walk. Seeing it from this angle, I am no longer sure.

I spin in a slow circle, scanning the terrain. Where else would he have gone? Is he crouched in some foliage somewhere, spying on a beast, prepared to attack? I don't want to startle him from a hunt, but I wonder where he is right now.

A rustle sounds behind me, and my first thought is Lucifer. I turn, my heart thudding, but there is no one there. My second thought—another snake. I scour the grass for any signs of movement but find none.

Relax, I tell myself, but my breathing is fast, and my stomach is revolting again. I've walked too far without food, but I can't let myself turn back now. I move forward, picking my way down the ridge until I find a rock to sit on. There is no protection from the wind on this hillside, and the wind cuts through my coats. I think of Adam being more exposed to the climate than I am. Is he regretting his actions now? Is he wishing he'd stayed with me until I felt better?

I slide down until I'm sitting on the cold ground, my back against the rock. Burrowing in the coats, I watch for any movement. I pull a green-brown leaf off a nearby bush and bite off a piece of it. The leaf is dry and tastes mostly like wood, but I chew and swallow, then eat another. My thirst compounds, but I want to watch for a while longer before venturing toward the river again.

Pulling my knees up, I wrap my arms around them. If I start back now, I'll make it to our dwelling before the sun sets. Or I can wait here and hope that Adam will see me on his return. The moments drag on while I wait.

Adam lay flat on his stomach as the rustling grew louder behind him. He didn't move, barely breathing, and he listened as the hoofbeats came closer. There were at least a dozen deer coming right toward him.

His body tensed as the first deer passed by him, close enough to touch. He let out his breath silently, inhaling again. He'd wait until all the deer but one had passed him. Then he'd capture the last one in the group.

Another set of hoofs passed near him, and he moved his head slightly to look for the next deer. The deer walked by him, more intent on what was up ahead than on what lurked on the ground.

When the final deer passed, Adam rose silently to his hands and knees. He reached for the sharp stick that he brought. The deer had stopped at a grouping of bushes, their mouths busy eating the berries.

His palms felt damp as he watched the animals feed. They were not aggressive as the snake or leopard had been. These deer were docile, reminding him of the ones in the garden.

Eve's words came back to him. In his mind, he saw her curled up on the ground, cold and hungry and feeling weak. He didn't know what was wrong with her, but worry consumed him. He'd thought if only he could pull Elohim back into their lives and find out the direction they were supposed to take, he and Eve would be safer, happier. But now he realized it was up to him.

Elohim wasn't going to deliver slain animals at their feet. He wasn't going to reverse the seasons or force the plants and trees to bloom out of order. This world was created in order, and it would remain in order.

One of the deer turned with a start, and the other deer shifted. They stopped eating and lifted their heads.

Had one of the deer seen him? One of the animals stepped back, sending a snapping sound into the air. In one fluid motion, all of the deer bolted through the bushes.

Adam scrambled to his feet and leapt toward them, his fingertips just brushing the last deer to clear the bush. By the time he made it through the bushes, the animals were out of sight. Adam looked around, his breath coming fast. There had to be another way to hunt deer. They were too alert and skittish.

He moved back to the other side of the bushes and discovered a good growth of berries. He ate a few of them quickly, then knotted more into the edge of the skin coat so that he could bring them back to Eve.

Most of the grove was already in shadow, and he knew he didn't have much time if he wanted to get back to the dwelling before dark. Leaving Eve alone probably hadn't been the best idea, but if eating fish was making her ill, he had to find something else.

Her sharp words echoed through his mind. He *had* been praying a lot, constantly, but he would do anything to prevent Lucifer from returning and coercing Eve into learning from him. Adam squatted and examined the disturbed earth where the deer had walked. He traced his fingers along the discernible indents left by the deer hoofs. He was learning to pick out the evidence of travel that animals left behind—their various prints, tufts of fur, or other remains.

The wind stirred the leaves littering the ground. It had been windier above the valley, but now its strength had reached him. He rose and continued in what he hoped was the right direction, moving through a grouping of trees as quietly as possible. When he reached a narrow stream, he paused. Surely the deer stopped here to drink.

He stayed within sight of the stream as he moved carefully through the trees. It wasn't long before he was rewarded. First he saw the brown-red fur moving through the stark branches, heaving in and out as the deer bent to drink or to sniff the leaves and other bits of brush on the ground.

Holding his breath and keeping still, Adam counted the deer he saw. There were nine of them, although he was sure that there had been more back at the bushes. Some must have moved on, past the stream.

Adam's heart thudded as he watched the serenity of the deer. He estimated how close he'd have to be to capture one without letting it bolt out of his reach again. With his senses alert, he took a careful step forward, then another, working his way around a couple of trees. The sharp stick gripped tightly in his hand, Adam took one more deep breath and leapt toward the nearest deer.

For an instant, he couldn't believe that he had reached the deer, and one hand clenched the fur of its upper back. Just as the deer's muscles contracted beneath his grip, Adam drove the stick into the deer's neck with his other hand.

The animal bolted, dragging Adam with it, the stick still embedded. He grabbed on with his other hand and held on as the deer dragged him into the stream, its muscles stronger than Adam expected.

When Adam's knees hit the water and scraped against the rocks, his grip faltered, and the deer slipped away. He scrambled to his feet, not taking the time to examine his injuries, and plunged through the stream after the deer. The beast was fast, but Adam could see that he'd injured it enough that the deer was slower than its herd.

Adam pushed his own muscles to keep moving, to stay on the deer's trail as it trampled through the trees. Then silence rose over Adam's labored breathing. He slowed then stopped when he reached the deer, lying on its side, its body trembling.

Exhilaration and regret collided in Adam's body. He sank to his knees, keeping his eyes on the failing beast as its side rose and fell with each breath. He stayed in one spot as the deer took its final breaths.

When all was still, Adam whispered a prayer of thanksgiving to Elohim. Then he rose and pulled out the stick. His eyes burned at the sight of the majestic creature lifeless on the ground. Bending, he lifted the deer into his arms, then moved it over his shoulder.

Adam turned back and crossed the stream, balancing the deer as he stepped on the wet rocks. As much as taking the animal's life pained him, he was determined to make good use of it and to reach Eve before nightfall.

31

And I will put enmity between thee and the woman, and between thy seed and her seed; it shall bruise thy head, and thou shalt bruise his heel.

—Genesis 3:15

The dark creeps across the valley, moving closer to where I huddle on the ridge. Doubt rings through my mind, becoming louder and more deafening. Why did I follow Adam? What if he doesn't make it back to the ridge before nightfall? The wind pulls at my coats, and I adjust them higher along my neck, trying to carve out more warmth from the animal fur.

My mind blurs with the waiting, and I drift off into dreams of nothingness. But the wind always cuts across, waking me up time and time again. I realize that my strength is fading, and without any recent nourishment, I might be too exhausted to make it back to our dwelling before dark.

When the valley is half-consumed by shadow, I stand, my hope waning with the diminishing light. I pause a few more moments, then start up the ridge. My breathing comes fast with the effort, and when I crest the hill, I turn a final time.

That's when I see a movement in the trees below me. I hold my breath as I watch, my heart pounding. I am sure it's him. It has to be.

A moment passes, then another. I lose sight of the moving figure; then it emerges from the trees at the bottom of the valley. Relief pours through me. Adam is starting up the incline, some sort of large animal slung over one shoulder.

His pace is determined as he strides up the hill. When he lifts his gaze and sees me, he pauses. I can't read his expression from this distance, so I wait until he gets closer. My heart clenches as I realize he's carrying a deer. I clasp my hands together as Adam climbs to the top of the ridge. He's breathing heavily, but his expression seems happy.

"I just couldn't wait alone," I say.

Adam slides the deer off his shoulder and sits down next to it, taking several deep breaths. He stares out over the valley, and I notice that his hands are stained with blood. There are bruises along his forearms, no doubt from capturing the deer.

The deer's eyes are open and unseeing, a small sprout of horns atop its head. It's a young male.

I wait in the silence for Adam to speak. The sun sinks behind us, turning the already-cloudy day colder. I remove the bear skin from my shoulders and hand it over to Adam.

"You wear it back to the dwelling," he says. His tone is flat, and although I'm glad he's speaking to me, my throat tightens with emotion. He still hasn't looked at me since we've been sitting.

Reluctantly I pull the coat back on, sneaking another glance at him. He doesn't shiver, but he must be cold. The wind is sharp, and dark is approaching fast.

I wait for Adam to stand first, but he continues to stare out over the valley. After a few moments, I say, "It will be dark soon. We should make our way back in case the moon doesn't cut through the clouds."

When he still remains silent, I say, "Can I help you carry the deer?"

He finally turns his head, and my stomach sinks as his gaze searches mine. I want to know what he is thinking.

"You didn't rest as I asked you to, and now you expect to have the strength to carry the deer?"

I open my mouth to answer, but he cuts me off. "You won't help carry the deer, Eve. I may spend too much time praying, but I don't expect my wife to carry a heavy beast."

"I didn't expect you to—"

"I know," he says, letting out a sigh. "But you were right."

I blink back my surprise.

"Elohim is probably tired of being pestered anyway. We need to do what we can for ourselves, making our best effort, and pray that Elohim will fill in the rest."

I nod, exhaling a silent sigh of relief. "I think Elohim has blessed us already," I say, gesturing toward the deer.

"I think you're right," Adam says, his tone softened. He stands and holds his hand out. I gratefully accept his help as he pulls me to my feet. The touch of his hand is warm and reassuring.

"How are you feeling?" he asks.

"Much better," I say.

Adam unties a knot at the edge of his skin coat. "I found berries." He gives me a handful, and I eat them. They are a bit dried and withered but sweet enough.

"Are these from that valley?"

"Yes," Adam says. "The deer were gathered around the bushes. That's how I noticed the berries."

"This valley might be a good place to explore further."

Adam nods once. "There's at least one herd of deer

roaming the area and plenty of trees that might bloom fruit when the winter season is over."

I hope this means Adam is considering allowing some distance between us and the Garden. Hope renews itself in my heart. We've made it this far, this long, and now Adam has caught a deer. I steal a look at its lifeless body. In the garden, I would have been repulsed to even consider eating the flesh of any of the animals, but after many moons of eating fish and after my stomach's reaction this morning, I look forward to a new meal.

He picks up the deer and settles it over his shoulder. Then he looks at me, his gaze cautious. "Ready?"

We walk together, Adam breathing hard from the weight he is carrying.

"Was it hard to capture the deer?" I glance behind me, but the ridge now conceals the valley.

"Not nearly as hard as a bear," Adam says, his tone light. His mouth turns up at the corners. "No claws."

I laugh, and laughter settles over me, warm and comforting.

When we make it back to our dwelling place, the moon is high in the sky. I know that Adam must be exhausted from carrying the deer the entire way, but he insists on removing the skin and preparing the flesh while I create a Fire.

I eat a few more of the berries, staving off just a bit of the hunger that wrenches through me. I am sure Adam feels even more hunger than I do. He works quickly in the light of the Fire. He is now more adept at preparing an animal because of the experience with the bears and the leopard.

As the deer flesh heats up over the Fire, I am grateful that fish won't be our meal tonight, nor for many days to come.

Adam stared up at the black sky as Eve slept next to him. Bright spots of light peeked through the spaces between the clouds. *Stars.* There were so many of them. The potential for other worlds out there seemed endless, and Adam wondered what was going on in those other worlds.

Were there other humans in other spheres praying to Elohim as well? Was Elohim able to hear and answer every prayer? Had other peoples spiritually fallen and were now cut off from their Maker?

Eve turned to her side, and Adam felt a pang in his heart. He needed to take better care of his wife. Instead of spending the days on his knees, he should be building a more permanent shelter, and to do that, he needed trees.

He slipped out of the coverings, leaving Eve asleep, and walked in the chilly air to the dark and silent altar. He paused, staring at it for several moments. Then he lifted his gaze toward the garden. It felt distant, especially in the dark, and from another existence only remotely related to what he was facing now. Frustration swept through Adam as he remembered the warmth, the plentiful fruit, and the sun-filled days inside the garden.

Yet, even before Lucifer arrived, Eve had become impatient within the confines of the garden.

If it had been up to him, Adam realized, they might have lived there forever. He blew out a breath, disappointed in himself and his lack of strength. Eve would be the one who would suffer the most, and she already had physical ailments, so he needn't complain.

His gaze fell on the altar's bulky shape. The rocks seemed to shift in shape, but that was impossible. Rocks didn't move on their own. The hairs on the back of Adam's neck rose, and a shiver trailed along his arms.

He took a step forward, squinting in the dull light, trying to make out why the altar looked different. Then he realized that someone was sitting on the ground, leaning against the altar. The figure rose to standing, rising in height above Adam.

"Good evening," the low voice said.

The figure was too tall to be Lucifer. Apprehension slid across Adam's skin. "Who are you?" He didn't know whether to step closer or to run back to Eve and protect her.

The being watched Adam, not in a hurry to explain himself. His arms seemed too long for his body as he clasped his hands in front of him. He wore a dark-colored skin coat, reminding Adam of Lucifer.

"Who are you?" Adam asked again, letting his voice grow louder. He didn't want to wake Eve, but he didn't like the presence of this being.

"I am your brother," the being said.

A chill brushed across Adam's skin. He'd heard the phrase before, and although this wasn't Lucifer, the person's presence felt like a disturbing intrusion. "My brother? Where are you from?"

"The outer world—the world of knowledge." The voice came soft yet deep.

"Are you an outcast?" Adam asked, taking a small step back. He wasn't entirely sure what this person wanted.

The laugh was raspy and thick. "Aren't we all?"

I am, Adam thought. "When?"

"You don't remember? You were there."

Adam took another subtle step back. "So you chose to follow Lucifer?"

The air was heavy with hesitation. "*Follow* isn't the description I'd use."

Adam's heart sank. This being was connected to Lucifer somehow. Where Lucifer was, Adam didn't know. Lucifer had been out of sight since the great Fire. Tendrils of fear crept over Adam's skin. Even with Lucifer absent, there seemed to be no shortage of other beings.

"Adam?" Eve's voice cut through him.

He turned to tell her to stay back, to remain where she was, but he saw no one.

Her voice came again, calling "Adam?" but this time it was on his right side. Adam spun, again seeing nothing. His gaze went back to the stranger, but no one was near the altar. "Where are you?" Adam called out, his breath coming fast. "You can tell our brother Lucifer that your kind isn't welcome here. I won't have his minions coming near me or my wife."

His words were met only with silence. He took a deep breath and said, "Wherever you are, leave us alone."

There was no sound, no movement, no breeze.

Adam hurried to where he'd left Eve asleep. Relief pulsed through him as he saw her burrowed beneath the coats, still asleep. He climbed in next to her. This would be the last night they'd stay in this place.

32

Unto the woman he said, I will greatly multiply thy sorrow and thy conception; in sorrow thou shalt bring forth children; and thy desire shall be to thy husband, and he shall rule [with] thee.

—Genesis 3:16

Three Moons Later

I inhale the softened air outside our shelter. The sharp cold has left, replaced with the scent of brown earth and green leaves. Winter season is finally gone, replaced by frequent mist. We have been in the valley now for three moons, and I have loved the abundant trees, the roaming beasts, and the decreased winds.

It has also been three moons since we've seen Lucifer or any one of his minions that Adam told me about. Although I still feel that Lucifer might be watching and waiting, he has not appeared to either of us.

There is a new thing that troubles me now. I stoop where the dirt is soft on the side of the shelter and draw lines in the dirt, counting back to the last time that I bled. The days number more than two moon cycles, or two bleeding cycles. I press the back of my hand to my mouth to stop the gasp from escaping.

But the gasp escapes.

I glance in Adam's direction. He leans toward the Fire, turning the skewer of deer flesh.

I wonder what has happened to my woman's cycle. Elohim told me that it would prepare my body for bringing forth children. So why has it stopped? Is something wrong?

Sliding my hands up my arms, I shiver although the day is mild. My hands move back down and rest on my stomach. The nausea hasn't stopped, although it has lessened, and I'm more hungry than usual. I eat nearly as much as Adam does now. My stomach protrudes slightly, and I know it's due to overeating. We had so little before that now I can't seem to let even a morsel escape my notice.

The smell of the cooking deer sends hunger pangs through me, as if I haven't already eaten plenty today. The wind shifts, and a billow of smoke trails in my direction. The scent is soothing and calms my stomach and the tension throughout my body.

"Eve?"

I open my eyes, not having realized that I closed them.

"Yes." It comes out almost a whisper.

"Are you ill again?" His voice sounds tired but patient. I have been "ill" for so long that I wonder if ill is all I'll ever be.

"Only hungry," I say, but there is no laughter in my voice. I meet Adam's gaze, and his look is as sober as I feel inside. My breath exhales, and I want to tell him about my absent woman's cycles. I don't know what he will think or how he will react. Maybe it has something to do with our intimacy. Have I somehow ruined my body's natural health?

I don't realize that Adam has moved until he is right next to me. His arm slides around my shoulders, and I find myself leaning against him. "Adam," I whisper, knowing he can hear me and is waiting for me to speak. "Something is wrong."

He doesn't pull away but only tightens his hold. And waits. As if he's known something all along.

"My blood cycle has stopped." The words hang in the air for a moment, unanswered.

With his other hand, Adam touches my chin and raises it. I blink once, then twice, surprised to see a smile on his face.

"It's as I've suspected."

"What is?"

"That you are with child."

I stare at him, disbelieving what he is saying, yet realizing that it might explain so many things. "How can you know?"

"Because you have been ill," he says. "And now you are always hungry." His hand moves behind my neck, and his forehead touches mine. "Your body is providing for two."

"Two," I say. It's not a question. I try to wrap my mind around *two*. "Do you mean I am carrying a child?" Of course that's what he means, but I must hear it spoken, confirmed, from his lips.

Adam starts kissing me, first on my forehead, then on my cheek, then on my lips. I cling to him, wondering if this is really happening—that we've created another life, one that is growing inside of me.

My stomach rumbles with hunger, and Adam pulls back with a laugh. His eyes are on mine, and I stare back, wonder coursing through my heart and mind.

"So all of this . . . illness . . . is not going to bring me death?" I say, feeling foolish that I might have thought so. The light fades from Adam's eyes, and I realize what I've said. Bringing forth a child may not bring me death, but it will bring sorrow and pain, as Elohim told us.

But there is no time for me to dwell on what will surely

come. At this moment, I let the relief and joy flood through me. We have fulfilled Elohim's commandment. This is the beginning of multiplying and replenishing the earth.

Adam kisses my neck and draws me against him.

"I am so hungry," I say, and he laughs into my hair. I have to shove him away so that he will release me.

I cross to the cooking Fire and turn the speared food, inhaling the rich aroma. I can practically taste the food in my mouth. Adam comes up behind me, wrapping his arms around my torso. I wriggle away, and he grabs me again from behind.

Giving in, I turn around and slide my hands up his chest and around his neck. "All right, you get your way," I say before kissing him.

When we finally eat, my mind is cloudy from kissing Adam and from thinking of the changes going on inside my body. I have certainly felt many of them, but it's hard to comprehend all that must be occurring. My hand absently rests on my stomach as if to protect what is growing there.

I wonder how large the child will grow. My breath catches when I remember what Elohim told us about how the child will leave my body. My hand stills over my stomach, and I press in slightly. I can feel no protruding shape, but I know from Elohim's explanation that my stomach will expand.

As the light fades into night, I find myself more tired than usual. Now I understand why. I'm the first to enter our shelter and nestle beneath the deer skin in the sleeping place. The deer skin is thinner than both the leopard and the bear skins, but it provides surprising warmth. Although the days and nights are no longer as cold as they were during the winter season, I relish in the added warmth.

I am just falling asleep when Adam's hand slides across my stomach. I inhale sharply. Heat pulses through me at his touch, but there is more significance now. I feel as though there are two beings connecting, Adam and the person who lies beneath my skin—the person we have created together.

"Adam," I whisper, "I wish we could stay like this forever."

His breath brushes my neck. "We will . . . as long as it's possible. And when our bodies return to dust, our souls will be together in Heaven."

I turn toward him. He encircles me with his arms, and our bodies seem to blend. Tonight, there is new life growing between them: our own life, our own creation, our own beginning.

Adam stood before the altar newly constructed in the valley. His heart was filled with joy for Eve's condition. He let her sleep this morning while he made his way to the altar for morning worship. She hadn't been sleeping well, and now he knew why.

He couldn't stop the smile from forming on his face as he knelt in the moist earth. "O Elohim, unto thee I pray. Eve is with child, and my gratitude is eternal. Lead me, in thy righteousness, and make my way straight."

When Adam finished his prayer, as in the moons past, he waited for a long time, listening and feeling until the soft warmth spread through him. It was the way Elohim communicated with him now, and Adam would accept whatever Elohim offered. If Adam kept his mind focused on the things of Elohim, all else faded.

Today the feeling was more intense than usual, confirming that Elohim knew of the child. Adam couldn't wait to tell Eve.

He rose to his feet, his heart expanded. Eve still hadn't emerged from the shelter that they'd built of branches and woven leaves. It offered a nice protection from the changing weather. They were starting to collect skins to line the walls, adding more protection between themselves and the elements. Today held the promise of warmth, and Adam knew that by midday he'd shed his bear coat.

He crossed to the cooking area and started the morning Fire. He and Eve had found that the animals they used for consumption tasted better heated over the Fire. As the Fire gained strength, still contained in the circle of rocks that Eve had arranged, he checked on the garden of cultivated herbs.

Eve tended to the garden more than he did now, but he enjoyed examining the plants and turning the soil. With the winter harshness gone, the herbs were thriving, and some of them would be ready to harvest soon. Today he could remain at the dwelling, but tomorrow he'd have to hunt again.

He heard Eve before he saw her. She emerged from the shelter, humming. The eastern light caught in her hair, creating a bronze arch around her smiling face. His gaze slid to her stomach, and he imagined, after only one day of comprehending that she was with child, that he could already see growth.

Her gaze caught his, and Adam thought he'd never seen her look more beautiful. Her smile widened as he continued to stare at her, and then she laughed. He knew she found his open gawking amusing, but he couldn't help it. It didn't take him long to cross to her and capture her in his arms.

She leaned into him, and he inhaled the sun in her hair. "Elohim knows about the child," he said.

"Of course he does," she said with a laugh and held onto him tighter. "He probably even knows if it's a male or female."

Adam exhaled, wondering himself. "How long until the child comes?"

"Elohim said nine moons."

Adam leaned away from her, his gaze moving down

with hers. She guided his hands to her stomach and said, "It has already been a couple of moon cycles. By next winter season, we'll be a family of three."

Adam kissed her forehead. "How are you feeling this morning?"

"The same, yet better because I know *why* I'm feeling tired and ill," she said in a soft voice. "You already built the Fire?"

"I knew you'd be hungry," he said, smiling.

"I am." She encircled his neck with her arms and kissed him softly. She broke away all too soon. "Thank you." She held his gaze, then led him by the hand toward the cooking Fire.

33

Because thou hast hearkened unto the voice of thy wife, and hast eaten of the tree, of which I commanded thee, saying, Thou shalt not eat of it: cursed is the ground for thy sake; in sorrow shalt thou eat of it all the days of thy life.

—Genesis 3:17

I'm pulled from sleep by a sharp pain in my stomach. The pain is worse than any discomfort I have felt so far in this state. I sit up, but the pain only deepens. I hold my breath until it subsides. Finally, I lie down again, hoping to find more sleep. The sky outside our shelter is purple with the early morning, promising another hot day, just as the last few have been. I love the warmer weather but find that I tire easily in it.

Then my stomach twists again, lower and deeper this time. It's not hunger: I've known hunger plenty of times. The pain radiates hot and fast through my stomach. My only thought is to get out of the shelter, to walk around, to see if the pain will lessen.

I try not to wake Adam as I leave. He is usually awake before me in the morning, busy improving our shelter or cleaning the skins from an animal caught the day before. We have an excess of dried and smoked animal flesh now. When the next winter season arrives, we'll be more than prepared.

I walk out of the shelter into the early morning air. It's cool on my skin, yet I know it will soon be warm, then too hot to stay beneath the sun. The pain subsides, and I take several grateful breaths. It's gone now. I know it can't possibly be time for the child to arrive. It's been only five moons, and Elohim said producing a child would take nine. My stomach has grown, pushing my skin out, and I marvel at the tiny being who is maturing there.

Looking around at each familiar part of the dwelling, I notice ripening fruit on the nearby trees. They are the most beautiful fruit I've ever seen—more beautiful than even the fruit in the garden because they are not plentiful here, so they are greatly cherished. After enduring our first winter season, relocating our dwelling place several times, and learning that Lucifer is not the only being on this earth trying to thwart our worship of Elohim, I take pleasure in the smallest of things.

I walk to the nearest tree and tug off one of the green leaves. It's cool to the touch, and I bring it to my nose to inhale its slight fragrance. It smells fresh and alive. The air is already beginning to warm as the sky lightens, changing from purple to pale blue.

The pain returns with force. This time it shoots heat up my torso and down my legs. I bend over, clutching at my stomach.

Dizziness swallows me, my vision becomes murky, and I reach for a branch to find steadiness. "Adam," I call out—or I think I call out. I'm not certain that any sound has escaped my lips.

I gasp as my knees sink to the earth. The pain is overwhelming, and I can't see or hear. I can feel only the pain as it fills every sense. I cry out again and again for

Adam, but I'm afraid I am only mouthing words that he can't hear.

I'm on the ground beneath the tree. I don't know how long I writhe in pain until I feel Adam's arms around me, lifting me and carrying me. When he sets me down, the pain finally turns everything black.

I awake, my body on Fire. I twist and cry out, trying to escape the flaming heat.

Adam's cool hands grasp my arms, and his voice cuts through the haze in my mind. "Eve, drink this."

His voice settles over me, and I realize there is no Fire licking at my skin. But there must be a Fire nearby; I feel so hot. Something touches my lips, cold and wet, and I open my mouth obediently. Water fills my throat, and I cough it up.

Adam reaches behind me and holds me as the water slides down my neck and chest. "Try to drink again. Come on, Eve."

His voice sounds hoarse, desperate.

I open my mouth and manage to swallow once, but I am shaking so much that the water spills more than I can manage to drink.

Adam's hand is on my cheek, then on my forehead. I can't seem to open my eyes; the lids are just too heavy. I'm not sure if it's day or night or if we are outside or in the shelter.

"Put out the Fire," I say, my own voice raspy through my trembling. "It's too hot."

There's a pause in Adam's caresses. "There is no Fire," he says. "The burning is from within your body."

My eyes open now. Adam's face is before me, his skin

pale and moist, as if he's been perspiring. "What is . . . burning me?" I push Adam away and look down.

I start screaming when I see the blood between my legs.

34

Thorns also and thistles shall it bring forth to thee; and thou shalt eat the herb of the field.

—Genesis 3:18

Silence. This is the sound of my sorrow, of my unwanted blood—a silence so deafening that even my own heartbeat is drowned out.

My grief has become a physical pain that I could have never imagined. The child is gone. Born too early. She didn't even take a breath.

The leaves that were once beautiful and brought me comfort now seem placid and aloof. The rich earth is no longer moist and welcoming but dry and harsh. I feel as though it is pushing me away, rejecting my presence.

Adam stands beneath the heavy-laden branches, waiting. His eyes are half-lowered, but I know that he is watching me. He's giving me the time I need to say good-bye.

The moment has come, and though I could put it off until tomorrow or the next day, since I know Adam will wait until I'm ready, I decide that I will never truly be ready. I must put one foot in front of the other and then do it again.

Somehow my body moves, somehow my legs function, although my heart has nearly stopped.

I see the flowers first. The flowers are only small buds of yellow that peek from their long stems, but I know their potential. They'll crown the burial site long after we are gone. They will die during the winter, but Adam says the flowers will bloom full again in the next season.

Only a few paces away, I pause, then take another step until I am only one step away. My knees bend, and I sink to the earth. There is still a distance between the carved-up earth and me. I feel the sob start low, then press its way upward, but I force it back down. Now is not the time for this loud grief. I will bid farewell quietly. I will bid farewell in peace to the child that I never knew or was allowed to call by name.

Reaching forward, I smooth the dirt that is already smooth by Adam's hands. I pull off one of the flower buds and cradle it in my palm. Then I lean down, putting my forehead to the dirt. Only a hand span separates me now from my daughter's body.

Adam says her soul is with Elohim now—that she is looking down on us.

I want her to be proud of her mother, but I also want her to know how much I miss her—how much I will always miss her. I will never see her first step or hear her first word. I will never feel her arms around my neck or be able to kiss her cheek.

My eyes burn.

But still I don't let the sob out.

I lift my head and inhale the scent of earth and flower. It will be the new smell that I'll remember her by, not the smell of grief and despair. Then I look at the sky, searching for anything—any sound, any movement that might indicate she is there, watching.

Yet only the breeze and the rattle of leaves disturb the silence.

I exhale ever so slowly. Then I stand, my legs still weak, but at least I am standing. I want to collapse onto the earth, press my face in the dirt, and never open my eyes again.

It's as though Adam knows my thoughts. His hand slides into mine, and his other hand goes around my waist. He doesn't try to pull me away from the burial site but just stands next to me. *With* me. He has lost a child too. His hands have smoothed the dirt countless times.

How long we stand together I am not sure, but perspiration grows between my shoulders and our palms. I can't breathe in this place any longer. It's too heavy with grief. We must move on, as much as I've loved it here.

I turn to Adam and whisper, "Let's go as far as we can—away from this valley, away from the garden, away from everything we've known."

There is no hesitation. He simply says, "Yes."

Then I slump against him. He holds me up since I can no longer manage alone. Then ever so gently, as if he's ready to stop at a single word of protest, he leads me away.

I stare at the ground, putting one foot in front of the other, each step widening the separation with my daughter. I begin to breathe again, in and out. Adam and I don't head back up the ridge toward the garden, from where we first arrived. We continue east through the valley. I don't know how far we'll go, but every step takes me closer to where I want to be.

When Adam stops, I am reluctant to stop as well. Behind us, I can still see the valley that we climbed out of.

"It's nearly dark, Eve," he says, his voice quiet and careful.

The shaking in my body starts now that we've stopped walking. "I don't want to stop. If I stop, then I won't be able to leave."

"We'll never forget her." He draws me into his arms. "Leaving doesn't mean we have to forget."

I am so cold and shaky. If it weren't for Adam helping me, I might fall to the earth, like a butterfly that's lost its wings. "Why did she have to be born too early?" I have asked this question many times, and every time the answer is the same, but I need to hear it. Over and over.

Adam answers again. "Elohim knows why, and so we need to put our faith in him."

I believe the words, but I still have questions. "Doesn't Elohim trust me with her? Doesn't he want our daughter to be with us?"

"Elohim trusts *you*," Adam's voice is soothing but firm.

"I would have taken good care of her," I say, my voice breaking.

"I know," Adam whispers into my hair. "And you will be a good mother to our other children."

I can't think of other children right now. It's too painful to consider that I might go through this loss again. I don't think I can survive it.

With Adam's arms around me, I try to suppress the pain, but it remains below the surface of my skin. We spend the night on top of the skins that we have carried with us. I fall in and out of sleep, and I know that Adam does too. We seem to wake each other up time and time again.

I am relieved when the sun breaks through the morning dark. It means that I have survived the first night away from my daughter. Feeling calmer than I expected, I can truthfully tell Adam that I'm ready to continue on our journey.

Adam checked the position of the sun in the sky. It was near midday, time to stop for a rest. Eve quietly plodded beside him, growing more and more quiet with each day. He'd stopped asking her if she was sure she wanted to leave their valley dwelling. Her reply was always yes, but still he wondered.

"We should rest until the heat of the day has passed," he said, turning to look at her. Her face was pale despite the time spent in the sun, and she had a delicate darkness beneath her eyes.

"All right," she said, her voice barely above a whisper.

Adam led her to a group of trees that grew close together. They'd traveled for many days already. They'd traversed over hills and through valleys, and now they were in a sparse area much like the region just outside of the garden. Trees were not plentiful here, and it would not be an ideal place to settle. Although Adam didn't think he'd have to worry. Eve had indicated no desire to settle. She simply walked in silence next to him.

Eve fell asleep quickly in the shade, and Adam stayed next to her, one arm supporting her head. He was exhausted, but worry overrode the ability to sleep. He missed his wife— missed her laughter, her bright eyes, and her affectionate touches.

They had not been intimate since the child had been born. Without Eve saying anything, he knew that she wasn't ready for the possibility of another conception. It was too soon. Adam smoothed her hair back from her face, which was moist from the oppressive heat. He couldn't wait until the seasonal heat lost its strong grip. The winter was an extreme, more uncomfortable than this endless heat, but both the cold and the heat had their challenges.

They were nearly out of food, and Adam would have to hunt again soon. So far he hadn't seen any promising herds of deer in this part of the wilderness. He could only hope that the more east they traveled, the more options they'd come across.

EVE

He started to say a silent prayer, one of many. Watching
Eve endure the pain of birth, and trying to help her after,
tore at his heart every time he thought of it. Even worse had
been seeing the small, lifeless body of their child. He wasn't
even sure how much Eve comprehended when they buried
the babe beneath the soil. Eve hadn't been herself since the
death. He hoped that leaving the dwelling and starting anew
would make a difference.

His prayers increased as he prayed for a safe journey,
that his wife might be healed in her heart, that they might be
blessed with more children.

He must have fallen asleep while praying because when
he opened his eyes, the sun had moved significantly in the
sky and Eve was watching him.

"I am afraid," she whispered. Her blue-green eyes
seemed to pierce right through him, and he couldn't quite
read her expression.

He reached over and touched her cheek. "So am I."

"What if our daughter died because of something I
did?"

Adam lifted up on one elbow. He didn't like Eve's
question, but at least she was talking. She had grown thin
since the death, and her cheekbones seemed to jut
prominently from her face. "You didn't do anything wrong,
Eve."

"How can you know? Did Elohim tell you?" her voice
trembled, and Adam wanted to avoid her breaking down in
sorrow.

"Elohim knows of our pain and grieves with us."

She looked away, blinking rapidly. Moisture slipped
from her eyes and traveled down her cheeks. "He could have
stopped it, but he didn't."

Adam sat up fully and reached for her hands, but she
moved them away.

"Maybe there are some things Elohim can't stop in this world," he said.

Her voice rose. "He has more power than Lucifer. He can stop anything he wants."

Adam knew she was right, and he also wondered why Elohim hadn't prevented their daughter's death. Maybe they wouldn't find out the answer now, or even later, but they would in time. "We must have faith."

"Stop telling me that." Instead of anger in her voice, her voice was dull and lifeless—which was almost worse.

He waited a heartbeat, then two. "How much farther do you want to travel, Eve?"

She wiped at her cheeks and heaved a sigh. "I don't know." She looked at him, and the pain on her face tore into Adam's heart. "I just know that I couldn't be there anymore. Not with her lifeless body beneath the soil . . . when she should have been in my arms, living and breathing."

Adam touched Eve's shoulder, and when she didn't pull back, he wrapped an arm around her. "She will always be ours," he said. "When our bodies return to dust, we'll see her again."

Eve's thin arms went around him as she leaned against his chest.

He kissed the top of her head, then drew away.

"What if . . . what if it was something that I ate? Or what if I didn't eat enough? I wasn't eating very much when I felt so ill."

"Shh," Adam said, taking her hands. "Only Elohim knows what happened."

Her eyes closed as she whispered, "What if it was our intimacy? What if it hurt the baby?"

Adam stared at her until she opened her eyes. "Were you in pain when we were intimate?"

"No," she said, still whispering. "But I worried about it."

"You must tell me when you worry about such things,"

he said. "You know that I'd never want to cause you any pain."

"I know," she said. "But I'm still afraid. What if the same thing happens to our next child?"

Adam looked down at his hands, muscled and browned by the sun. There were many things he could do with them—build, hunt, cultivate—but he couldn't protect a child born too soon.

Eve hung her head. "I didn't know the sorrow would be like this."

I didn't either, he thought. *I didn't either.*

35

In the sweat of thy face shalt thou eat bread, till thou return unto the ground; for out of it wast thou taken: for dust thou art, and unto dust shalt thou return.

—Genesis 3:19

The dreams are back. Dark and still. Whispered words that I can't quite grasp. But I know it's him. I know he's close.

And I don't care.

Let him take my soul—if I have one left.

Each day I walk with Adam, following him through trees, across grass, over rivers. When he takes my hand, I feel nothing. When he looks into my eyes, I see nobody. When he speaks to me, I hear only the dry wind pushing through the leaves above.

The child that I left behind has created a numbness, a dark hole that grows from my stomach and spreads throughout my body until I am nothing but the hole itself. Something presses against that hole, and I sense what it is. Or *who* it is.

Lucifer is watching me. It's as if I can see him in every shadow, in every crevasse of rock, but he is gone the moment

I turn my gaze to look. I wonder if Adam feels Lucifer's presence or if he is walking aimlessly for his own reasons.

I'm not sure how many days we've been traveling. It's still hot, and the leaves are still green. Maybe one moon, or maybe two moons.

When Adam tells me that he needs to go hunting, I barely reply. I haven't paid attention to our food supply, and I eat very little of whatever Adam hands me. He tells me to rest and leads me beneath the shade of a tree.

I watch Adam walk away, his strong back hunched, his steps hurried. I know that he doesn't want to leave me alone, but there is no choice since I can't help him in the hunting. Together we'd scare any beasts away.

Adam may worry that I won't be safe alone, a worry that is justified, but I'm not afraid to be alone. In fact, I feel alone whether or not I'm with Adam—whether or not I'm praying or listening to Adam pray. The hole that has become me leaves no room for anyone else.

It's because of this that I know that as soon as Adam retreats, I will have a visitor. I have felt his presence for too long and seen him in too many of my dreams to doubt that he will take this perfect opportunity.

I wait for Lucifer to arrive, knowing that he is waiting too. Sitting beneath the tree, I lean against the trunk. I close my eyes as if sleeping, even though I don't expect sleep to come.

At first I think I feel a touch on my arm, but it's only the high grass. I wait some more, concentrating on breathing evenly, in and out, and then something blocks the sun.

I open my eyes, and my heart jolts, although I shouldn't be startled. Lucifer is smiling down at me. He looks different, or maybe I just think he looks different because I haven't seen him in so many moons.

His hand is held out toward me, and I reach for it before remembering that he can't help me to my feet. His smile widens as if he just realized the same thing, but I know that with him, all things are intentional.

"Eve." The single word drops from his lips like a slow raindrop. Wind seems to swirl around me, making me hot and cold at the same time.

I stare up at him, wondering what he's been doing in his absence yet not daring to ask him anything.

"Lucifer," I say. It's been a long time since I've spoken his name aloud, although it seems all too easy to speak.

"You are traveling the earth in search of happiness?"

How does he know my most intimate desires?

I blink, and the world seems to come back into focus—the grass that reaches toward the sky and the fallen angel standing before me, dressed in an almost-black fur from his waist down. His torso is bare but not perspiring as Adam's would be from walking around in the heat. Lucifer looks as if the season has no power to affect him. His lean, muscled arms hang to his sides as if he's relaxed, but I can feel the tension from him.

"Why have you sought me out?" I say, speaking more words together than I have in many days.

"I have never lost sight of you, my dear Eve. You should know that." He tilts his head slightly, amused.

I look away from him and stare at anything that *isn't* him, but it seems that he fills up every place around me. "Why did you set that Fire?" I finally ask.

Irony is plain in his voice as he speaks. "I did not intend for it to grow so large."

I snap my gaze up at him. "I can't believe that. You had every intention."

His lips curl. "Perhaps . . . perhaps it's good to learn that your brother has all the power he will ever need."

"The power of destruction," I say. This statement doesn't appear to bother him.

"The power of *knowledge*," he says. "And I am here to

restate my offer. I haven't forgotten you, and you won't be able to forget me."

"Is that why I've been dreaming—" I cut off my own words. I don't want him to know, but it's too late.

"Yes," his voice soothes. He steps closer to me. I could reach out and touch his coat if I wanted to. His eyes are so dark, darker than any night sky I can remember.

It's hard to breathe, but I'm not afraid. Adam is gone, yet I know that I wanted this . . . this meeting with my brother. After so much time spent in the wilderness, I have many questions. I can almost hear Adam warning me to stay away, but I push his voice out of my head.

Rising to my feet, I reach behind me, steadying my hands against the tree trunk. We are standing beneath a tree, a different tree but together again.

Lucifer's fingers touch my cheek. There is no warmth, no soft flesh, only a shiver, but still I feel it. "I dream of you too."

I close my eyes and exhale.

Will he go away if I don't open my eyes? Do I want him to go away?

"You still have a choice, Eve," he says, his whispering close to my ear. "This world is full of pain and sorrow. I can take that away from you."

I bite my lip, my throat raw, to keep the sobs from surfacing. "How?"

"Come with me, and I'll show you."

My eyes stay shut. Looking at Lucifer might convince me to follow without question. Not looking at him allows me to consider only myself.

The breeze stirs around us, bringing the scent of wood and grass and water—the scent of Adam—reminding me. "What about Adam?" I say.

Lucifer's hand slides to my neck, and I imagine his breath on my cheek. "We'll come back for him later."

I think of Adam holding me when my child was born, of his grief combining with my own, of his quiet words during my restless sleep, of his hands stained with dirt from digging in the earth. I think of my daughter and her too-small body buried so far away—in the ground. Dust. She is dust now.

Is this what I have to look forward to—sorrow that doesn't seem to end until Adam and I return to dust with all of our children?

A sob builds in my throat.

Children.

Will there be more children? Adam says Elohim will surely bless us with more. I think of my lost daughter and how every part of me cries out to raise her, to care for her.

Leaving with Lucifer might take away that pain, but it would also take away any future joy.

"No," I say. My voice is only a whisper on the wind. I open my eyes. Lucifer is so close, looking as if he could devour me like a hungry beast—a desperate beast.

"No." My voice is stronger now. Elohim may have given Lucifer the power to bruise my heel, but Elohim gave me the power to crush Lucifer's head—the power to reject him, the power to say no. "My choice is Adam, as it has always been. My choice is our children, no matter the pain or sorrow."

Lucifer lets out a groan that sounds like a growl, and I lift my hands as if to ward it off.

He doesn't touch me but steps back, and I feel the distance between us like a much-needed drink of water. The strength leaves my body, and I collapse to the ground with a cry as my arm scrapes against the trunk. Squeezing my eyes shut, I wait for Lucifer's revenge, but there is only the sound of the wind.

After a moment, I open my eyes.

He is gone.

Clouds, low and dark, have gathered in the clear sky, and my body starts to shake.

Adam ran as the light streaked across the sky. Something was wrong, and it wasn't the fast-moving storm. He didn't slow when the mist pelted him, a mixture of water and winter cold. He carried two rabbits in his hands, but until he knew what was wrong, he'd wait to hunt for more.

The tree where he'd left Eve to rest looked twisted and lonely against the dark gray sky.

Another burst of light illuminated the surrounding terrain. He should have been able to see Eve by now, leaning against the tree, waiting for him, but the area beneath the tree was barren.

Adam pushed his legs faster, wishing he were already there. His breath came in gulps interspersed with inhaling drops of water. "Eve!" he called out, doubtful she could hear him over the roar of the storm, but he was desperate enough to try.

Only a few paces were left. Then he was there, beneath the rattling, dripping branches. His heart thudded and skipped a beat as he saw her curled up on the ground, her hands covering her face.

"Eve," he rasped out. What had happened to her? He shouldn't have left, but the sky had been clear and the wind mild when he'd departed. Dread pulsed through him as he imagined the worst. Was she still breathing?

He knelt beside her and grasped her wrists, pulling her hands away from her face. There was resistance to his touch, and there was warmth in her body. He leaned over her, too afraid to believe, but when her eyelashes fluttered against her cheeks and her eyes opened, relief poured into every part of his body.

"Adam," her mouth said, but no sound came.

He didn't need words—not yet. He needed her to be

alive and well. Gathering her in his arms, he sat against the tree, her body nestled against him. With one hand, he grabbed a skin coat he had discarded earlier in the heat and wrapped it around the both of them.

The wind pulled at their hair and coats, making a high-pitched keening sound interrupted by rumbling from the clouds and shots of light streaking across the sky.

Eve shuddered in his arms, but she wasn't crying . . . or speaking . . . yet. Adam just held her tight, his chest constricting at the thought of his wife being in danger for even one moment. She was barely a remnant of her former self: he hadn't heard her laugh since their daughter was born. She hadn't even smiled.

The storm didn't fade until it was almost dark, and then the light remained suspended between the gray of the storm and the twilight of the evening.

"He was here," Eve whispered.

The sound startled him. He'd become used to his wife's silence. At first Adam wasn't sure if Eve was speaking or if the wind created the sounds. But when he looked down, her eyes were open. He didn't need to ask who *he* was. Adam tightened his hold around her trembling body.

"I shouldn't have left." His skin burned with self-incrimination.

A sigh escaped her. "I needed to talk to him," Eve said, her voice a little stronger. "Without you."

Adam drew away, feeling stung. With the movement, the deerskin coat fell off her shoulders.

"Listen to me first," Eve said, her expression pleading.

But he didn't want to hear her explanation, even if it meant she was finally speaking again—even if it meant the sorrow had temporarily left her eyes, replaced by urgency. He wanted to leave, to walk away, to put space between them so he could think. After all that had happened, all that Lucifer had destroyed, she had *wanted* to speak to him?

He released her and moved so that she had the deerskin coat to herself. She didn't readjust it over her shoulders. She just let it sit around her waist. He resisted the urge to fix it.

Her hand touched his, and he looked down at it as if it were something foreign on his skin.

"I wanted out of this sorrow," she said. "I wanted someone to understand."

"But *I* understand," Adam said, the frustration building. "It's my sorrow too." He swallowed against the tightness in his throat. His whisper came out hoarse. "She was my daughter too."

Eve's eyes reddened. "I know. I'm sorry. I didn't know how to bear such a burden."

"Together," Adam said. "You and I *together*."

"Lucifer offered me another way," she said in a quiet voice.

"Of course he did." Fear shot through him. Had Eve made a covenant with Lucifer? *Have I already lost her?* If so, then why was she still here, with him? To say good-bye?

"I didn't take it, Adam," she said. "I don't think that I ever really considered taking it." She looked down. "Maybe I did, or maybe I just wanted to hear that I still had a choice." Moisture dripped down her face, and she didn't make a move to brush it away.

"We've always had choices," he said in a quiet voice. "But the choices leading to Lucifer are not the ones we seek."

She let out a breath and raised her red-rimmed eyes to meet his. "He was persuasive, and he promised that he could make the pain and sorrow of this world go away. He told me that I wouldn't have to feel *this* anymore." Her hand went to her chest.

He stared at her hand. "What was the price?"

"You," she said. "And our future children."

It was the first time that Adam had heard Eve speak of

future children as though they might be a possibility. A small bit of hope grew inside him.

"I thought of all the souls that are dependent on me—on *us*—who are waiting." She brought her hand to her face and finally brushed away the wet. "I will never forget our first daughter, and I don't want anything to make me forget. I don't want to forget how much I wanted her or loved her. I can't let Lucifer take that away from me. It would be like losing her again."

Adam placed his hands on each side of her face, gently stroking her cheeks with his thumbs. "We'll never forget, but not forgetting doesn't mean we have to stop living."

Her arms went around his neck. "I told him no. I realized that no matter what sorrow this world brings, my love for you is stronger than all of it." She moved closer. "I told him that I choose you always, forever."

Adam held Eve tight, breathing her in, her fragile parts and her strong parts. Without each part, she wouldn't be his—she wouldn't be Eve, the mother of all living.

36

And Adam called his wife's name Eve; because she was the mother of all living.

—Genesis 3:20

I never want to leave Adam's arms, and I bury myself in them as he sleeps. Lying beneath the full moon with the sound of a nearby stream, everything seems quiet and peaceful. But I know that although I have rejected Lucifer again, he won't give up.

I won't give up either.

Adam has been so patient, so understanding, that the guilt sits hard in my stomach. He is too good. He has waited for me long enough. I haven't allowed any intimacy, my fear like a wall between us. I can see it in his eyes as well, the fear of the unknown, but there is also the spark of faith.

If I am ready, he is ready. This I know, but I need to also have faith in Elohim. Faith in myself that I have made the right choice. Faith in us.

The moonlight plays across Adam's features, his cheekbones, nose, and chin. His eyelashes are thick and dark upon his cheeks, his brow relaxed in sleep. We have not found a place to dwell yet and continue to spend each night in a different place, but I feel settled inside.

There was a time when I wondered if I'd come out of the darkness that engulfed me—if I'd be able to see again, to love again, to feel again. It wasn't until I was at the lowest point and allowed Lucifer to come back into influence that I realized what I had been giving up.

I had been giving up Adam—who was warm, strong, dedicated, faithful—who was my husband. And for what? To exist in the depths of despair as some kind of proof that I wasn't happy about my daughter's death when living and bringing more children to the earth would have manifested my love for her and would have proved that I was worthy of her love.

In the farthest corner of my heart, I wonder if she was taken because I wasn't worthy yet, because my faith was not strong enough, and because I was willing to consider Lucifer's offers.

No, I breathe out. *Don't think that. Her soul is where it needs to be. And your soul is where it needs to be—separated from her for now.*

My refinement has just begun. I am only part of the woman that I hope to be when this mortal probation is over. When I meet my daughter in the afterlife, I want to be worthy of her praise.

Adam's steady breathing is soothing, and I reach my hand up to touch his face. I try not to wake him, but when his eyes slowly open, I know what I want. *Him. Us. Together.*

I lean up on my elbow and slowly kiss him. It feels like an eternity since I've allowed myself this pleasure. Pushing past the fear and the unknown, I let him take me into his arms. To start a new beginning.

⚜

The air has grown increasingly heavy. The incessant heat has released its hold, but there is a new touch to the air. It seems to weigh on us and slow us down.

When Adam asks if I want to stop for a midday rest, I answer, "No. I feel there is something that we must see and that it won't be long now."

Of course, I could have been saying this for days and days, but there is something that feels different about this day. The sun is the same, the high clouds are no different, the breeze is light, but my heart beats strangely off rhythm, as if it's sensing something new.

The trees we are walking through thin, and we make our way around large rocks. The rocks seem as though they are guarding or protecting someplace. Parts of them are covered in green growth. "What is that?" I ask, running my hand along the dry texture.

"They look like small herbs," Adam says, peering closer. "Dried herbs."

A bird, large and white with gray, flies overhead. It screeches against the sky.

"What kind of bird is that?" I point to it, although Adam is already following it with his gaze.

"I haven't seen it before," he says in a quiet voice, and I think that he feels it too: a change, a difference.

"Come on." I grab his hand, suddenly impatient and not wanting to examine tiny herbs on large rocks. We move around the rocks together, hand in hand, then stop when the earth seems to fall away in front of us.

We are at the top of a ridge that drops straight down. The large rocks have kept it hidden from view. My heart plunges as I gaze downward, as if my body were moving down with my gaze, falling in the air.

An expanse of pale earth stretches from the bottom of the ridge until it meets blue.

Adam and I stare at the blue that's much larger than any body of water we've ever seen. "It's the sea," he says.

The word *sea* enters my soul and surrounds me, and I whisper it to myself. "The sea."

The blue ripples like a river, but instead of endlessly moving forward, it pulls back. Then it moves forward again—and then back. The vast body of water extends as far as I can see, until it meets the sky above, where the sky blends blue with the water, stretching even farther, stretching forever.

It's as if we've reached the end of the earth.

"Is this the end?" I ask in a whisper. I don't know why I am whispering, except for the fact that it seems my normal breath is gone.

"If it is, it's incredible," Adam says. He releases my hand and moves away from me, walking along the ridge. I follow, keeping my gaze on the vast waters. I want to get closer to them, to touch them, but the ridge is too steep.

We walk for several moments in silence, just staring at the blue. There are crests of white as the ripples turn and plunge back into themselves.

When Adam stops, he waits for me to catch up. "I think we can get down here."

I study the descent with some doubt, but it looks safer than the place where we first stood.

Adam starts down the ridge, then turns and holds out his hand, a grin on his face. I grasp his hand, threading my fingers through his. I don't realize I'm holding my breath until I nearly have to gasp for air. I gingerly take a step, then another. I am so focused on the immense stretch of breathing water that I miss a step and stumble into Adam. He steadies me and pulls me close.

Arm in arm, we walk down the ridge toward the blue.

The sea breathes and moves as one, as a vast body changing its formation, then changing back.

About halfway down the ridge, the smell hits me. It's unlike anything I've smelled before. It's a warm smell that I can literally taste—it's rough yet clean, sharp yet smooth.

"Can you smell the waters of the sea?" Adam asks, his eyes bright with anticipation. "Think of all the living fish below the surface."

"Not more fish," I say, and he laughs.

Then the sound of an approaching storm reaches my ears, but as I look above the waters and across the sky, I see no clouds.

"What's that sound?" I say. It's quiet yet all-encompassing, reverberating down to my feet.

Adam is looking around too, and when our gazes meet with the same question, he says, "It must be the sound of the waters." With his free hand, he points to the white tops. "There is a lot of strength in that water as it pushes back and forth."

We continue down the ridge, and something tugs at my heart, whispering. *This is your home.* I shiver as a breeze passes over me, touching my skin in a caress. This is a sight I could wake up to each morning.

Adam's hand tightens in mine, confirming that he feels the same way.

37

And Adam knew Eve his wife; and she conceived, and bare Cain ...

—Genesis 4:1

Nine Moons Later

Adam stretched his back, pleased that his day's labor was nearly finished. The garden of herbs that he'd plotted and cultivated was coming along fine in the warm weather. He felt grateful for a mild winter season compared to what they'd experienced inland, but he was most grateful that any day now, he and Eve would welcome a new child.

If the movement within his wife's stomach was any indication, this child would be born alive and strong. Joy pulsed through him as he thought of Eve's happiness. Her face had taken on a serene quality, and she seemed at peace more than ever before, including when they lived in the garden. Since arriving at this place, the land of vast, blue waters, they'd created a permanent dwelling—one that pleased them both.

Adam pulled up a few young roots, deciding to add them to the evening meal. In his most recent hunt, he'd acquired an adult deer, so he wouldn't have to hunt for a while. He didn't want to leave his wife when she was close to bringing forth the child.

Nine moons, Elohim had told them in the garden. Without the sun setting, Adam knew tonight would be the full-moon phase, the ninth moon since Eve believed she'd first conceived. Over the past few days, every part of Adam's body had been tense with anticipation—for Eve, for the child, and for how he could protect them both.

Carrying the bundle of herbs, he headed for their shelter. It was more elaborate and sturdy than anything he'd built so far. With time and practice, he was figuring out how to create more than one living space and how to fit together branches and arrange animal skins so that he and Eve were protected from the elements.

As he passed the herb garden, the wind picked up, carrying the scent of cooking. Eve had already started the evening meal, it seemed.

She would be surprised to see him back earlier than usual.

Halfway between the herb garden and the dwelling, Adam passed by the altar—where he spent each morning praying. Elohim had been generous, he knew, although it had taken him time to realize that Elohim had been watching over them all along.

Lucifer was always nearby, lurking in the trees, sometimes near the vast waters. He hadn't made an effort to penetrate their dwelling yet, but Adam knew he would continue to wait for an opportunity—one that he and Eve didn't intend to ever give him.

Adam ran his fingers across the altar as he walked by. The sturdiness of the rock formation seemed to transfer its strength to him. Even in this lone wilderness, there was much beauty to be found. And much love.

He saw the curls of smoke first. The smoke was blacker

than usual. Adam increased his pace without really knowing why, but as his heart thumped, possibilities came to his mind.

Then he heard Eve cry out his name.

He looked around, trying to see where she was. No one was by the cooking Fire, and he could see that the animal flesh was overcooked, nearly black. "Eve!" he called out as he began to run.

She didn't answer back, so he ran straight for the shelter, dropping the herbs he carried.

Bursting inside, he couldn't see anything at first. The interior was dim, and his eyes had to adjust from the brightness outside. Then he heard a soft cry—not his name, more like a moan.

"Eve? Where are you?" he said, his heart pounding in his chest, making it difficult to speak.

"Back here," her voice came to him in the dimness.

The sound was from the second living space, which connected to the front area. Eve was in the place where they had their soft bed of skins.

He stumbled through the shelter, holding his breath. By the time he reached the back area, his eyes were nearly adjusted to the dimness. Eve was crouched next to their bed of skins, her hands on her stomach, her gaze staring through him, wide and unfocused. He wasn't sure that she saw him.

A shot of both fear and wonder coursed through Adam. The time had come. He knelt beside her, murmuring her name. "What can I do?"

Eve was breathing rapidly, and she gripped his arm tight. Adam didn't dare move, although he knew there would be bruises from the pressure of her fingers. Her face and arms were moist, covered in perspiration, and her hair hung in damp tendrils about her face.

She continued to stare forward, but at least Adam knew

she was aware of his presence. Her body started to shiver, and her eyes clenched shut.

Adam felt her scream almost before he heard her. Eve's scream extended from her, vibrating through his body. She grabbed for him with her other hand. "Hold me up," she gasped. "The child is coming."

The dark curls crown his round face, warming my heart.

Our son.

Born and alive.

I lean against Adam, whose arms encircle me as we recline against our bed of skins. Our son is at my breast, his body warm against my own, and he and I are surrounded by love, by Adam.

"We are a family," I whisper. I have never felt safer, more protected, more content, or more at peace. The joy is almost incomprehensible, almost painful because it expands within me, and I feel that it might escape me at any moment.

Adam's chin rests on my shoulder as he watches our son, who is eating and somehow sleeping at the same time. I close my eyes, exhaustion consuming me, but I don't want to sleep—not yet.

I am grateful that my husband returned from the herb garden early to find the meal burning and me in the throes of pain. The memories of pain are already fading, and I silently thank Elohim for that. For a moment, I wonder if my soul was really in my body at the time.

It was as though this was happening to someone else and I was observing as my body became a medium for bringing forth a child. I could not feel hot or cold or even hear Adam's words of comfort. All I knew was the pain. It was its own force, claiming and controlling me.

And now it seems far in the past.

To be replaced by the sweetest gift of all.

My eyes open, and moisture runs down my cheeks.

My son's hands are so small, his tiny fingers each with their own nail. Dark lashes touch his round cheeks, and I marvel at his small ears, his faint eyebrows, his feet, his toes . . . all that has been created and has grown inside me.

Adam sighs, enveloping me in the sound. His sigh tells me that he is content too. We'll worry about other things tomorrow, but tonight, there is only us.

Three of us.

Disbelief and joy course through me. At one time I thought this day impossible, especially after losing our daughter. Only now I realize that my heart has healed, day by day, as this new child grew inside me. And his birth—his perfectness—has at last healed the deepest sorrow. It has replaced the anguish with hope and love and promise.

"What should we call him?" Adam whispers, his breath against my neck.

I look down at the tiny living, breathing child and marvel at his existence, at his creation. "Elohim has sent him to us," I say. "He is our first son."

"The first son we have created," Adam says, his voice quiet, reverent. "How about Cain?"

"Cain," I repeat, testing out the sound of it. The child stirs in my arms, his small noises touching my heart. "I think he heard me."

Adam chuckles, his chest vibrating against my back. "He did."

"And perhaps he approves," I say. "Cain is a strong name."

"One that will never be forgotten."

I nod. "We'll raise this son in joy and protect him from all that we can."

"Yes." Adam strokes my arm. Then his fingers meet

mine as we touch Cain's small fist. "We'll teach him in righteousness, and he'll grow into a man who will be a strong leader and who will be remembered throughout the generations."

Adam's words are comforting, washing over me like the sea, and my heart turns to prayer. I pray that this son of ours will embrace Elohim and bring us great joy. I can't imagine anything more sweet as I touch his dark curls against his forehead. His presence has already filled me with unspeakable gratitude.

I lean down to kiss his brow, his skin warm against my lips.

"I love you, my sweet child," I say. "In this life and forever."

Acknowledgments

The story of Adam and Eve is certainly a timeless one, and, I believe, an eternal one. Although my rendition has plenty of fictional world-building aspects, I hope that the selfless nature of our first parents shines through. While researching, writing, and subsequently editing this story, I was struck time and time again by the remarkable events that took place in the Garden of Eden and before and after the Fall.

Many thanks to my husband, Chris, for being patient when I tell him I've finished a book but then dive right into the next one.

This manuscript has seen a myriad of readers and editors, including those in my fabulous critique group, which consists of Jeff Savage, Lu Ann Staheli, Robison Wells, Annette Lyon, Sarah M. Eden, and Michele Holmes. Thank you!

Early readers of the manuscript were essential in developing the story. Thanks to my parents, Kent and Gayle Brown, for looking over this story in its roughest form.

As with all my work, this manuscript passed through several stages of editing. Angela Eschler, Kelsey Allan, Mindy Holt, Micala Downs, Melissa Marler, and Julie Wright all added valuable feedback. I can't thank them enough!

My final thanks go to my agent, Jane Dystel, for her encouragement and for keeping me on the right track.

About H. B. Moore

H. B. Moore is a *USA Today* best-selling author and a 3-time Whitney Award winner for Historical Fiction, 3-time Best of State winner, and 2-time Golden Quill winner. She has more than a dozen historical novels written under the pen name H. B. Moore, including The Moses Chronicles and The Omar Zagouri Series. Under Heather B. Moore, she writes romance and women's fiction. She's a coauthor of the Newport Ladies Book Club series. Her romance works include *Heart of the Ocean*, *The Fortune Café*, the Aliso Creek series, and A Timeless Romance Anthology series.

Author website: www.hbmoore.com
Blog: MyWritersLair.blogspot.com
Twitter: @HeatherBMoore
Facebook: *Fans of H.B. Moore*

www.ingramcontent.com/pod-product-compliance
Lightning Source LLC
Chambersburg PA
CBHW060858250626
47159CB00008B/2788